LOVE CAME
CALLING

By the Author

Edge of Awareness

The Courage to Try

Imperfect Truth

Love Came Calling

Visit us at www.boldstrokesbooks.com

LOVE CAME CALLING

by

C. A. Popovich

2018

LOVE CAME CALLING
© 2018 By C. A. Popovich. All Rights Reserved.

ISBN 13: 978-1-63555-205-8

This Trade Paperback Original Is Published By
Bold Strokes Books, Inc.
P.O. Box 249
Valley Falls, NY 12185

First Edition: May 2018

Credits
Editor: Victoria Villasenor and Cindy Cresap
Production Design: Stacia Seaman
Cover Design by Tammy Seidick

Acknowledgments

I'd like to gratefully acknowledge all the hardworking folks at Bold Strokes Books who help me give my books a home and fulfill my dream of writing. Victoria Villasenor and Cindy Cresap, editors extraordinaire, thank you for helping me make this work so much better. I especially want to thank Victoria for her extra push and encouragement with this manuscript. She guided me to "dig deeper" and "make it matter." Painful but necessary lessons.

Thank you to my friend and retired English teacher, Fran, for her invaluable feedback and suggestions. And to her wonderful book club members who never fail to offer their beneficial thoughts and ideas. To Carsen Taite, awesome BSB author, I thank you for taking time to answer my legal questions. Thank you to my friends and fellow BSB authors Friz and Kris, for your listening ear and helpful suggestions. Thank you, my friend Chris, for allowing me to bounce ideas off you. And thank you to Sandi for your support and recommendations. I'm grateful for all the ways you're in my life.

Finally, thanks to all the readers of lesbian romance. Your support means everything.

To Sandi.
Thank you for calling.

CHAPTER ONE

Joslyn Harlow sat on the wooden rocker facing the snow-covered ice and appreciated the partial view of the Ice Bridge to Canada. She enjoyed watching the snowmobilers follow the tree-lined pathway she'd helped create, and it usually marked the busiest part of the winter season for her cabin rentals. The snow sparkled in the sunlit expanse, and the peaceful scene strengthened her resolve to keep the cabins she'd inherited on Drummond Island in the Upper Peninsula of Michigan. The three acres of waterfront property had grown in value after falling drastically during the recession and forcing her father to remortgage. It was hers now, and she had plans for the place. If she could keep the cabins rented for a couple more months, she could refinance the existing high-interest loan. Just two more months and she could finally put her business degree to use for the birth of her lesbian resort, Harlow's by the Bay. Her dream. She stood, dusted the snow off the steps, and headed to her office to review her finances. Half an hour later, her concentration was interrupted by the jingling of the bell on the lobby door.

"Hello. Anyone here?"

Joslyn looked up from her desk toward the sound of a male voice. She shoved her ledger into a drawer and locked it before moving to the front counter. She didn't recognize the burly man wearing a black snowmobile suit. "Hello. Can I help you?" She smiled, wondering about his confused look.

"Yeah. I wanna know where Jack is?"

She tried not to squirm under his glare. "I'm not sure who this Jack is you're looking for, but I'm Joslyn Harlow, the owner of these cabins, but please call me Josie." She waited hoping he'd elaborate.

"The owner, eh? I don't think so. I know the owner, and he ain't you." He looked side to side, examining the room.

"Could I ask your name, sir?" Josie figured being polite would get her further than revealing her annoyance.

"I'm Abe Bernstein. Jack and I were huntin' buddies, but I've been downstate takin' care of some business. I'm back now, and I want to talk to Jack about buyin' this place." He stomped some snow from his boots and wandered to the wall covered in pictures. "Yeah. I remember this." He pointed a stubby finger at one of the photos.

"I'm sorry, Abe, but I'm not sure who Jack is. Those pictures are of my grandfather when he built this place. They're my cabins now, and I'm not interested in selling them, but if you want to leave your name and number, I promise to contact you first if I ever do sell."

Abe turned back to her and narrowed his eyes. "Your grandpa, huh?"

"Yes. My grandfather, Harold Patterson."

"I'll be in touch. Don't you worry." He turned, pushed the door open, and banged it shut before hopping onto a snowmobile and riding away.

Josie sighed and went back to her office to finish updating her books and figure out her next move, but first she opened her wall safe and took out the deed to the property. It was there in black and white. Her father had left everything to her in his will, and she'd had the deed recorded and title transferred. The property was legally hers. Abe was an odd guy, and gruff, but he seemed puzzled and frustrated at not finding whoever Jack was, not really threatening. Still, she noted the time and date of Abe's appearance on her calendar and an hour later, pushed aside any uneasiness as she locked her office and outer door.

Josie tossed the pile of towels, the final load for the day, into the oversized washing machine. The group of Canadian guests had been a welcome surprise when they'd pulled into the parking lot right after sunup with three trailers full of snowmobiles. She'd finished plowing the twenty-by-twenty-foot parking lot merely half an hour before their arrival. The first week in February generally began the busiest time during the winter, but this lucky group found her with two cabins available. It didn't matter why they were there, or why they hadn't bothered to make reservations, because it meant she'd be able to pay the tax bill easily next month.

She added bleach and soap to the washer and then headed to the woodshed. She wanted an ample supply of firewood in case her guests wanted to warm up and relax in the main lodge when they returned from their snowy ride. The tiny cottages had electric heaters, but the chilled snowmobilers found the main lodge with its massive stone fireplace ideal. She loaded the firewood rack and set up the forty-two-cup coffeemaker. She filled a second smaller one with water and set two baskets filled with hot chocolate packets next to it, along with a few stacks of Styrofoam cups. She circuited the large open room and shifted the leather couch and chairs to face the fireplace and made sure the worn wooden end tables were within easy reach for cups. She scanned the room a last time, assuring visibility of the large signs declaring the room alcohol-free. Her father had dealt with numerous drunken guests over the years and had demanded the visitors keep their booze in their cabins if they wanted to drink. Josie planned to keep that requirement and hoped she wasn't naive to believe a group of lesbians would be respectful of it.

She interrupted her chores to pour herself a cup of hot chocolate and take a moment to reflect on her life since the death of her father four months ago. A twinge of guilt twisted her gut when she realized she'd let the time slip away without seeing Nooko. She smiled at the memory of the Ojibwe word for grandmother, *nookomis,* and how, as a child, she'd shortened it to *nooko.* Josie wasn't full-blooded American Indian, but her nooko was an Ojibwe elder. She'd been fairly steady on her feet with the use of a cane while they stood greeting friends at the funeral, but when she'd talked to her since, she'd noticed a weakness in her voice she'd attributed to grief.

Her grandmother had hinted the last time they'd talked about the empty bedroom in her two-story bungalow located in the Lower Peninsula, and Josie knew her intimations were partly based on her progressing immobility. She wondered if Nooko would consider moving back to Drummond Island with her, once she got her renovated resort off the ground. Tomorrow she'd call and make a plan to visit her. Maybe she'd even get a chance to spend an evening at the local lesbian bar for a hookup. She'd been working to keep the cabins rented to the exclusion of any fun since her father's death, and she missed the physical connection with a woman. She knew her prospects for a suitable bed partner were better downstate, so maybe she could find time to hook up with a beautiful lady and relieve some stress.

❖

"Good morning, Nooko. It's Joslyn." Josie would have preferred to use her cell phone than be tethered to the corded landline, but she'd learned not to place much faith in the wireless connection from the island. She sat on her bed, leaned back against her headboard, and stretched out her legs as she watched the morning sun begin to brighten the eastern sky. *Maybe being stuck by the window isn't such a bad thing.*

"Oh, it's so good to hear your voice, honey. How are you?"

"I'm good. Everything's going well here. I thought I'd give you a call before my guests get up. How're you feeling?" Josie shifted her phone to her left ear and grabbed her coffee cup.

"I feel fine, dear. Do you have a full house this month?"

Her grandmother always referred to all the cabins being rented as a "full house." "I do, Nooko. I just filled the last two yesterday. A group of snowmobilers, and they're having a ball. How's the weather there?"

"It's cold and snowy." She exhaled loudly. "I'm not even bothering to have the driveway plowed. I can't drive anymore anyway. I don't know what I'm going to do with your grandfather's Jeep. Did I ask you if you wanted it? I can't remember. I know your father didn't want it."

"I'll take a look at it next time I'm there. I wanted to talk to you about when." She worried about her nooko being trapped in the house in an emergency.

"You come anytime you want to, honey. You know you're always welcome. I haven't been upstairs…in a while. The extra bedroom may need a little dusting, but it's yours whenever you want it."

Josie hesitated, hearing the message beneath her words and the weakness in her voice. She made an instant decision. "I'm thinking of wrapping up the season at the end of this month. Fishing doesn't get going until April, so how does March sound for me to come visit?" She set her coffee cup on her nightstand and stood to gaze out the window, already beginning to plan ahead.

"Oh, yes, that would be lovely! I'll plan on it."

"Sounds good. My lodgers are up now, so I better go get the coffeemaker started. I'll give you a call tomorrow, and we can plan some more." Josie didn't mention her calls would continue to be daily until she could figure out a way to keep her nooko safe.

She quickly set up the coffeepot she kept in the lodge and went to her office to review her schedule. She had no bookings for April despite the excellent fishing that time of year, so she calculated that she could afford to spend the time with Nooko if necessary. She had one group booked for the beginning of March, and reservations for her first lesbian group weren't until May. She looked forward to reconnecting with her nooko before beginning her new endeavor in earnest.

CHAPTER TWO

Come on, Kelly. It'll be fun, and we could all use a relaxing getaway."
Debby leaned back in her chair. Her brown eyes sparkled.

Kelly Newton took a bite of her sandwich and considered what her friend and coworker had told her about a newly opened lesbian resort located on an island in northern Michigan. The owner advertised it with furnished cabins, private decks, and a huge fireplace and hot tub in the main lodge. The latter nearly made her decide on the spot as she tipped her head from side to side to stretch her neck. She needed a vacation to clear her mind and help with her decision to change jobs. She gazed about the lunch area where they sat at one of the small round tables. *Getting away for a while would be heaven.* She began a mental list of preparations before turning to face Debby. "I don't know, Deb. I'll think about it. You and Alex are going for sure, huh?"

"Yep. I've put in for a two-week vacation starting the end of May, and I've convinced Kristen and Jaylin to come along. Jaylin said she might be able to get Maria and Dana to join us, too. We're almost ready to confirm our reservations. We're going to sit by the water, or the fireplace, depending on the weather, and unwind." Debby speared a piece of chicken from her salad and popped it into her mouth.

"I'd like to support this lesbian-owned place. She just opened, huh?"

"Yes. We'll be her first lesbian group." Debby grinned.

Kelly took a deep breath and exhaled to release the tension in her shoulders. "I could sure use a holiday. We're stressed to the max around here." She pictured herself sitting in a peaceful cabin on a remote island until the cabin picture morphed into a wooden shack with drafty windows, leaky roof, and a moldy bathroom. "It's new, though, right?"

Debby sipped her water before answering. "Right. The woman's family has owned the cabins for years, so they're not new, new, but she's remodeled them. She's a descendant of the Ojibwe American Indians. She grew up on Drummond Island and wants to make a go of the place. It's called Harlow's by the Bay. Look it up. She's got a website with great pictures."

"Thanks. I'll check it out and let you know what I decide. I've got to get back to work. See you later." Kelly dropped off her used tray and lunch dishes in the kitchen and wrenched her thoughts from lounging in a hot tub to juggling the nurse's schedules to cover the new patients arriving. She'd only been back at her desk moments before she was dealing with another staffing issue.

"But I worked a twelve-hour shift yesterday." Megan, one of the new registered nurses, leaned on the counter opposite Kelly and tapped on the schedule. "I'm only staying until five today." She glared a challenge at her.

"When you hired in last week, I reviewed the schedule thoroughly with you. Our influx of patients requires all of us to put in a few extra shifts. At least for a while. I need you to work twelve hours today. You'll get tomorrow morning off, and Rachael will fill in. We have two new aides starting tomorrow, too. I'm sorry, but there are three new residents who need to be checked in, reviewed, and have treatment protocols set up."

Kelly pinched the bridge of her nose and turned away from Megan to face her computer screen, hoping she'd take the hint. She heard her huff as she stomped away. If this kept up, her decision to leave the nursing home would come sooner rather than later. The thought reminded her she hadn't heard back from the VNAA, Visiting Nurses Association of America, regarding her application. It didn't sound ideal, carrying a bag and working out of her car, but she couldn't stay in the stressful environment of the nursing home much longer. She'd been with Serenity Care for twenty of her twenty-five years as a nurse, and she'd seen it change as healthcare changed. The number of patients had grown throughout the years, and the facility had developed a reputation for being one of the best in the state. The aging population, growing number of seniors needing care, and the increasing number of people obtaining health insurance had resulted in more patients than healthcare workers to care for them. Janis Smith, the administrator, did an excellent job of managing the nursing home, but it had become increasingly difficult for her to find the required staff to care for the residents. Her nurses were overworked and in danger of burning out, and Kelly was thinking of walking away after twenty years. What did that say about the situation? Kelly shut down her computer and headed to check on their newest patient. She'd just finished taking the ninety-year-old's vitals when one of the aides poked her head in the door.

"Hey, Kelly. Janis asked me to let you know she wants to see you in her office when you're done here."

"Thanks, Jean. I'm almost done." Kelly frowned, wondering why the administrator wanted to see her. She hoped she wouldn't tell her there were more residents being admitted. They were out of room. She recorded the patient's critical information into her laptop before heading to Janis's office.

"Thanks for coming, Kelly. Please sit for a minute." Janis indicated the empty chair opposite her desk. "I have something I need to discuss." She leaned back in her desk chair and rolled her shoulders before continuing. "As you're aware, we've taken in quite a few new residents this year. You've been with me since the beginning, and I value your experience and opinions." Janis shifted in her seat and leaned forward before continuing. "A few of our aides told me they've had to constantly alter their patients' bath schedule because the nurses insist their tasks are a priority."

Kelly blew out a breath and shook her head. "I've talked to every new nurse about scheduled vital checks and medication distribution. I thought they all understood. Why didn't the aides come to me about this?"

"I believe it's because you're the nursing supervisor. They figure you don't have time…I don't know. I just know we need everyone to be as efficient as possible with our budget constraints, understaffing, and all these new patients."

"I'm sorry you had to get involved with this, Jan. I'll call a staff meeting this afternoon, or tomorrow morning, or both if needed, and make sure everyone can work together to make the best use of time." Kelly forced herself to shut the door gently as she left the office. She went directly to her station, sent out an email regarding a staff meeting, and made a note to remind herself to contact VNAA about her application first thing in the morning.

❖

"No openings in the area at all?" Kelly paced from one end of her kitchen counter to the other and switched her phone to the other ear as if she'd hear something different from the other one. "So where do you have openings? Illinois? But I live in Michigan. Is there any chance of something opening up anytime soon? I see. Thank you." She turned off her phone and flopped onto her couch. She had a hard time believing the only spot available with the Visiting Nurses Association turned out to be in Illinois. She leaned her head on the back of the sofa and squeezed her eyes shut. For a fleeting moment, she considered taking the out-of-state position and pondered the feasibility of the daily drive. Perhaps it would be less stressful than what she was dealing with now. She stood, grabbed the eggs from the refrigerator, and took out her frustration by scrambling them.

Kelly finished eating her breakfast before going to her barn to feed her horse. "Hey, boy. It looks as if I'm not changing jobs anytime soon." She filled his grain bucket and tossed a couple of flakes of hay into the feeding corner of his stall. She picked out a pile of droppings and flung it onto the manure pile before double-checking his water bin and heading back to the house. She took a few minutes to wash up, finish a cup of coffee, and reflect on her conversation with the VNAA representative. Maybe she'd just have to make the best of the nursing home. *Maybe it'll get better once the new employees settle in.* One thing she knew for sure, she'd join her friends on a vacation getaway. She sighed and grabbed her briefcase before leaving for work.

CHAPTER THREE

Josie slogged through the foot of snow leading to her grandmother's front door and brushed the heavy late winter snowflakes from the doorbell. She made a mental note to find someone to keep the driveway clear as she pressed the button.

"I'm coming." Ruth Patterson peeked through the curtain before opening the door. "I didn't expect you until tomorrow. Come in, honey."

Josie stepped inside and enfolded her grandmother in a hug, surprised at how frail she felt in her arms. "I decided there'd be less traffic on Sunday, so I came today." She stepped back and held her grandmother's shoulders. "Do you feel as good as you look, Nooko?" Josie hadn't known what to expect when she'd locked up her cabins and packed to head south to her grandmother's, but her bright smile encouraged her.

"I'm fine, dear. I was on antibiotics for a few days, but I'm done now. Come, take your coat off. I'll make us some hot tea."

Josie watched her shuffle to her walker next to her couch. She grabbed the handles and smoothly moved toward the kitchen. She obviously felt more secure with the walker than her cane. This evident decline in her mobility in only a few months concerned her. Josie removed her boots and pushed aside what seemed to be a lifetime of her grandfather's and Nooko's coats, sweaters, and boots to stow her own winter garb. She'd bring her suitcase in later after she had a chance to assess her situation. She wandered through the living room noting the dust. The carpet hadn't been vacuumed in a while, and dankness indicated the windows hadn't been opened in a long time. She sighed deeply, realizing her nooko looked good, but probably couldn't be left alone much longer.

"I'll get the cups while you tell me why you were on antibiotics."

Josie retrieved two mugs and a box of tea bags from the cabinet and set them next to the stove, where her grandmother had put a kettle on to boil.

"Thank you, dear. I had a cough that wouldn't go away. The doctor wanted to be careful because of my age, I guess. I spent a few days in bed, but I'm fine now."

"How'd you get to the doctor?" She took a deep breath, trying to dispel the remorse for not even knowing her nooko had been sick, let alone not being there to help.

"My neighbor, Nancy, from across the street took me. She has the Meals on Wheels route here, so she checks on me every day." She patted Josie's hand as she spoke.

Josie watched her grandmother plop into one of the kitchen chairs. *At least she has someone looking in on her.* "You sit. I'll pour the tea. I'd like to talk about some things." She set the mugs on the table, considering her next words. "I have some plans for the cabins, Nooko." She waited for a response, but her grandmother just sipped her tea and watched her expectantly. "I've renamed the place Harlow's by the Bay, and I've advertised it as a lesbian resort. I've already got it booked for two weeks after Memorial Day." Josie stopped talking and waited. Her grandmother set her cup down before speaking.

"I always knew you were smart." Nooko smiled and regarded her for a long moment. "Your father never liked change. He worried about disappointing your mother and grandfather. When he and your mom took over the land, he promised to do his best to keep it up and keep it in the family. Your grandfather wouldn't have cared if he had to sell the place. Harold and I had a good life here." She gazed at the wall seemingly lost in memories. "He built this place, too, you know."

"I remember him being a hard-working man. I miss him, too." Josie sat quietly for a moment, not wanting to intrude on her grandmother's thoughts. "You probably know Dad took a loan out on the property about nine years ago. I've just about got it paid off now." Josie took her nooko's hands in hers and squeezed gently. "I can make this work. I know I can."

"I know you can, too, honey."

Josie blinked back tears, allowing herself to feel the love and support from her nooko. She took a deep breath and realized how apprehensive she'd been to tell her about her plans. Any misgivings she had about her nooko's support vanished. Now she had to make sure she kept her safe.

❖

Josie leaned on the plastic snow shovel and appraised the previously snow-covered driveway. She felt good about opening up her grandmother's world by assuring her a clear pathway out of her house, but a nagging feeling warned her she wouldn't be able to take advantage of it. She bent to stretch her back, realizing she'd gotten used to her snowplow and hadn't had to shovel in years. She put the shovel in the garage and swiped off a dust-covered side window of Nooko's twenty-year-old Jeep with her gloved hand. She peered inside, admiring the condition of the interior, but doubted it would run since it'd been sitting idle for the ten years since her grandfather's death.

"Nooko?" The warm air of the house was welcome, and Josie went in search of her grandmother. She'd left her sitting at the kitchen table with hot tea and toast and instructions to call her if she needed to get up. She frowned at the walker unmoved from where she'd left it within easy reach. Her chest constricted as she hurried through the living room toward the bedroom. She stopped short when she passed the bathroom and heard a groan. "Nooko!" She knelt on the tile floor next to her grandmother, who was wedged between the toilet and sink cabinet, the toilet paper holder the only thing keeping her from sliding to the floor. She rushed to the bedroom and grabbed all the pillows from the bed. Her grandmother whimpered, and Josie shoved the pillows beneath her for support and wrapped her arms around her waist. She gently pulled her up and pivoted to sit her on the toilet seat. "Do you hurt anywhere? Are you dizzy?" She checked her arms and legs, but a growing bruise on her wrist appeared to be her only injury.

Nooko shifted on the closed toilet seat and shook her head. "I don't know what happened. I don't feel dizzy at all. I just lost my balance somehow when I twisted to flush the toilet. I can walk." She reached for the counter to push herself up.

"Just stay right there, Nooko. Don't try to get up yet. I'm going to get your walker." Josie sprinted to the kitchen to retrieve the walker. *Not good.* She'd have to rethink leaving her nooko alone, even briefly.

Josie settled her on her couch with ice on her wrist. "How does it feel?"

"I'm fine. Quit fussing over me."

"Nooko. You fell in the bathroom. What would've happened if I hadn't been here?" Her throat went dry imagining her nooko lying on the floor for days.

She merely sighed, her eyes tear-filled and her lip trembling.

"I'm not comfortable leaving you alone here anymore. Especially since I'm hours away. I've got Dad's bedroom cleaned out and we'll move all your things in there." Josie paced the length of Nooko's couch and ran her fingers through her hair.

"Honey. I'm not going anywhere. Harold and I lived in this house for forty years. All my memories are here." Nooko swiped away her tears and crossed her arms in front of her as if protecting herself from Josie's insistence.

"You fell. Remember?"

"I told you Nancy is right across the street. I have her number taped to the wall next to the phone, and this fall was just an accident. I reached too far. I'll be more careful, I promise."

Josie sighed in frustration. She wasn't convinced this was Nooko's first fall. "Okay, Nooko. How about if we make it only for a little while. Consider it a trial period only until after my first group in my new Harlow's by the Bay leaves." She hoped she'd conveyed her seriousness.

"All right. If it'll stop your worrying." She relaxed back into the couch as if relieved. "But for how long?"

"They've booked two weeks starting the twenty-seventh of May. If you feel up to it, I'll get you back here by the end of June."

"I'll try it, dear. For your sake."

Later that evening, Josie activated the new GPS emergency call button she'd purchased and plugged it in to continue charging the battery overnight. She'd make sure her nooko wore it at all times. Josie felt better knowing she'd be close to her and could be monitored for a few weeks. The fact that she'd barely protested suggested she might be a little more frightened than she let on. *And lonely.* She'd see just how much care Nooko needed, and deal with her long-term care later if necessary.

She wrestled with images of Nooko falling before sinking into a restless sleep.

CHAPTER FOUR

Kelly pulled out her patient notes and nestled her briefcase under the desk at the nurses' station. It looked like another long day with new patients to assess and nurses to train. She took a deep breath and headed to the tiny room that housed the staff coffeepot. She grabbed a warm blueberry bagel from the unexpected local bakery bag next to the coffeemaker. The day looked better.

"Good morning." Megan stood next to Kelly's chair with a cup of coffee in one hand and bagel in the other. "I brought the bagels this morning." She grinned. "A peace offering. I'm sorry for my grumpiness yesterday. I appreciate you calling a staff meeting, because I didn't mean to be difficult."

"Thank you, Megan. I'm glad we're all on the same page now. We're getting so busy, we need to work together and communicate well."

"I agree. I'm off to begin dispensing meds. Do you have time for lunch today?"

Kelly hesitated. A new friend would be nice. "Yeah. Sounds good. Stop by on your way to the cafeteria."

"See you then."

Kelly waved to Megan before checking her next patient's chart and collecting the needed supplies.

"Good morning, Mrs. Grist. I've got your heart medications for you." Kelly smiled and gently squeezed the eighty-year-old's hand. *Warm. That's good.* "How're you feeling today?" She clipped the pulse oximeter on her finger waiting for a reply. Her patient merely turned to look at her and smiled. She'd stopped speaking a long time ago, though no one knew why. "You're smiling. That's a good thing. Your oxygen level is perfect." She patted her arm and recorded her vital signs before making sure she swallowed her pills. "Your aide, Pat, will be in soon to help you to the bathroom. Make sure you push the call button if you need anything." Kelly pointed to the button built into the bed railing and made sure Mrs. Grist could reach it before leaving for her next patient. She leaned against the wall outside the door to check her list. Only two more. *Things may be settling down around here.*

Her phone pinged and she glanced at the readout. Janis? *Can you come to my office ASAP?* Kelly said she'd be there after her next patient and slid her cell phone back into its case. Whatever Janis wanted must be important to interrupt her rounds.

Kelly knocked softly before entering Janis's office. "Reporting as directed." She grinned, expecting Janis to at least chuckle, but she frowned at her and indicated the chair opposite her desk.

"Have a seat. I know you're busy, so I won't keep you long, but this is important." She toyed with her pen for a second before continuing. "As you know, we've been overcrowded and understaffed for a while now. I found out two days ago that the owners have finalized plans with a corporation to sell this place." Janis paused, looking uncharacteristically uncertain.

"What is it, Jan? You look…spooked."

"I'm sorry, Kelly, but we've been gobbled up by the growing move toward corporate ownership of healthcare facilities, and there's not a damn thing I can do about it. Our little nursing home is now part of a corporation buying nursing homes and assisted living places all over the state." She leaned back into her desk chair and sighed.

Kelly sat quietly absorbing the news. "So, what's it mean for us, specifically?"

"I don't have all the details yet, but I've been put in the position of having to decide how to distribute our resources."

"Of which I am one." Kelly didn't think her job was in jeopardy. They were filled to capacity with residents, and she had the most seniority of the nursing staff.

"Yes. You are." Janis opened her laptop and typed for a minute before turning it around to show her a list of names. "This is a listing of places this company now owns. There are a few brand-new buildings they want operational by the end of this summer, and they need a senior staffing nurse to oversee the implementation for each one." She pointed to one name on the list. "This one, Woodland Care Center, is scheduled to open in June. It's the closest to your house, but still too long a distance to commute, so I'm assigning you to it with the condition they provide you lodging."

"What?" Her stomach twisted, and she swallowed to dislodge the lump in her throat. "Jan, I have a house and a horse and a life here. I can't just move to…where is this place?"

"It's in the Upper Peninsula."

"The Upper Peninsula? That's a five-hour drive!"

"Six, actually. But it isn't a permanent position, Kelly. I only need you to be there to get them up and running. We've worked together for twenty years and you're valuable here. They're willing to send several support staff to cover things here, if I'm willing to send my senior staffer to help get one of their other places ready. It's a trade-off, and I don't want to lose you, but I have to ask you to please take this assignment. It's only for a few months. The place should be autonomous by October. Will you please think about it?"

Kelly stood, circled behind her chair, and leaned on the back. Her thoughts whirled, and she fought to calmly sort them out before speaking. "What about my vacation plans? I'm taking two weeks off in the beginning of June." She thought about the lesbian resort located on Drummond Island, in the same location as her new job. It would give her a chance to check out the area.

"Not a problem. You can still take your vacation, but I do need an answer soon in case I have to find someone else."

Kelly turned to leave the room without a good-bye, feeling like she'd been ambushed, but stopped with her hand on the doorknob. She'd wanted a change, and maybe her sister, Tory, would be excited to stay at her house and care for Pogo for a few months before beginning college in the fall. Maybe she could look at it as a creative challenge. "Fine. But if I have trouble making arrangements for my house, that will change things."

"Hell. I'll take care of your house and your horse if you take this position." Janis smiled weakly, but Kelly saw the spark of hope in her eyes.

❖

Kelly saw Megan sitting at a corner table as soon as she walked into the cafeteria. She waved before going through the food line and wondered how much she should disclose about the reason for being late. Janis hadn't said to keep anything a secret, and the staff would have to find out soon about the changes.

"Hi. I thought maybe the boss kidnapped you." Megan smiled and pulled a chair out for her.

"No, she just wanted to let me know about some changes coming down the pike."

"Ah. The corporate takeover?" Megan took a bite of her sandwich and looked at her expectantly.

"I guess you already know about it. I didn't until Jan told me. It sounds as though this corporation's taken over quite a few facilities." She bristled at the news that Megan knew about this before she did.

"Hm. I know I'm glad to have gotten in here before the shake-up. One of my instructors at Eastern Michigan University recommended it. She knew I wanted a long term care facility position, and this one's rated as one of the best in Michigan."

Kelly took a bite of her salad, considering how much to tell the newly hired nurse. "Has Janis said anything to you about work assignments?"

"She just told me when I hired in that the owners were in talks regarding the possibility of a buyout by a corporation. She said it wouldn't affect me much except with regard to who signs my paycheck."

"I suppose it'll be up to Janis to let everyone know what's going on, but I've been reassigned for a few months to a new place in the Upper Peninsula. They need someone with experience to help train the staff."

Megan looked thoughtful as she took a sip of her coffee. "You'll be great at it." She smiled and lifted her cup in a toast.

Kelly smiled back, glad to feel Megan's support. "Thanks. It probably means you'll be even busier than you are now, but Janis believes she can get extra help to make up for the loss."

After lunch, Kelly started thinking ahead, a feeling of excitement bubbling deep inside. Janis had taken her by surprise with the request for a temporary transfer, but a small whisper of relief at the change settled some of her unrest. She found herself looking forward to undertaking the challenge. Her contribution could be consequential. She'd be a major contributor to the development of what would probably be a state-of-the-art facility, but first, she'd take a much needed break. "Hi, Debby. Have you got a minute?" Kelly opened the pharmacy door a crack to peek inside.

"Sure. Come on in."

"I'm on my way back from lunch, but I wanted to double-check our vacation plans. Are we all set for the twenty-seventh?"

"Yep. You should probably call and verify you'll be there, though. I've got the number here." Debby pulled a piece of paper out of her desk and handed it to her. "The owner's name is Joslyn Harlow. We confirmed our reservations last week. I was going to check with you tomorrow to see what you decided."

"I'm getting the hell out of here for a couple of weeks, for sure. Thanks for the number." She went back to her station to prepare for a long afternoon, but the afternoon was now filled with excitement for an upcoming, much needed break, and planning for the unanticipated changes.

CHAPTER FIVE

Josie parked in front of the lodge, troubled by the sight of the porch chairs turned upside down. *What the hell?* She jumped out to open the passenger door for Nooko. "Here we are." She made sure she had her cane and was steady before leading her to the porch.

"I'm a little stiff from the ride, dear." She took the few steps one at a time. "I'd forgotten how beautiful the view is from here. May I sit a minute?"

"Of course." Josie uprighted the chairs, pulled two cushions from a bin against the wall, and nestled them on the rockers. "Here you go. You sit while I unload the car and turn the water pump on."

Josie checked on her grandmother a couple of times in the half hour it took her to carry in their luggage and supplies. Nooko leaned back and rocked, gazing out at the water. Josie began to sit in the second rocker when she heard the phone. "I'll be right back." She glanced at Nooko, already beginning to doze in the chair, before hurrying to the front desk.

"Hello, Harlow's by the Bay, may I help you?"

"Hello. My name's Kelly Newton, and I want to confirm my reservation. Is this Joslyn Harlow?" Kelly's mellow voice floated over the phone line, and Josie wanted to hear her say her name again.

"Yes, this is Joslyn. When is your reservation?"

"I'm hoping you have it. My friends confirmed theirs for the twenty-seventh of May through the tenth of June. I believe it's under the name Debra Johnson."

"Oh, yes. I've got a reservation for six confirmed and one maybe for those dates. Are you the maybe?" Josie hoped so. She looked forward to meeting the body behind the voice.

"I guess I am. Please count me in. I need a vacation."

Josie's breath caught when she heard Kelly laugh. She could listen to that all day. "You're all set. You'll be in cabin number four. And please, call me Josie. My grandmother is about the only one who calls me Joslyn anymore."

"Josie it is. Thank you and I'll see you on the twenty-seventh."

"Sounds good." She didn't want to hang up and quickly thought of something else to say. "Oh…Kelly? One more thing. Are you bringing a dog?"

"A dog? No. Why?"

"Just checking. Your friends are bringing…let's see…a dachshund, a border collie mix, and a lab mix, so if you were bringing one, I'd give you the spiel about leashes and cleaning up after them."

"This ought to be fun. See you soon."

Another laugh from Kelly and Josie hung up the phone, sure she was grinning like a fool. *Yes, Kelly Newton. See you soon.*

Josie returned to the porch and took the seat next to Nooko, who was awake and looked contented. "I just had another reservation confirmed for next week. We'll have four of the six cabins full for two weeks, and the other two for one week. I'm going to make a cup of hot chocolate. You want one?"

"Oh, I'd love one. Thank you."

Josie loved seeing the sparkle in her nooko's eyes. Already, she looked brighter than she had when Josie had shown up at her place, and she knew she'd made the right decision bringing her here. She was also glad they'd stayed in Nooko's house longer than she'd planned. It gave Nooko time to pack items important to her and Josie time to close up her house properly. "Be right back." She filled two mugs with hot chocolate and delivered them before heading to check on the firewood. Everything looked as she'd left it. Her concern over the upended chairs lessened when she found the tarp over the wood rack secure. *Could've been a windstorm. Or a critter.* She continued surveying the circumference of the lodge and found nothing else amiss. She shook off her concerns and went back to join Nooko on the porch.

"Are all of your guests coming next week lesbians?"

"Yes. I've advertised as a lesbian resort, and I think I'll do well. There's only one other one I found on the west side of the state quite a few miles south. I want to show off our beautiful island and the Ojibwe history here."

"I want to help. If you're going to keep me hostage here, I get to do some work, too."

"How 'bout if you get settled in first? We'll get you unpacked, and then we can talk about what you might be up to doing." Josie smiled, stood, and handed Nooko her cane. She followed her into the lodge, staying close enough to support her when she wobbled. She settled her on the couch facing the fireplace. "You relax for a minute. I'm going to get us a snack to go with some tea."

"Thank you, dear. Everything looks wonderful in here." Nooko gazed around the room smiling. "Can we have a fire in the fireplace?"

"I think that's a great idea. I'll get it started after I get our refreshments." Josie put a kettle of water on the stove, sliced pieces of cheese onto a plate, and grabbed a box of crackers. She placed the cheese and crackers in front of Nooko on the coffee table and lit the fire in the fireplace before retrieving their tea and settling next to Nooko. "Comfortable?"

"Oh, yes. This is such a comfortable room. I remember Harold and me sitting together on this very couch. He built that fireplace, you know." Nooko looked like she was struggling to keep her eyes open. They sat in companionable silence enjoying the soft glow of the flames and the occasional sputter of the burning wood.

"Grandpa did an excellent job. It's a great fireplace. I know I'm pretty tired. You ready to head to bed?" Josie rested her hand gently on Nooko's thigh.

"Yes, honey. I suppose we'll have plenty of time tomorrow to get settled." Nooko pushed off the couch and swayed slightly before steadying herself with her cane.

"We have over a week before our guests arrive. Like you say, plenty of time." Josie led Nooko to her room and tucked her in bed before heading to finish unpacking.

Josie finished before dark and went to check on the cabins. She'd look closely at them in the morning, but she knew she wouldn't sleep with her lingering trace of concern over the upset deck chairs. She walked through each cabin checking the window locks, bedrooms, kitchens, and heaters. She flushed the toilets and ran water in the sinks. She finished before midnight, and after looking in on her grandmother, fell into bed hoping for dreams of her *maybe* woman.

❖

"What time are all your friends coming?" Nooko asked.

"They're not my friends, Nooko. Only women who've made

reservations to stay here." Josie reviewed the placement of the tables she'd set up for games for the third time. "Do you think they look inviting? Maybe I ought to move them closer to the fireplace."

Nooko sat in one of the leather chairs next to the fireplace in the spacious room, looking right at home. "Everything looks lovely, honey. They're going to love it. What time are they arriving?"

"I told them check-in is any time after eleven. They're coming from pretty far south, so I don't expect them until afternoon." She moved one of the tables aside and pulled the other leather chair to face her grandmother, glad for a chance to relax for a minute. She'd been working hard to make sure the place was perfect. "By the way, have you ever heard of a guy named Abe Bernstein? He came by in February looking for someone named Jack and wanting to buy this place." She'd been unable to shake the creepy feeling he'd left her with, and now that she had a minute, she remembered to ask her grandmother.

Nooko frowned, clearly concentrating. "No, dear. The name doesn't ring a bell. I can't imagine who he is. Maybe he had the wrong place?"

"He recognized the pictures on the wall, so I thought maybe he was a friend. How about the name Jack? He referred to Jack as the owner."

"No, again. I never heard Harold mention a Jack or an Abe, and I knew all of his buddies. You know how turned around people can get up here. He might've been lost. He said he wanted to buy the place, huh?"

"Yep. I know my dad never said anything about selling, so I don't know what the guy was talking about." Josie made a mental note to talk to the island's conservation officers about Abe. It would give her a little peace of mind that someone besides her knew about this guy. "I guess I'll just wait and see if he comes back. I'm going to the office to make sure everything's in order."

She pulled out her reservation book when she got to the front desk and put out a sign directing guests to ring the bell if she wasn't at the counter. She made one more walk-through of each cabin before heading back to the lodge and waiting for her first lodgers at Harlow's by the Bay. She stopped to stand on the porch for a moment and took a deep, settling breath. She gently ran her hand over the doorframe before taking a step inside to offer a silent thanks to her grandfather and parents, who afforded her this opportunity. Her dream was finally coming true.

❖

"Welcome. I'm Joslyn Harlow, but please call me Josie." She smiled at the couple as they walked through the door hand in hand. "No problem finding the place?"

"None at all. I've got a GPS in my car and we had no trouble."

Josie checked off each name on the register as the women introduced themselves. The hazel-eyed woman smiled, and Josie relaxed in the presence of her serenity. Her partner stepped up to put her arm around her waist, and the gesture sent an unexpected flood of longing surging through Josie. She shook off the unusual feeling and continued checking them in. "Are the others on their way?" she asked.

"They're right behind us. We all decided to drive separately, but we left pretty much at the same time."

"Good. You're all set. Kristen, Jaylin, and Railroad, you'll be in cabin number two. I can show you where it is now, or you're welcome to relax in the lodge if you want to wait for the others."

"Relaxing in the lodge sounds good to me." Kristen spoke and turned toward Jaylin, who nodded and smiled. "We'll just take our dog for a short walk before we go in."

"The main room is through there." Josie pointed toward a door to her left. "Or you can just go in through the front doors on the porch. My grandmother is staying with me temporarily, so you'll see her there." Josie settled into her desk chair but didn't wait long before the other couples arrived. "Dana, Maria, and Frankie, you're in cabin number one, and Debby, Alex, and Abby, you're in cabin number three. Jaylin and Kristen are waiting in the lodge for you. You can go through that door." Josie smiled and indicated the same door she'd shown Kristen and Jaylin. *So far, so good.*

Josie leaned on the check-in desk and reminded herself that this was really happening. She now had three of her cabins occupied by *her* lodgers. Not her father's or her grandfather's, but hers. She stretched to her full height and allowed herself a moment of pride. She did this. She was making it work. One deep breath and she updated her record log, anticipating the arrival of Kelly Newton.

CHAPTER SIX

It was close to six o'clock when Kelly pulled into the parking lot of Harlow's by the Bay. She stepped out of the car and stretched before appraising the area and log building nestled among gigantic pine trees. She'd barely managed to catch the 5:10 p.m. ferryboat crossing, and the spectacular view of the island as it pulled into the dock took her by surprise. Her research of the island hadn't prepared her for the reality of its natural beauty. *Maybe this work assignment won't be so bad.* She'd been pleasantly surprised to find the new facility where she'd be working was on Drummond Island and only a few miles from Harlow's by the Bay. She'd have time to scope it out before starting work there.

She dragged her suitcase out of the back seat of her car and headed toward a door with a wooden, handcrafted office sign above it. "Hello?" she called out before noticing the note next to a bell, so she hit the plunger twice and waited. She scanned the room, glancing over the pictures of what looked to be the original construction of the building. She admired the colorful Indian blanket tacked to the wall behind the counter with two large dream catchers on either side of it.

"Hello. You must be Kelly Newton," a woman said as she emerged from another room. "Sorry, I was in the back getting some pamphlets for your group. I'm Josie."

Kelly clutched the handle of her suitcase tightly at the unexpected urge to touch Josie's beautifully smooth complexion. Her dark eyes shimmered like her black hair in the soft light. Then she smiled, and Kelly's knees nearly buckled. She swallowed hard, willing her voice not to quiver. "No problem. I was just admiring your beautiful dream catchers. It's nice to meet you. I'm not too late, I hope."

"Oh, no. Not at all. I knew you were on your way. Your friends are all in the lodge waiting for you. Here's your key to cabin four. Would you like me to show you where it is, or do you want to stop in the lodge first?"

"I guess I better go check in with everybody so they know I made it." Kelly eased her grip and rolled her suitcase as she followed Josie. *Geez, you'd think I'd never seen an attractive woman.* She tried to focus and shake the feeling off.

She nearly stumbled when they entered the lodge, rendered speechless by the expansive room. "Oh my God. This is fantastic." She parked her suitcase against the wall and hurried to stand in front of the huge blazing wood fireplace. She turned twice, allowing the warmth to radiate through her, chasing away some of the stress of her life. "This and a hot tub? I may never leave." She turned again and found herself face-to-face with Josie. The warmth of the fire paled to the heat generated from her gaze. Kelly took a step back, surprised by her intense reaction to Josie.

"I'm glad you like it. And yes, the hot tub is through the doors in the back. There's bottled water and towels on the shelf against the wall next to it. You can't miss them." Josie smiled again, and butterflies took up residence in Kelly's belly.

"Hey, you," Debby called from her chair at one of the game tables where she sat with her partner, Alex, and a couple Kelly didn't recognize. Alex's dog lay on the floor at her feet, nose to nose with a dachshund.

She waved to Debby before turning back to Josie. "Thanks, Josie. The hot tub will be my first stop after I drop off my suitcase. This lodge is beautiful, by the way." She returned Josie's smile, pleased by the flicker of interest reflected back.

"Thanks. My grandfather built it, as well as the cabins. My grandmother's on the couch." Josie motioned with her chin toward a regal looking elderly woman seated on one end of a well-worn leather couch. Her bright brown eyes reflected intelligence and her smooth skin, a shade darker than Josie's, held a healthy glow. A cane leaned on the armrest next to her and Jaylin's fluffy dog, Railroad, rested her head in her lap.

"It's a good thing you allow dogs here." Kelly chuckled. "I'm not sure any of my friends would've come if you didn't."

"You might be right. I'd say nine out of ten inquiries I get from callers is about my pet policy. I love dogs, so it's all good. I just need to make sure they're kept under control for the few people who dislike them. I've introduced my grandmother to everyone already. Do you want to meet her?"

"Sure."

Josie led the way over. "Nooko, this is Kelly Newton. Kelly, this is my grandmother, Ruth Patterson."

Kelly took her hand in hers, resisting the urge to check her pulse. It would take a while to unwind and leave work behind.

"It's good to meet you, Kelly. I hope you have a wonderful stay here with us."

"Thank you. I'm sure I will. I'm already enjoying the fireplace." She turned to Josie. "Nooko?"

"Nookomis is the Ojibwe word for grandmother. I couldn't pronounce it when I was a kid, so I called her Nooko. Still do." Josie shrugged and smiled at Nooko, who smiled back at her with obvious affection.

"Ah. I used to call my grandmother Gram, most likely for the same reason. I'm going to drop my suitcase off and freshen up a bit. I'll see you later, Ruth." Kelly liked the woman's gentle energy and easy smile. It would be nice to talk to her more during her stay.

"I'll walk you to your cabin," Josie said.

Kelly stopped to say hello to Debby and meet the other couple at the table before following Josie out the front door. Again, she was struck by the beauty of the area. "Wow. This is a gorgeous view. I love the way the sun sparkles on the water like diamonds."

"Sit for a minute. It's the perfect time of day for it." Josie gestured to one of the rockers. "In the winter, the entire expanse of water is frozen solid, and many of the island residents create a path lined with evergreens for snowmobiles to travel to and from Canada. It's called the Ice Bridge to Canada. Quite a sight."

Kelly watched the emotions play across Josie's face as she gazed at the water. Pride, serenity, and a fleeting sadness that surprised her. She studied her profile for a moment, stirred by her intensity. This woman was obviously intelligent and strong. And quite beautiful. The island was a verdant paradise, but why was she living here alone with her grandmother? *But maybe she's not alone. Her partner might be working or out of town.* She'd only just met Josie Harlow but was already seeing her as a mystery she yearned to solve. She rocked a few minutes, enjoying the quietude until fatigue from the long drive replaced her curiosity. "It's a beautiful evening, but the trip up here just caught up with me. I only stopped once to eat a sandwich and fill up my gas tank. Combined with the stress of work, it's kicked my butt."

"Come on. I'll show you to your cabin." Josie grabbed her suitcase and carried it effortlessly off the porch.

Kelly suppressed an unexpected desire to take Josie's hand as they strolled toward the cabin. She'd passed the row of cabins when she drove in and knew which one was hers by the hand-carved wooden numbers above each door, but she welcomed the opportunity to spend some time alone with the charismatic owner.

The well-designed small space inside the cabin felt cozy rather than cramped. The kitchen window located above the sink offered a clear view of the water through a few saplings sprouting spring leaves. She peered inside the bathroom as she passed it. Clean and dry. Her fears abated, she rolled her suitcase to one of the two bedrooms. A smaller version of the dream catchers in the entryway hung on the wall above the head of the double bed. The patchwork quilt and matching throw rug and curtains looked handmade. A small reading lamp sat on a wooden nightstand wrapped in birch bark on one side of the bed. She could imagine sleeping soundly encased in the room's tranquility. "This is a fantastic little cabin. You obviously take good care of the place."

"Thank you. The property has been in my family for years. Generations, really. My mother made the dream catchers. She insisted each bed had to have at least one." Josie's tone softened and turned wistful when she spoke of her mother. "I hope all your dreams here are pleasant ones. As well as your experiences. I'll leave you to unpack now. Check back with me if you can't find the hot tub." Josie stopped at the doorway and smiled, looking like she wanted to say more, before turning and walking out the door.

Kelly organized her toiletries into the small bathroom cabinet, hung her clothes in the tiny closet, and left the rest of her clothes in her suitcase before putting on her swimsuit under a pair of sweatpants and T-shirt. She filled the miniature refrigerator with the few items she'd brought and made a mental note to ask Josie for the location of the nearest grocery store. *Time to go soak in the hot tub.*

"Hey, Kelly," Kristen and Debby both called to her as she passed through the huge room in the lodge.

"Hi, guys. I'm headed to the hot tub. Anyone want to join me?"

"Nah. You enjoy it, but stop by on your way back. We're planning our adventures for tomorrow." Debby grinned and waved her on before turning back to the numerous pamphlets spread across the table.

Kelly hoped Josie would overhear and show up, though she hadn't been with her group of friends. *She's the owner. She's not going to jump into the tub with me.* She'd obviously been single too long, if she was fantasizing about someone she'd met twenty minutes ago. She settled into the tub and allowed the hot bubbling water to relax away the stress of nursing schedules and staff meetings. Her thoughts strayed to her friends and their enthusiasm. She'd settle in with them later. Her first priority was to unwind and try to relax. She allowed herself a brief image of Josie beneath her, supporting her in the frothing warmth. *This is not relaxing!* She shifted to distract herself and enjoy the feeling of having no patients to assess and nowhere to be but where she was. She sighed, finally feeling the tension abate.

CHAPTER SEVEN

Josie rose from her stool to stand by the door wall overlooking Sturgeon Bay. Her new guests had looked content when she'd checked on them, and Kelly had been heading to the hot tub. She took a moment to try to figure out her intense reaction to Kelly. She never allowed herself to feel anything more than sexual desire for a woman, so she wondered what it was about Kelly that had her wanting to know her, to take the time to find out who she was inside. *I've only known her for an hour.* She shook off her pondering to absorb a moment of peace.

The towering pines and hardwoods would obscure the panoramic view when the leaves fully matured, but now she gazed past them, absorbing the serenity of the scene. It'd been a few weeks since she'd been able to take time to relax in her studio to sketch or indulge in the craft her mother had taught her of creating dream catchers. She'd never put her things on display in the main lodge, though, preferring to allow her mother's memory to take center stage.

Her few sketches of the island's flora and fauna, as well as her miniature dream catchers, were relegated to the walls of the studio. Once her mother's sanctuary, and now hers. She lost herself for a few minutes in memories of her mother in the seat she'd just vacated, head bent over her task, concentrating on each step of her process. She kept the room off-limits to all visitors, just as her mom had. It was her refuge, a place to unwind and nourish her imagination. Her thoughts strayed to her latest lodgers, and she wondered if Kelly would like her creations. The idea surprised her. Kelly was a beautiful woman, but her attraction to her could never be acted on. She wouldn't take a chance of tarnishing the name of Harlow's by the Bay by hitting on one of her lodgers. Her fantasies of her blond hair splayed across her pillows and her intelligent blue eyes sparkling up at her, darkening as they kissed, would have to stay in this room. Along with her own handiwork. She locked the door and headed to check on firewood.

The sun was starting to fade by the time she finished restacking the wood on the rack. She had no idea how the wood pile had fallen over, but it brought back the memory of the upended porch rockers. She stomped back to the lodge with an armload of logs, unable to shake the feeling that something was off.

The group had pushed two tables together and six of her seven guests sat talking and laughing, with her grandmother seated in the middle. She placed a couple large pieces of wood on the waning fire to revive it before heading to the jovial group. "Can I get anyone anything? You all appear to be having fun." She wiped her hands on her jeans, remembering she'd just stacked firewood and not wanting to look grubby.

"Hello, dear. We just finished a round of hot chocolate, so I don't need any." Nooko looked to the women seated on either side of her, and they all nodded their assent. "I've been telling your friends stories about the island and the powwow coming up next weekend. We should all plan on going."

"Absolutely, Nooko. There're flyers in the pile of information I gave you guys. The powwow is one of the most popular events of the year around here." Josie grinned, pleased her grandmother felt relaxed with their guests. Maybe it would convince her to stay. "Is Kelly still in the hot tub?"

"Yeah," Kristen said. "She's got one at home, and she spends most of her evenings in it."

"I'll go check on her. Holler if you need anything." Josie stopped in her office to make notes regarding the dates and times of the upside down rockers and the upset firewood. She didn't notice the envelope on the floor until she turned to leave. She opened it carefully.

It isn't much fun having to restack firewood, is it?

She put the note in the safe with shaking fingers, chills raising the hair on her arms. She'd call the conservation officer in the morning, but her concern over Kelly in the hot water of the whirlpool urged her to hurry. Debby had said Kelly had a hot tub at home, but she was responsible for everyone staying here, and she wanted no accidents. She stepped into the tub area and swallowed a surge of panic. Concern over the note intensified her anxiety. She had a hard time believing only mischievous kids would leave a note. She raced to the edge of the tub, scanning every inch of water.

"Looking for me?" Kelly stepped out of the corner of the room with a towel wrapped around her. "This is a fantastic space, Josie. I love the composite decking. And the bench around the spa is great."

Josie took a deep breath, trying not to show how worried she'd been. "Thank you. I spent a lot of time researching the best way to build this. I wanted it to be easy to get in and out, comfortable, and safe. I'm glad it works well for you." Now that she'd verified Kelly's safety, she took the time to enjoy the view. She'd pulled her hair back into a ponytail and pinned it up, away from her neck. Josie resisted the urge to touch her tongue to each water droplet, or perhaps bead of sweat, trickling down her neck to her bare shoulders. She noted the straps of her bathing suit, grateful for the extra layer which made it easier to dispel the image of her naked body beneath the oversized towel. Before her imagination moved to puckered nipples and smooth warm skin, she stepped back toward the door. "I'll leave you alone. I just wanted to check on you."

"Thank you. I'm a nurse, so I can usually gauge my limits. I'll walk back with you and see what my friends are up to. I left them strategizing for the day tomorrow." Kelly unwrapped her towel and bent to dry her legs. She draped it around her neck and slipped on a pair of deck shoes.

Josie swallowed hard and held the door open for Kelly. *She's gorgeous.*

"Are you going to join us now?" Debby stood with her hands on her hips and spoke from across the room.

"You better go get in on the plans. Just call the main phone if you need anything. It rings in my room, too. Have fun." Josie stopped to check on Nooko, who appeared to be having the time of her life, before heading to her office.

"Hello. Anybody here?"

Josie jumped at the unexpected male voice and hurried to the front desk. "Mr. Bernstein. Good evening. What can I do for you?" She felt her heartbeat in her ears, and she willed her jaw to relax.

"I've come back to see if you're ready to sell yet. I can make you a hefty offer." He leaned on the counter looking relaxed and confident.

"Thank you, but I'm still not interested in selling, and I'll be getting the authorities involved if there're any more of your pranks or threatening notes. The Mulligan place off South Alton road is for sale. I can give you his number." Josie hoped he'd take the number and leave. She wanted to get her nooko settled in for the night, and she wanted this guy far away from her land.

"Nope. I want *this* property, and I don't know nuthin' about any pranks. Think about changin' your mind. I'll be back."

"Wait." Josie refrained from reaching for him. "Can you at least tell me why you want my property so badly?"

She didn't think he was going to answer until he stopped with his hand on the door handle and turned back toward her.

"Let's just say that it'll be worth your while to sell to me. My reasons are my own." He pulled the door open and walked out, letting the door slam closed behind him.

Josie locked the door and hung up the closed sign. Apprehension over Abe's visit compelled her to double-check the lock on her safe and deadbolt her office before dimming the lights for the night. She'd stop in town the next day, pick up some motion sensing security lights, and report him to the conservation officer, who she knew would contact the sheriff's department.

She headed to the lodge, determined not to let her guests know she was rattled. "Ready to turn in for the night, Nooko?" Josie stood between her grandmother's chair and Kelly's. She caught the faint scent of coconut shampoo. Kelly must have showered after the hot tub, and now she'd have the fantasy of running her hands over her soapy body to dispel.

"I'm a bit worn out, but I love all of your energy." Nooko addressed the group as she grasped her cane and stood.

Kelly reached to take her hand. "We'll see you in the morning, Ruth. Sleep well."

Josie wrestled back tears when the group of women all stood to give her a hug good night. It looked as though her nooko was going to be just fine here. *I can deal with some jerk. What matters is my dream coming true and taking care of my family.* She hooked her arm through her grandmother's. Nothing would stand in her way.

❖

The group quieted and settled on the couch and leather chairs to enjoy the fireplace after Ruth and Josie left.

"So, what adventures did you guys decide on for tomorrow?" Kelly asked. She propped her feet up on a footstool.

"I'm trying to talk everyone into going walleye fishing," Maria said. Her dark eyes sparkled.

"And Debby and I want to check out the hiking trails," Alex said.

"I wouldn't mind checking out the trails, too. I'm sure to get some great photos." Jaylin looked to Kristen as she spoke.

"I don't suppose I'd get away with spending two weeks in a hot tub, huh?" Kelly grinned.

"No," her friends answered in unison. Conversation continued as they talked about the variety of options. There was plenty to do, but if all they did was hang out and talk, Kelly would have been fine. It felt amazing to know she didn't have to think about anything but relaxing for the next two weeks.

"Everything all right out here?" Josie grinned as she strode back into the room.

Kelly laughed at her friends' exuberance and to cover her reaction to Josie. She'd exchanged her jeans and sweatshirt for a T-shirt and a pair of sweatpants. She looked relaxed and even sexier, and Kelly ached to run her hands over the soft-looking material covering her firm rear. She willed herself not to stare at her breasts when she sat across from her. "Everything's fine. They"—she pointed—"don't think I should spend my whole vacation in a hot tub."

"I have to agree because you'd miss out on all the island has to offer. I hope you plan on attending the powwow with us, at least," Josie said.

"Oh, yeah. It's next weekend, right?"

"Yep. It'll be fun." Josie gave her a small smile. "Well, I'm going to make my last walk around the place. So, I'll wish you all pleasant dreams, and if you need anything, please call." Josie stood and started toward the front door.

"Wait. If you don't mind, I'm ready to call it a day. May I walk out with you?" Kelly asked.

"Of course. I'll walk you to your cabin."

There was a chorus of good-byes and gentle teasing about turning in early, along with promises to eat breakfast together. It was true, Kelly was tired, but she also wanted a moment with Josie.

Kelly pulled her denim jacket tighter around herself as they walked to the cabin, the late spring chill making her shiver. "Thanks for letting me join you. I wanted a chance to let you know how nice I find this place. I'll admit I was skeptical when Debby first told me about it, but it's great."

"Thank you, Kelly. I appreciate your input. So, you're a nurse. Where do you work?"

"In a nursing home in Novi. I've been there twenty years."

"You must enjoy what you do to have stayed there so long."

"I do, I love being a nurse, and it's a good nursing home." She didn't feel it necessary to get into how overworked and understaffed they were.

"I just read in our local paper there's a new rehabilitation center slash nursing home opening here on the island. A pretty big one, too."

"I actually know about that one. I'll be working there temporarily to help train the staff. I start right after my vacation here. They seem to be popping up on every corner these days. I guess it's due to our aging population." Kelly smiled, thinking about Ruth.

"I certainly hope that's not the only reason you came to stay here." Josie looked concerned.

"No, not at all. It was just a lucky coincidence." Kelly placed her hand on Josie's arm to try to reassure her. "I planned on this vacation before I was reassigned."

Josie didn't pull away. "Good. I know there're quite a few families on the island with elders in need of help with their care. My grandmother agreed to stay with me for a few weeks, but I'm not sure she'll be able to live on her own much longer." A frown creased Josie's smooth forehead.

"Do you have any siblings who might be able to help?" Kelly removed her hand and put it in her pocket.

"No. I'm an only child. I've lived on the island most of my life. I left to go to college when I was eighteen, but moved back to help with the cabins after graduation."

"I'm fortunate, I suppose. My parents are doing well in Florida, and I've got a brother in Lansing and a sister getting ready to go to college." Kelly wasn't entirely sure what else to say. It wasn't a situation she'd have to deal with, though she dealt with plenty of families at work in a similar situation. "Here's my cabin. Thanks for the company, and I guess I'll see you tomorrow." Kelly hesitated, confused by the desire to kiss Josie good night.

"Yes. I'll see you tomorrow. Sleep well." Josie walked backward for a few steps, her expression unreadable, before she turned and waved over her shoulder.

"You, too." Kelly watched Josie as she turned and walked out of sight. *Why is she still single?* Kelly knew it was her wishful thinking that Josie was single. She very well might not be, but she hadn't seen anyone other than Ruth at the lodge. Josie's lover could be away, or maybe they didn't live together. She decided speculation would get her nowhere. She'd just have to ask Josie. She was done dating unavailable women. She wanted someone to settle down with and share a life. She sat on the small couch in her cabin and propped her feet up on the coffee table. Longing for Josie to sit next to her and snuggle was fruitless fantasy until she found out if she was available. She picked up a book and set it back down. Between the long drive, the hot tub, and the stirrings Josie elicited, she was pooped. It had been a good day and she intended to enjoy every one of her vacation days. She turned up the heater in the living room and got ready for bed.

CHAPTER EIGHT

Kelly checked her GPS for the third time before disconnecting it in frustration and pulling into a gas station to find a map. "Hello?" She leaned to search the empty space behind the counter. "Is anybody here?" She turned back toward the entry door at the sound of the bell.

"Well, hello." A tall auburn-haired woman, lean and hot in a beige uniform, stood grinning at her from the door. She stood three inches taller than her in her leather work boots. "Luke's out back. He'll return in a minute." She offered her right hand and Kelly took it. "My name's Barbara, but please call me Barb."

"It's good to meet you, Barb. I'm Kelly, and I'm looking for a map." She released Barb's hand to turn and look for Luke.

"I'm sure Josie had maps of the island for you at the lodge, didn't she?"

"How did you know I was staying there?" Kelly shifted from foot to foot, slightly uncomfortable with Barb's familiarity.

"Drummond Island might be two hundred fifty square miles, but there're only about a thousand year-round residents, and I'm one of only a few conservation officers. I pretty much know all of the rental property owners, and I guessed you're probably from her group." Barb flashed a smile, softening her angular features. "Where do you need to go?"

"It's a new nursing home opening in June."

"Ah. Just keep heading east on 134, the road you came in on. It'll be called East Channel Road, too. You'll see the facility on the right just before you get to the road to the airport."

"Thank you. I planned to use my GPS, which ended up sending me on a wild goose chase."

"Yeah. It happens often on the island. Put in the airport's address and you'll be fine."

Kelly left the station without meeting Luke, but she wouldn't soon forget the sexy conservation officer. She began to wonder about Drummond Island as she walked back to her car. First Josie and now Barb. Two of the sexiest women she'd met in a long time, and she had to drive three hundred and fifty miles to find them.

She drove another ten minutes before she saw the facility's large granite sign. Kelly understood why the company had chosen this site as she followed the winding driveway to the one-story brick building nestled in a stand of pines. The area exuded serenity. She took a moment to appreciate the fresh air and peacefulness before proceeding to the entryway. The doors opened to an enormous, fully carpeted common room, with a grand piano positioned in one corner. Comfortable-looking upholstered couches and chaise lounges faced the piano, and a large screen TV, affixed to the wall, was easily visible from anywhere in the room. A number of tables with chairs strategically placed for easy access filled in the middle with plenty of room for wheelchairs.

She continued past the unoccupied desk she presumed would be the check-in point for visitors, and the scent of new carpeting faded as she wandered through the empty tiled hallways. She peeked inside the swinging doors leading to the kitchen and noted the stainless steel appliances. *No expense spared here.* The empty hall, lined with empty rooms on either side, had a well-positioned wide hand rail on both sides and nurses' or aides' stations located on each end. The building's design consisted of two squares with an adjoining hallway. The rehab portion of the facility on one side and the long-term care portion on the other. She wondered how long it would take to fill the numerous rooms.

She retraced her path toward the maintenance room, disturbed by the lack of personnel. *Where's the security in this place?* She pulled out her phone when she returned to her car and tried Janis's number. She'd been warned about the spotty cell phone service, and the warnings held true. She was supposed to be on vacation anyway. She'd deal with the unlocked doors when the time came. The building was new and clean and appeared to be ready for residents. She found herself looking forward to the challenge of starting up a new facility. She'd be part of bringing safe, reliable care to those who needed it. She drove back to the lodge feeling optimistic and with thoughts of a soak in the hot tub.

The first thing Kelly saw when she pulled into the parking area was Josie, who was facing one of the cabins and waving her arms over her head.

"Hey, Kelly." Josie trotted toward her.

"Hi, Josie." Kelly unsuccessfully tried to ignore her solid body and the slight sway of her breasts.

"I just wanted to let you know I've installed a few security lights around the place this morning. I'll let everyone know when I see them, but I'd appreciate it if you'd let them know when you talk to them."

"Sure. Must be what all your gesticulating out here was about."

"Gesticulating, huh?" She chuckled. "Yeah. I'm testing the range of these things."

"Have fun. We're all meeting in the lodge soon to review our plans for the day, so I'll tell the group. First, I'm heading to the hot tub."

"Enjoy. Oh…by the way…there's no spotlight in the hot tub area. Only two around the outside perimeter."

She smiled and Kelly's breath caught. She really needed to find out if Josie was single. She didn't pay much attention to the cruiser pulling into the lot as she went into her cabin to change. Thoughts of the new facility ran through her mind, and as much as she was trying not to think about work, she couldn't help it. A long soak could clear her head and leave space for the fun she could have today with her friends. Fun was something she hadn't had in way too long.

❖

"I don't know where he came from, Barb." Josie and the conservation officer sat in Josie's office. "He only told me his name, Abe Bernstein, and he wanted to buy the place. He said he used to hunt with someone named Jack who owned this place. I told him I didn't know who Jack was, and I was the owner. Then he left in a huff. When he came back the second time, I told him again that I didn't want to sell and mentioned the Mulligan place for sale. He said he wanted this property but didn't say why. He gives me the creeps."

"Huh. I wonder if he's looking for Jack Moor. He used to own the hardware store in town, but he sold out years ago. I'll certainly keep an eye out for anybody suspicious, but it'd be a good idea to make a report with the police. They can send a patrol by a couple of times a week for you." Barb sat in a chair opposite Josie and rested an ankle on her knee.

"Sounds good. Abe also said that it would be 'worth my while' to sell to him. He's an oddball."

"What were the dates you found the disruptions?" She pulled a notepad and pencil out of her shirt pocket and made notes. "Got it. I'll make sure the state police have this information. On a lighter note, congratulations on your first group here."

"Thanks. They just arrived yesterday, but they're a great bunch. My grandmother loves them."

"Kelly sure is a looker. Do you know anything about her?" Barb lowered her foot and leaned toward Josie.

"Not much. I know she's a nurse, and she's here alone with a group of friends. When'd you see her?" Josie frowned.

"This morning. I ran into her at Luke's gas station. She was looking for the new nursing home up on 134. I guess it makes sense if she's a nurse." Barb stood and put her notepad away. "I'd better get back to work. I'll be sure to keep an eye out for anything suspicious for you."

"Thanks. I'll walk you to your car. Hey, don't forget the powwow this weekend." Josie waved as Barb drove away. Her unbidden reaction to Barb's interest in Kelly bordered on protective or possessive, maybe jealous, and was totally unlike her. She shook off the unfamiliar reaction and headed to the lodge to check on Nooko.

❖

Kelly stepped behind the privacy screen to change into her jeans and sweatshirt. The warm water had relaxed her to the point of grogginess, so she splashed her face with cool water from her water bottle before heading to the lodge. Ruth sat in one of the leather chairs facing Josie on the couch.

"Where is everyone?" she asked.

Josie indicated the empty seat next to her. "I don't know. Nooko and I've been here drinking tea and talking about the powwow. We haven't seen anyone."

Kelly took Ruth's hand and squeezed gently. *Warm.* "It's good to see you again, Ruth."

"It's good to see you, too, Kelly. Did you sleep well last night?"

"Like a baby. I love how dark and quiet it is here." She sat on the opposite end of the couch from Josie and put her feet up on the coffee table. "And this sure beats working." She tipped her head back and closed her eyes. "I suppose they'll be here eventually." She opened her eyes and turned toward Josie. "Do you have plans for this afternoon?"

"Just sitting here feels pretty good for now." She toed off her shoes and propped her feet up next to Kelly's. "I finished installing motion detectors on the parking lot and porch lights today. Let me know if they disturb you, please."

"Sure. You've been busy. You put in security lighting, huh?" Kelly wondered if Josie was worried about something specific. It seemed like an awfully safe place, out in the middle of nothing as it was.

"Yes. It was something I'd planned to do weeks ago, but I just didn't get to it. It lowers the price of my insurance, too."

"Ah. Makes sense." She closed her eyes and rested her head on the back of the couch, but restlessness soon had her shifting again. "I didn't drive all this way to sit around. As good as this feels, I'm going to take a walk to the water. I haven't seen it up close yet." Kelly sat up and bent to put her shoes back on. She couldn't remember where the girls had said they'd go today, but she was okay with being on her own.

"Take Kelly on a tour, honey," Ruth said. "Show her the boats and the fish cleaning hut. And don't forget the path along the water by the leaning pine."

"The leaning pine?" Kelly asked.

"It's an old pine tree grown out over the water. Good idea, Nooko. Will you be okay here alone?"

"I'll be fine. Your friends will be here soon. I'll keep them company." Ruth waved them away.

"I'll pass on the fish cleaning hut," Kelly whispered.

Josie chuckled. "No problem."

Kelly slid her hands into her jean pockets, surprised to again want to grab Josie's hand as they walked. She looked forward to seeing the sights Ruth had been so excited about, and pushed aside the unfamiliar feelings. They could be dealt with later.

Chapter Nine

"This is gorgeous." Kelly stepped over a fallen branch on the path as she and Josie reached the water's edge. The water sparkled in the late morning sunshine, and she watched a few small fishing boats bob on the gentle waves. "It's peaceful." She took a deep breath, catching the scent of fish and fresh water grasses.

"Yeah, it is. I never get enough of it."

Kelly turned to Josie and caught her pensive gaze. "You said you grew up on this island. Did you always live on this land?"

"Pretty much. We lived in a small Indian hutment for a few years after I was born. But we moved to this lodge when my grandfather finished building it. I only have vague memories of the Ojibwe community." Josie smiled and pointed toward a small bench Kelly hadn't noticed nestled in the brush.

The view was even better from the new spot, and as they sat quietly, Kelly had the surreal feeling of being transported back in time to when canoes lined the wooded shore. "I wasn't sure what to expect when Debby suggested this vacation. I just wanted to support a lesbian-owned establishment and get away for a while. I had no idea this gem existed."

"Had you never heard of Drummond Island?"

"Oh yes. But I always thought of it as far away up north where they get five feet of snow. I guess I've pretty much lived in my own little world of work and riding my horse." She shifted on the seat and her leg nestled against Josie's.

Josie glanced at their legs but didn't move away. "Where do you ride your horse?"

"There's a fairground near my house where I ride in barrel racing and gymkhana events. Debby and Kristen participate as well. I love it."

"So, you're a nurse who loves to ride her horse and...lives alone? No one special in your life?"

Kelly hesitated, surprised at the personal question, but intrigued. "No. No one special. I was going to ask you the same thing. Why do you live here alone with your grandmother?"

Josie chuckled. "I'm totally single and have no plans to change."

Kelly stifled her unexpected disappointment. She wanted to know, and now she did. Josie was single but unavailable. "No desire to find a love to spend the rest of your life with?"

"None whatsoever. Is that what you're looking for?" Josie's tone held only curiosity, no judgment.

"It is. I love my horse, and I love my friends, but I feel there's a piece missing. I want someone to come home to after work. Someone special to feel next to me in bed and to wake up with in the morning. Someone to share a love and a life." She scanned the expanse of water and wondered for the umpteenth time if maybe she was expecting too much. "Don't you ever get lonely?"

"I'm too busy to get lonely. I've spent my life either working at the cabins or going to school. I've dated some, but found I'm not relationship material. You ready to head back? Your friends might be looking for you." Josie stood, surprising Kelly with her abrupt withdrawal. *I guess that subject's off-limits.*

"You're right. Thanks for showing me all this. It's nearly as good as the hot tub." Kelly took one more look over the water before following Josie back to the lodge. When they got back, she decided to head to her cabin for a minute or two to chill out. She'd kind of hoped for a connection with Josie, and now that she knew that was out of the question, she wanted to push away the defeated feeling before she rejoined the group. *It's not like I've lost a soul mate. Geez.*

She smiled at Josie when she went her own way, hoping she didn't look as disappointed as she felt.

❖

The group of women had pushed three tables together and sat on either side with Nooko on one end.

Josie stopped to watch the interaction for a moment after Kelly went to her cabin and wondered if she would be back to join her friends. She shook off a cloak of melancholy, realizing that even if Kelly wasn't a guest at Harlow's by the Bay, she'd have to keep her at arm's length.

There was no way she'd get involved even for a night with someone set on commitment. There was no *one and only true love* for her. Kelly was sexy and enticing, but totally off-limits.

She fought against the bombarding memories. She understood about missing pieces. Her own anguish at the abyss left by the loss of her mother barely compared to the devastation it caused to her father. The love they'd shared and all their future plans had been snatched away in an instant by a senseless accident. She wouldn't take a chance of living through such loss. If she never allowed herself to fall in love, she'd never have to go through the pain of losing it. Or of putting someone through the devastation of losing her. Loneliness she could live with; that pain of loss, she couldn't.

She concentrated on her other lodgers and her nooko. "Hi all." She stepped behind her grandmother and rested her hands on her shoulders. "Looks as if you're all enjoying yourselves."

"Did you have a nice walk, Joslyn?" Nooko smiled the innocent smile Josie recognized when she was holding something back or plotting something.

"I did, and Kelly loved the leaning pine. Thanks for suggesting it." She ignored Nooko's sly smile.

"You saw Kelly?" Debby asked.

"Yeah. She was in the hot tub earlier. I took her by the water, and then she went back to her cabin. By the way, I wanted to let you all know I installed a few security lights on the property. None in the hot tub area but around it, and day and night sensors on the porch lights, so please let me know if they bother you."

"Oh, we will," Kristen said. "So far everything's great. We're going into town tonight to one of the restaurants you recommended. The ten percent discount coupon you gave us is great."

"I'll go bang on Kelly's door and let her know what time we're leaving. Be right back." Debby kissed Alex lightly before heading out the door.

"Are you comfortable, Nooko?" Josie worried her grandmother was pushing herself to try to help at the expense of her own comfort.

"Oh, yes. I'm enjoying everyone's company. Did you know Jaylin's a veterinarian? And Debby's a pharmacist and does barrel racing. And Dana and Maria own their own businesses, like you. I'm getting to know everyone, dear. Why don't you join us?"

"Maybe I will later. Right now, I'm going to stop in the office. Just call if you need anything." Josie appreciated the group being so kind to her nooko, but she doubted they'd want her around all day, every day. She'd need to find something to occupy her.

Josie checked the locks on the doors and checked for any signs of tampering with her safe. The note from Abe and his visits disturbed her. She couldn't figure out why he wouldn't take no for an answer. She couldn't prove he was responsible for the upturned chairs and tipped-over firewood, but she was convinced he was behind the incidents.

She stopped at the two empty cabins to make sure they were ready for the occupants arriving Saturday, and she hoped this group was as easy as Kelly's. From the front, the cabins looked to be in good shape, she walked to the back door of the first one and froze. The bottom corner pane of the multipaned door window was broken out. She pushed the unlocked door open and fleetingly thought perhaps she should call for help. She surmised there'd be no reason for anyone to harm her, and it could've been bored kids creating mischief. She'd have to replace the window before Saturday, though. She shouted as she entered, just in case, but froze in shock when she looked around. The place was a mess. The kitchen drawers had been pulled out and set on the floor, their contents strewn from one end of the kitchen to the other. The plates were removed from the cupboards and spread over the kitchen table, though thankfully they hadn't been broken. The bedsheets and covers had been taken off the beds and thrown to the floor. She didn't see anything taken, only messed up. The unbroken plates set haphazardly on the table were weird, and the drawers had been set on the floor, not flung and destroyed. *Very odd.* She hurried to her office to call the police and Barb before grabbing her camera to head back to take pictures. It was early evening before she returned to the lodge after taking plenty of photos. The police had said to leave things alone until they could come out the next morning, so she had.

Nooko sat alone in one of the chairs by the fireplace. A healthy fire blazed spreading warmth throughout the room. She gave a silent thanks to whoever stoked it before leaving for dinner. "Hey, Nooko. Everyone gone?"

"Oh, hello, dear. Yes, they just left. They asked me to go with them. Can you imagine? I thanked them, but I knew you had baked chicken for us tonight. Can we eat now?" Her nooko stood and grabbed her cane.

"Let's eat out here tonight." The temperature had dropped outside and the fire felt heavenly after spending time in the cool cabin.

She filled their plates and relaxed with her nooko.

She washed dishes and cleaned up after dinner before allowing herself to reflect on the damage to one of her cabins. She made sure Nooko was settled in front of the fireplace before she went to her office. The vandalism could certainly have been done by kids, but the more she thought about it, the more she considered it the work of Abe. He'd denied any pranks when she'd confronted him, but he would. Even if she could prove he was here, probably the most he could be charged with was trespassing and maybe breaking and entering for the cabin. She reviewed the pictures she'd taken and locked them away in the safe before locking up and heading to bed.

CHAPTER TEN

No. I didn't find anything missing. Whoever did this just tossed things around. It's what makes me think about mischievous teenagers. But I believe you have a note in your files about a man named Abe Bernstein who I believe may be responsible for this. I'd appreciate it if you look into it." Josie gave a statement to the police officer, hoping he'd hurry. She wanted to finish readying the two empty cabins for her upcoming lodgers, but she hadn't touched the mess or fixed the broken window in fear of disturbing any evidence. She fidgeted and waited for him to finish his notes. She worried Kelly's group might return from their outing and see the police car in the lot.

"I'll file this report and make sure we send a cruiser out to patrol daily. Let us know if you have any more trouble." He gave her a copy of the signed paperwork before leaving.

Josie breathed a sigh of relief and quickly replaced the broken glass pane as soon as she got to the cabin. Nooko had told her the couple with the dachshund had gone fishing and the others had taken the other two dogs hiking and swimming. She supposed Kelly had gone hiking as well, but she'd taken her own car. She allowed herself a short fantasy of joining Kelly in the hot tub when she returned. She'd never imagined anyone loving the hot tub as much as she did, but Kelly's enthusiasm for it even beat her own. She continued the daydream of bubbling water and Kelly stretched beneath her writhing in orgasm for a few more minutes before getting back to work. A little harmless fantasy couldn't hurt as long as she kept it as only a fantasy.

She took a break for lunch and returned to the lodge to check on Nooko. She went to the kitchen first, thinking she might be fixing sandwiches, but she was nowhere to be seen. She checked her bedroom and bathroom, quickening her pace as memories of finding her on the floor surfaced. She opened the door to the hot tub area puzzled by the sounds of laughter drifting out of the room. She peeked in the door to see Kelly standing in the middle of the six-person tub supporting Nooko, who floated on her belly giggling. Both women laughed as Nooko splashed and kicked. Kelly glanced up at her and winked, and a flood of longing flowed from her head to her toes.

"You guys are missing lunch, you know." Josie stood with her hands on her hips in mock annoyance. "I'm making turkey sandwiches to go with fresh coleslaw. You're welcome to join us, Kelly. I'll be in the kitchen." She grinned and shook her head as she left. The excitement at the thought of sharing a meal with Kelly took her unawares. And the look of innocent joy on Nooko's face was something she didn't remember seeing in a very long time. It made her heart warm. It wasn't long before they joined her.

"This is great. Thanks for inviting me." Kelly pulled a chair out for Nooko before sitting at one of the tables in the lodge.

"You're welcome. Thanks for entertaining Nooko."

"It wasn't entertainment, dear." Nooko spoke, looking serious. "It was exercise. Kelly's a nurse, you know, and she has a list of strength and balance movements for me to try."

"That's great, Nooko. You'll have to show them to me so I can help you when Kelly goes home." She set out paper plates and a tray of sandwiches on the table. "Help yourself." She put a sandwich on one of the plates and cut it in half before placing it in front of her grandmother.

"How come you're not out fishing or hiking with the others, Kelly?" Josie asked.

Kelly scooped some coleslaw onto her plate and furrowed her brow. "I'm not into fishing, but I love the idea of floating on the water with my face to the sun, cooled by a soft breeze. I could get into lying back gently rocking with the waves, listening to the lapping of the water against the side of a boat."

Josie squashed the picture in her mind of Kelly lying with her arms stretched and her head in Josie's lap as the warm tendrils of sunlight skimmed over her naked body, the ebb and flow motion of the boat matching their rising passions. She cleared her throat and squirmed in her chair. "Sounds pretty nice to me."

"Me, too." Nooko smiled, looking wistful. "I wouldn't mind a little boat ride."

"Let's go after lunch. It's a beautiful afternoon, and your group's only using one of the boats." Josie looked at Kelly, thrilled at her smile and enthusiastic nod. It had been a spontaneous offer, but they both looked so happy she'd gladly have made it again. "Good. You guys lucked out with the weather, by the way. It was rainy and cold this week last year."

Kelly grinned. "It wouldn't have mattered to me if you still had a foot of snow on the ground. Maybe not a foot of snow, but I needed a break before starting my new position at the new nursing home facility a few miles from here."

"It's a long way from home for you, isn't it?" Nooko asked.

Kelly nodded and swallowed a bite before answering. "Yes, it is, but it's only temporary, and I was looking for a change, so it'll work out for the best. The company's leased a small apartment for me, so I don't have to commute."

"Does that mean you'll be close by?" Nooko sat up straight and held her fork in the air, waiting for a reply.

"Yes, I will, Ruth."

"Oh good. We'll still be able to see you, then." Nooko went back to eating as if nothing happened and everything was settled.

Josie finished her sandwich, delighted to know Kelly would still be nearby after her vacation but worried about Nooko's apparent attachment to her, given that she'd be leaving when her contract was finished. Still, it would be nice to have a new friend around. She ignored the little voice in her head that wondered if friendship was all she really wanted.

The sunlight sparkled off the clear water of the bay as Josie pushed the rowboat away from the dock. She began slow strokes with the oars, steering them along the shoreline and pointing out the vegetation as they glided across the water. She watched Kelly reach to steady Nooko when a wave rocked the boat, and Nooko grabbed the sides of her seat. She smiled a silent thank you when she caught her eye across her grandmother's head. Kelly shrugged one shoulder as if to say it's no big deal, tipped her head back to the sun, and closed her eyes. *She's beautiful.*

"Let's show Kelly the leaning pine tree from the water's side." Nooko sat up straight and pointed toward the shore ahead.

"Here we go." Josie rowed them closer to the shore and grabbed a branch overhanging the water to hold them in place.

"It's lovely out here." Kelly turned to the shore where Nooko was pointing enthusiastically. "And the pine tree is pretty cool. I love the way it supports itself with its roots and suspends over the water while reaching toward the sun. Thank you for showing me this, Ruth. Is there significance to this tree?"

"There is for me. Joslyn told me there really are some pine trees, somewhere, that lean toward the equator or something, but this one is special." Nooko's eyes sparkled as she watched the tree and continued. "It was right under there." She pointed toward one of the branches just high enough above the water for a rowboat or canoe to travel under. "That's where Harold proposed to me." Nooko tipped her head and smiled softly. She looked lost in a magnificent memory.

"That does look like the most romantic spot on the shore. I understand why you accepted his proposal."

"Oh, I didn't accept. Not right away, anyway. It was what happened after that made me say yes. He sat waiting for my answer and we started drifting away from shore. It was a lovely summer day, but the wind had picked up and he was having a hard time keeping us from floating away. He had to stand up to reach that branch to hold us in place. He was holding on to the branch for dear life while I was sitting in the boat slowly drifting away. I grabbed his legs and the boat floated out from under us." Nooko began laughing at the memory and tears rolled down her cheeks. "Well, Harold couldn't hold on to that branch any longer, and we both fell into the water fully dressed. That's when he did what he did, and I accepted his proposal of marriage." Nooko stopped talking and looked lost in her memories again.

Josie glanced at Kelly who looked as perplexed as her. "What did Grandpa do, Nooko?"

"He kissed me." Nooko pressed her fingers to her lips and closed her eyes. "Right after he dragged us out of the water to the shore. He just leaned over me and kissed me. It was our first kiss. I knew then that I would marry him and we'd spend the rest of our lives together."

Kelly took one of Nooko's hands between hers with tears on her cheeks. "Thank you for sharing that wonderful memory with me, Ruth."

"Yes, thank you, Nooko. I never heard that story." Josie pushed her words through the lump in her throat, overwhelmed by Nooko's story as well as Kelly's show of tenderness.

"Thank you for bringing me out here so I could see that spot again." Nooko sighed and gazed over the water.

"I'm going to turn us around to head back soon. I need to get the two cabins ready for our next group arriving this weekend."

"Are the new people going to be here for the powwow this weekend?"

"They're scheduled to be here, but I don't know if they're planning to go. They're a group of four from Canada." Josie guided the rowboat to the dock, stepped out, and secured it to a post with a rope before reaching for her grandmother. Kelly knelt on the seat as Nooko stood and steadied her from behind as if she'd done it a hundred times. "Thank you for your help." Josie spoke softly to Kelly as she stepped out of the boat. She concentrated on steadying Nooko to shake off the sudden flood of desire generated as their arms brushed.

CHAPTER ELEVEN

Kelly peered into the window trying to evaluate how comfortable she was going to be in the little apartment. The Realtor had told her the one-bedroom unit was available whenever she was ready. She used the key she'd been given when she stopped to sign the lease agreement to let herself in, but she was only five days into her vacation and had no intention of moving yet. She brought in her extra suitcase with her work scrubs and a few sweaters and jeans and put it in the bedroom.

She verified that the promised bedding and towels were in the closet before starting her tour, which turned out to be a short one due to the teensy rooms. She noted the apartment-sized green refrigerator and stove and lack of microwave. A small cupboard above the counter contained plates, glasses, and cups, and the two narrow drawers were filled with mismatched silverware. At least she wouldn't have to buy anything except her food. She sat on the solitary wooden chair and leaned her elbows on the scratched Formica top of the metal kitchen table. The table sat against an outside wall with a window overlooking a lush green space enhanced by a bird feeder on a shepherd's hook. She'd enjoy watching the birds, but sighed realizing she'd have to work to be comfortable there.

The fact Josie was only a short drive away lifted her spirits. Even though Josie wasn't relationship material, and she found herself having to suppress her attraction to her nearly every time they were together, they shared a comfortable, relaxed connection. Their walk along the water and short boat ride with Ruth were times when the stress of her job had totally melted away. She smiled at the memory of Ruth kicking in the hot tub and her determination to stay strong. She was an example of an elderly woman who'd likely never need a nursing home. She could be an excellent example for most of Kelly's patients. She checked the condition of the bathroom and the compact washer and dryer before she locked the door and headed back to the lodge.

She took a longer route back to spend some time alone and enjoy the scenery. She pulled off the road onto a deserted area by the water and watched the waves lapping onto the shore. She rolled down the car windows and breathed in the fresh air. She missed her horse. She'd checked in with her sister when she'd arrived on the island and was assured that everything was fine and she'd call if that changed, but Pogo was her baby. She missed him, and she had no doubt that he was missing her. In a few days, she'd be living in a little apartment, miles from home, and starting a challenging job that she hoped would turn into a rewarding experience. She felt a bit off balance and out of her comfort zone, and her inability to shake her attraction to Josie bothered her. She'd wanted a change and she got it. She'd take things a day at a time and call Tory to check on Pogo when she got back to her cabin. She turned and took the shorter way back.

"Hi, Kelly. Did you have fun exploring today?" Josie tossed a log onto the fire as she spoke. Ruth sat at her usual end of the couch with her hands toward the fireplace.

"I did. I checked out the apartment I'll be calling home soon. It's in a nice location." She couldn't think of anything more positive to say, so she poured a cup of hot chocolate and took a seat in one of the leather chairs near Ruth.

"Will you be joining us for the powwow?" Ruth asked.

"Oh, definitely. I'm looking forward to it. Is it far from here?"

"Not at all. There's a park just down the road where they set everything up. It's a beautiful wooded setting. Perfect for a powwow."

"Sounds great. I'm glad we could be here for it." Kelly sipped her hot chocolate and watched the muscles in Josie's arms as she tended the fire. Her perusal was interrupted by loud laughter and shuffling as her friends entered the lodge.

"Hey. There you are." Debby waved from across the room.

"We've got fish!" Maria set an overflowing bowl of filleted walleye on one of the tables.

"Wow. Would you like me to fry those up for you?" Josie offered.

"Oh yes. I'll help." Ruth grabbed her cane and started toward the lodge kitchen.

"I caught them all," Maria piped up from the other table. "I love your fish cleaning hut, and thank you for the offer to cook them. I certainly can help, too." She grabbed the bowl and followed Ruth into the kitchen.

Kelly moved to sit at the table next to Debby. "I thought you went hiking today."

"We did. Maria and Dana went fishing. Did you go check out your apartment?" Debby asked.

"Yep. It's small." Kelly tried to sound optimistic.

"Ah. At least it's only for a few months. And you'll be close to Josie." Debby grinned and wiggled her eyebrows.

"Josie is pretty hot." Kelly smiled. "But there can never be anything between us."

"Do you want there to be?"

"She and I have different ideas of what we want. I like her a lot, and Ruth, too. Maybe we could be friends, but nothing more."

"She seems honest and straightforward, and I like the way she looks at you." Debby reached for Kelly's hand. "Just be careful. I don't want to see you hurt."

"Thanks, Deb. I'll just enjoy my vacation and ogle her from afar. I'm going to my cabin to change before dinner. See you later." Kelly followed the longer wooded route to her cabin. She slowed her pace and breathed in the cool early evening air, taking a moment for reflection. What did she want with Josie? From Josie? She'd spent most of her vacation time so far with her and Ruth but didn't regret any of it. Was she pathetic to enjoy a relaxing soak in the hot tub and quiet time with a beautiful woman and her elder, instead of hanging out with her energy-filled, laughing friends? She didn't think so, as long as she was careful. Her draw to Josie worried her a little, if she was honest with herself. Josie was more than attractive; she was mature, intelligent, responsible, and tender with her grandmother. What she knew so far about Josie indicated she would definitely be someone she would want to date, and could possibly fall for. She continued to her cabin, resolving to enjoy the rest of her time away from work, and she'd appreciate Ruth's and Josie's company with no expectations.

She took the time to give her sister a call and check on her house and horse. Reassured that all was well at home, she dressed quickly and casually. That was another nice thing about this place. It was relaxed in a way being at home wasn't. *But then, that's what a vacation is about.* She couldn't forget this wasn't real world stuff. It was like summer camp; it would end, and they'd go their separate ways. Steadied, she returned to the lodge and sat with the others for dinner. Conversation was fun and light, and Kelly let herself simply enjoy the moment.

"This fish is fantastic. Thank you for sharing it with us, Maria," Ruth spoke from the makeshift head of the table the group had made by pushing three tables together in the lodge.

"Yeah. I agree. I haven't taken time to go fishing in over a year. I'd forgotten how good freshly caught walleye is," Josie said.

"You're welcome. I love fishing, so it was a treat for me. Tell us about the upcoming powwow, Josie."

Josie set her fork down before speaking. "The Ojibwe powwow is a spiritual event celebrating the history and life of the Native American people. You may not know, but powwows were restricted until World War Two because the dances were seen as war dances, but they're in fact an expression of the culture. There'll be all kinds of dancing, drumming, and music there."

Kelly watched Josie's dark eyes sparkle as she spoke of the event. *She's sexy when she's intense.* "Debby told me you're a descendant of the Ojibwe, right?"

"Yes. My mother was half Ojibwe." Josie glanced at Ruth and smiled. "But my grandmother is full-blooded."

"Cool." Jaylin spoke between bites.

"I can't wait to go." Kelly stood to stoke the fire.

"You don't have to do that." Josie rose but stopped when Kelly waved her hand dismissively.

"Don't be silly. You cooked the meal. The least we can do is help with some chores. I even plan to do the dishes."

"I won't argue," Josie said. "But you'll be *helping* do the dishes, if you insist. I'll not have the word spreading I make my guests work when they come here." Josie picked up a few of the empty plates from the table and took them into the kitchen.

"Is she truly worried, Ruth?" Kelly asked.

"My granddaughter worries over everything. Her mother was the same way, God rest her soul. My husband, her grandfather, built these cabins, and when he died, left them to our son-in-law, Joslyn's father." Ruth paused. "He was a good man but never recovered from his wife's death, and he made some poor financial decisions. When Joslyn inherited the cabins, she had a bit of a mess to clean up. I'm very proud of her for creating Harlow's by the Bay, and I know she'll be successful with it. Especially after meeting you all." She smiled and held Kelly's gaze.

Kelly had more questions than ever about Josie after Ruth's disclosure, but they were for Josie to answer. "I better make good on my offer. I'll see you guys later." She collected the last of the tableware and headed to KP duty.

"You really don't have to help with this, Kelly." Josie stood with her gloved hands in a sink full of hot soapy water.

"I want to. I'll dry." She picked up a dish towel from a holder on the wall and grabbed a plate from the dish rack. They worked in comfortable silence for a while. "I admire your grandmother."

Josie nodded. "She's a remarkable woman. She was a significant presence in my life as a teenager. I was upset when she and my grandfather moved south, but I couldn't blame them. My grandfather was offered a job as a manager at a large construction company in Tawas, so they had a house built and semi-retired there. Then my father and I only saw them on holidays. I visited them a couple of times when I was in college and spent a week with Nooko when my grandfather died."

Kelly refrained from pulling Josie into her arms when she saw the sorrow play across her face. She rested her hand on her shoulder instead. "I see how caring you are with her. You're a good granddaughter."

"Thank you. I know she loves me, and I love her. I'll do anything I can to keep her safe and happy." Josie took a step back, almost as though to put some distance between them. "We're done here. Let's go see what the group's up to. I'll take the garbage out on our way."

Kelly followed Josie out the kitchen through a back door. Josie put the black garbage bag into a large bin with a bolt-secured latch. The bin, located near the hot tub area, sat against the wall next to a metal door she hadn't noticed before labeled *Private*. "A storage room?" she asked.

"No. My studio. It was my mother's, but I use it now." Josie walked quickly past the door without saying anything further, and it was all Kelly could do to keep up. Josie's instant reaction to her interest in her studio even surpassed her swift response when she'd asked her about being single. She was clearly a private person, and Kelly wondered if she let anyone in.

Ruth sat alone on the couch in the expansive room when they returned, and the fire had dwindled to burning embers.

"Did the group go back to their cabins?" Kelly asked.

"They did. They asked me to tell you good night and they'd see you in the morning. It was a nice evening, wasn't it?"

"Yes, Nooko. It was. I'm glad you're enjoying our guests." Josie nestled a log on the cinders and poked the fire until it sparked to life. "I'm going to enjoy the fire a bit before I turn in. Can I get you anything?"

"I'm so full I don't think I'll need anything for a week." Ruth leaned back and rested her hands on her belly.

"I'm with you, Ruth," Kelly said. "I'm going to make a cup of tea before bed, though. You want one, Josie?"

"Sounds good. Thanks."

Kelly brought back the cups of tea and settled on the end of the couch opposite Ruth with her feet curled under her. Again, she wondered why this felt so much more comfortable than going out on the town. There wasn't much of a town to go out on, but she was fine with it. She sighed and sipped her tea.

"Are you okay, dear?" Ruth leaned toward her looking concerned.

"Oh, yes. I'm great, Ruth. I knew I needed a vacation, but I don't think I realized how much. I haven't relaxed this much in a long time."

"I'm so glad. I know Joslyn will be glad to hear it."

"Hear what?" Josie had gone to retrieve more firewood for the morning and walked in on their conversation.

"Kelly's enjoying her vacation by relaxing."

"Good. Things will get a little more exciting this weekend. We get hundreds of people streaming to the island for the powwow." Josie settled on the couch next to Kelly. Their thighs touched but neither moved away. "I'm glad you're enjoying yourself, and please let me know if there's anything you need."

"We're getting new people tomorrow, aren't we?" Ruth asked.

"Yes, Nooko. Cabins five and six will be full tomorrow," Josie said.

"A full house." Ruth grinned. "I'm ready to call it a day. What time are we heading to the event, Josie?"

"About noon. Our Canadian guests plan to be here by eleven, so I'll get them checked in and be ready to go as soon as they're in." Josie turned to address Kelly. "We can meet here at the lodge and you can follow me, if you want."

"Sounds good. I'll check with the group and find out their plans. Good night, Ruth. I'll see you tomorrow." Kelly rose, noting the cold spot where her leg had been nestled against Josie's. She walked the path to her cabin slowly, enjoying the warm night air. She looked forward to experiencing the powwow and spending some time with her friends. She had no regrets about how she'd spent her vacation so far, and she felt more rested and relaxed than she had in years. Maybe it was time to distance herself a little from unavailable Josie and play with her friends.

CHAPTER TWELVE

K elly sat on her porch sipping iced tea and enjoying the warm sunny morning while waiting for her friends to decide who was driving and how many they could fit in their car. She'd offered to drive, but her friends claimed Jaylin's vehicle had more room. They laughed and joked and discussed various versions, but since Kelly wasn't interested in piling in one car like a bunch of teenagers, they all decided it was best if Kelly just followed them. Sounds to her right drew her attention to Josie, who was helping Nooko into her SUV. Josie waved and grinned, and her belly fluttered.

"Do you want to ride with us, Kelly?"

"I'd love to. Thanks." Kelly waved to her friends, who were squeezed into one vehicle, and pointed to Josie's Jeep. She waited for their acknowledgment before she tossed her daypack into the back seat. She slid in and reached to squeeze Ruth's shoulder. "Good morning, Ruth."

"Good morning, dear."

"Thanks for offering a ride. All the others are going to follow in one car."

"Let's go celebrate life." Josie shifted the car into gear and they drove the short distance to the event with the group following close behind.

"Wow. This is amazing." Kelly jumped from the car as soon as it stopped, eager to look around. She turned in a circle, taking in the expansive open area located at the edge of the woods. White tents stood around the perimeter of the space with tables and chairs for anyone wanting to get out of the noonday sun. Dream catchers swayed in the breeze and jewelry sparkled in the light as they hung displayed on several of the tables. "Are those all for sale?"

"Mostly they are, but some folks bring their artwork to trade," Josie said. "Why don't you find us a spot to settle? The dancing's going to begin soon. We'll be right behind you."

The sound of the drum's reverberation kept pace with her heartbeat. Kelly followed the group to one of the tables under a tent and positioned their coolers and packs to claim the spot. Debby and the others took off right away to have a look around. Kelly turned to look for Josie and Ruth and gasped in surprise as Ruth exited the vehicle. She wore a beautifully beaded long black dress with rows of beads and dangling rods laced across her chest and shoulders. Another ring of beads hung just below the waist and swayed as she walked. She couldn't believe she hadn't noticed the dress in the car. It was stunning. "Ruth, you look fabulous. Is that a native type dress?" She cringed at her ignorance and hoped she hadn't offended Ruth.

Ruth laughed and her dark eyes sparkled. "It's an elder jingle dress. Just watch."

She kissed Josie on the cheek before turning and stepping in time to the drumbeats and moving to the center of the dancing area. Kelly watched as it filled with dancers in various forms of dress. Several of the men wore multicolored tunics and pants with feathers and headdresses. Some carried eagle feathers or sticks and stomped to the beat of the drum. The women hopped and danced as the items pinned to their dresses swayed and jingled.

Kelly watched Ruth pause and shuffle a few beats before lifting her feet for a few steps. "She's getting tired. Should we stop her?"

Josie leaned close to speak, and Kelly automatically reached for her hand, grateful she didn't pull away. "Nooko's an elder, and she hasn't been to a powwow in years. This is a great honor for her to dance today. I can't believe a few weeks ago, I was helping her up from the floor after she fell. She's doing quite well out there. Let's let her go as long as she's able."

Josie squeezed her hand before releasing it and standing to address the group, who had rejoined them and were all avidly watching the dancers. "This is called the Jingle Dress Dance, which was originally a medicine dance. All of the different dances you see, as well as the chants and music, are Ojibwe cultural expressions, and the powwow, through the drum, is a reminder of our connection to Mother Earth. The drum is a sacred symbol of the circle of life, the drumbeat our combined heartbeat. It's blessed by an elder and kept safe by a drum keeper who brings it to the powwow."

The drumming volume increased as well as the chanting, and Josie sat close as they kept a close eye on Ruth. She appeared to be having a ball as she promenaded alongside the few other elders in the circle of dancers. "I'm glad Ruth's able to be here, and thank you for bringing all of us." Kelly stopped herself from reaching for Josie's hand again. She sensed Josie wouldn't move away, but she didn't want to send mixed messages. They'd already established their vast differences. Josie wasn't interested in a permanent relationship, and she wouldn't settle for less. She caught the spicy scent of her cologne and stole a glance as her polo shirt stretched across her chest when she leaned back with her elbows on the tabletop and extended her legs out in front of her. The Harlow's by the Bay logo, printed in script just above the swell of her left breast, summoned to be traced with her fingers. She looked relaxed and sexy.

"I'm glad you all wanted to come along. Powwows are big events every year, but we don't have one on the island that often. There's an annual three-day powwow held in Sault Ste. Marie on their Sault Tribe powwow grounds. It's a huge area and great event. There are also powwows in St. Ignace, Michigan, and many other areas of the Upper Peninsula and neighboring states." Josie smiled and waved at Ruth as she circled toward them.

"You looked great out there, Ruth." Kelly moved to the back and side of her in case she needed support. But she didn't.

"Thank you. I had fun." Ruth sounded breathless, no doubt more from excitement than exertion.

"Let's get something to eat and drink," Josie said. "I brought some sandwiches and water, and I saw some bottled iced tea up by the entrance. You'll want to pick up some maple syrup while you're here. It's the best around. And the corn soup is a tradition not to be missed."

"I'm going to check out the jewelry and stuff." Maria stood and the rest of the group followed.

Kelly smiled at Josie and Ruth, who settled down with sandwiches and waved them off. She was strangely reluctant to leave, but chastised herself. She was supposed to be having fun with her friends, too. She linked arms with Debby as they wandered past the various tables.

"This is fun, isn't it?" Debby asked.

"Yeah. I had no idea what to expect, but it's great." Kelly took a sip of the iced tea she'd bought and picked up a pair of handmade moccasins from one of the tables. "These are nice. What do you think?"

"Very. Buy them."

Kelly paid for her new footwear, along with a jar of maple syrup, and followed Debby and Alex back to their table. "I'm glad we've had nice weather this week. And today is perfect." She tilted her face to the sliver of sun peeking through the leaves. She breathed in the fresh air and listened to the sounds of voices emanating from the various groups. The drumming had stopped for a break, but Josie had told them they'd begin more drumming and dancing within an hour.

"You and Josie make a striking pair." Debby sat across from her sharing an iced tea with Alex.

Kelly shook her head. "Nothing there."

"Maybe it'd be a nice diversion for you. A little roll in the hay with a sexy woman?"

Debby was grinning, but Kelly sensed her seriousness. She didn't want to divulge her fear. A fling with Josie had the potential to open her to heartache. She'd tried and failed before to avoid reading more into a relationship than what was there. It was better to never know what she couldn't have. "As good as it sounds, I can't do it, Deb. I'm done chasing after unavailable women. And she made it clear she's not available."

"Fine. But I still think you two are hot together." She reached and squeezed Kelly's shoulder. "And you deserve someone who thinks the world of you."

The sound of drumming and chanting interrupted any further discussion.

"Kelly? Hey there."

Kelly turned to the sound of the voice she'd only heard once before but wouldn't forget. "Hi, Barb. I guess I shouldn't be surprised you're here. How are you?"

"I'm good. Happy to see you again. And hello to your friends." Barb introduced herself to everyone before turning back to Kelly. "Can I buy you an iced tea or something?" She sat close to Kelly on the bench and reached her arm around her waist before quickly removing it. "Sorry. I don't mean to be presumptuous, but Josie told me you were here alone, and you're a beautiful woman."

"Thank you, Barb. I am here alone, and that does mean I'm single. I just finished an iced tea, but thanks. This is great." She turned her attention back to the dancing. Barb was attractive, and she could tell she was interested in her, but she reminded herself of her vow to take it slow. No more one-night stands leading nowhere.

"Yeah, I'm single, too, and this is great." She grinned. "And so is the powwow. We don't have one on the island often. I'm glad you made it for this one." She turned toward her, and Kelly tumbled into her hazel gaze.

"Maybe another iced tea would be nice." She stood and Barb rested her hand on her lower back to lead her to the vendor area. She leaned toward her as they walked, enjoying Barb's interest. It'd been a long time since she'd felt wanted by an available woman, and she looked forward to the possibility of spending time with her.

"How much longer are you going to be here?" Barb asked. She sandwiched Kelly's hand between hers for a moment before gently releasing it and retrieving their iced teas. She opened Kelly's bottle before handing it to her.

Kelly took a settling breath before answering. "Checkout is noon next Sunday." She took the bottle Barb offered and shivered as a current of desire shot up her arm when their fingers brushed. This woman was all kinds of sexy.

Barb smiled, took a step back, and bowed slightly. "I'd like to formally request the honor of your presence for dinner with me this Friday. About six?"

Kelly scrutinized Barb, searching for guile, but found only directness and honesty in her gaze. "Six o'clock would be great. Casual dress?" She doubted there were any fancy restaurants on the remote island, but she wasn't sure. Barb's soft chuckle answered her question.

"You'll be perfect in whatever you wear." Barb winked. "Jeans and a T-shirt would be fine. It'll be a long week for me until our date. I've got to get back to work, but you enjoy the rest of the powwow." Barb waved to a few people as she walked away from the festivities.

Kelly watched Barb leave, enjoying the sway of her hips and her confident stride. She found Barb forward but sexy, and she looked forward to their date to learn more about the self-assured conservation officer.

She tossed her empty bottle in a recycle bin and turned toward where Josie and Ruth sat. She stopped when she saw a tall, unshaven man in worn jeans and a flannel shirt towering over Josie. He was waving his hands and looked menacing. She watched for a moment before continuing to another table to sit and observe. He looked slightly threatening, but Josie only shook her head at him and leaned back in her chair. She stood abruptly when he turned toward the seated Ruth and scowled. She couldn't hear what he said, but he definitely didn't look happy. Josie stood and situated herself between the man and Ruth, and

Kelly waited. She wouldn't intrude, and she knew Josie could handle herself. But she'd be ready if it looked like Josie needed backup. The desire to protect her was strong, but she'd keep it in place, where it belonged. She wanted to be with someone who wanted her, not someone who wanted only a friend. But friends protected each other, too, right?

CHAPTER THIRTEEN

I've already told you I don't want to sell. I'd appreciate it if you'd quit asking and leave us alone." Josie stretched to her full height, which didn't bring her eye to eye with Abe, but she hoped it showed him she wasn't backing down under his veiled threats. But the way he looked at Nooko scared her. "We're trying to enjoy the powwow. Please, just leave us alone. I'm not selling, and I don't know who you think you are, but back off." She stood with her hands on her hips.

He lifted his hands in front of him before speaking. "Hey. I don't want no trouble. I just want your property. I'm sorry Jack's dead, and I wasn't ready to buy it when he was alive, but I am now. I just want you to sell it to me, and I'll be out of your life." Abe took a step back and lowered his arms.

"Is there a reason you want my property? There are many places for sale around the island that would probably sell for less." Josie relaxed slightly but remained wary.

"I want that property, and you need to change your mind about sellin'." He grunted, glanced at Nooko, turned, and stomped away.

"Who was that, Joslyn?"

Josie bristled at the frown lines on Nooko's forehead. No one had the right to upset her nooko. "He's Abe Bernstein, the guy I told you about who asked to buy my property. Did he look familiar to you?"

"No, honey. Not at all. He's a little scary." Nooko looked tired; her shoulders slumped slightly. "He's got bad energy."

"I know. I'm not sure why he's so persistent. I've told him every time he's asked I don't want to sell to him." Josie was unnerved after Abe's aggressive stance and scowl at Nooko. She searched the area for her group, considering heading back to the lodge, and then was puzzled by her flush of calm at the sight of Kelly walking toward them.

"Hey there. Everything okay?" Kelly asked.

"Yeah. Fine. I was thinking about heading home soon. If you're not ready, I can come back and pick you up later."

"No. I'm ready. I've got my maple syrup and moccasins, I've enjoyed the dancing and music, oh, and the corn soup was interesting. It was all terrific. Thanks for bringing me. I'll just let the others know we're leaving."

"The rest of the event is pretty much a repeat. Maybe a few new dancers, but Nooko's beat, so we'll wait for you in the car."

The ride back to the lodge was quiet, and Josie considered telling Kelly about Abe. She didn't want to worry her, but he would've been hard to miss towering over them, and Kelly had walked up quickly after, which meant she probably saw the whole thing. She glanced at Nooko in the passenger seat, who looked to be having a hard time keeping her eyes open. She decided to tell Kelly about him if she asked. Her nooko was safe, and she'd do whatever necessary to protect her. She parked and turned in her seat to speak to Kelly. "I'm glad you enjoyed yourself, Kelly. I didn't mean to cut your day short. I can drop Nooko off and take you back if you'd like."

"That's okay. I can always drive myself back if I want to go, but I've enjoyed myself, and I appreciate you being there to fill us in on the meaning of the dances. Thanks for the ride. Oh. Didn't the new lodgers in cabins five and six want to go to the powwow?"

"They decided they'd been to many of them already and they'd skip this one. They'll be heading back home on Monday. I guess one of them has some sort of family emergency. It's too bad. I think they'd have gotten along well with you guys." Josie shrugged.

"Yeah, too bad. Maybe I'll stop and say hello to them tomorrow. I'll see you two later." She patted Ruth's shoulder. "You take it easy for the rest of the day, and get some sleep tonight." She exited the vehicle and headed to her cabin with a wave.

"I'm going to change and rest a bit, dear. Kelly's right. I need to put my feet up." Nooko stepped out of the vehicle and headed to the lodge.

"Wait up, Nooko. I'll help you up the stairs." Josie rushed to her side and held her arm as she wobbled on the first step. "A little jingle dancing and you think you can do anything." She smiled to show she was teasing.

"Thank you so much for taking me. I had a wonderful time, and I did do well, didn't I?"

"You sure did. You were the leader of the group out there today."

Josie made sure Nooko was comfortable before heading to check the building. Her apprehensions were aroused since confronting Abe at the celebration. She started with the lodge and walked through each room. She checked behind the hot tub room and confirmed all the outside doors were locked. Everything was as they left it, so she shook off the unsettling feeling and went to her office to check for another note. She double-checked the safe and the lock on her desk drawer before inspecting the outside of the buildings. There was no note and nothing disturbed.

She sat at her desk and picked up the landline phone to call Barb. "Hey, Barb, it's Josie. I need to let you know that Abe confronted me at the powwow today."

"Sorry, Josie, I didn't notice. What happened?"

You were too busy seducing Kelly to notice. Josie shook off the thought and concentrated on telling Barb about Abe. "He didn't threaten me, but he sure pressed hard about me selling to him."

"I'll double my rounds in your area and make sure the other COs are aware of him. Let me know if he bothers you again."

"Thanks, Barb." Josie hung up and leaned forward, cradling her head with her hands. She took a deep settling breath and headed to her studio.

She peeked into Nooko's room as she passed it and found her sound asleep, looking relaxed and content. She opened the door wall when she got to her studio and breathed in the fresh air. She was nearly finished with a dream catcher she'd planned to give Kelly. She didn't want to examine too closely her desire to give her a gift. She told herself it was just gratitude for her caring attitude toward Nooko. Trying to keep her distance from Kelly was proving more difficult as the days passed.

Something about her called to Josie and triggered a fear she wasn't ready to let go of. She carefully threaded the rainbow colored beads on the three soft leather strips hanging from the willow hoop wrapped in fine yarn. She attached feathers on each end with secure knots while she silenced the voice in her head telling her this meant more than only a gift to a friend. She refused to admit to herself how much she'd been thrown at seeing Barb and Kelly together at the powwow. She knew how seductive Barb could be, and she worried she would charm Kelly into seeing her, then walk away. Josie had been honest with Kelly about her disinterest in serious dating, and she hoped Barb would be as well.

It was none of her business who Kelly chose to see, but she knew Kelly wanted more than what she, or Barb, had to offer. She repeated it over in her mind, willing her heart to listen.

She locked her studio door when she'd finished for the day and took the path alongside the hot tub area back to the kitchen. When she reached to unlock the door, she looked past the garbage bins and around the corner of the building but saw no one.

She went to wake Nooko and relax. It had been a fun but long day, and her energy waned. "You ready for dinner, Nooko?" Josie waited from outside her bedroom. She'd checked every door lock again to reassure herself. "We have leftover spaghetti, and I'll make a spinach salad." She knocked on the bedroom door. "Do you need a hand?"

"I'm coming, dear. I wore myself out dancing. I'm moving a little slow." Nooko opened the door and leaned heavily on her cane.

"Let's eat in the lodge again." Josie followed her grandmother closely until she sat at one of the tables before going for the food.

She returned to the table with two plates of spaghetti and a bowl of spinach salad, surprised to see Kelly and Nooko laughing and munching on pieces of cheese and apples. "I see you couldn't wait for dinner, Nooko." She smiled to soften the comment.

"Hey, Josie. I hope you don't mind. I thought I'd see if anyone was here and wanted a snack. I see you're about to have dinner. I'll leave you two alone." Kelly stood to leave.

"Please stay," Ruth said. "We have enough spaghetti, don't we, Joslyn?"

"We do. Would you care for a plate, Kelly?"

"Oh, thank you, but my group is planning to try the little restaurant with homemade pasties tonight. I'm looking forward to it. They're going to meet me here in a few minutes if they're not all worn out from the powwow today and running late. You go ahead and eat."

"Have you ever tasted a pasty? Not everyone knows what they are." Josie took a bite of her salad after she spoke.

"Oh, yes. I think of them as a pot pie, only folded in half and stuffed full."

Josie chuckled and finished her meal while listening to Kelly and Nooko discuss the powwow. It looked as if neither one would forget it for a long time. She took the time to observe Kelly as she smiled and laughed with her attention on Nooko. She watched her lightly rest her hand over Nooko's and gracefully tuck a strand of hair behind her ear. Josie lost herself in a fantasy of taking her in her arms and, starting with her lips, kissing her way down her neck to her breasts. Kelly glanced her way and tipped her head slightly. Her lips twitched to a half smile as if she were reading her mind. Josie picked up their empty plates and retreated to the kitchen.

She set the dishes on the counter and leaned over the sink as it filled with hot water. She willed her breathing and heart rate to normal as desire stirred her every nerve.

"Need help with anything in here?"

Josie heard Kelly's voice glide over her skin as tangible as a touch. She turned with her back against the counter as she took a step toward her.

"I thought I'd help with the dishes." Kelly took another step closer and reached past her to grab a dish towel.

Her arm brushed her hip and their breasts were inches apart. A need she'd never known before settled deep into a place Josie hadn't known existed. The heat coursing through her body consumed her reason. Her mind told her she had to resist the pull of this woman. She had a reputation to maintain, and Kelly wanted a commitment she couldn't give. But she released her grip on the counter behind her and leaned toward Kelly. The allure that was pure Kelly urged her closer until she felt the whisper of her breath.

"Or maybe I could help with something else."

Their lips met and tendrils of passion drew their lips together. *How can this feel so right?* She pulled Kelly against her, spun around, and pushed her against the counter. Their kiss deepened, and the feel of Kelly in her arms ignited the cravings she'd been denying for days. She lingered with her lips on Kelly's, wanting more but unsure of what. Carrying this into the bedroom for a quick roll in the hay somehow wouldn't be enough. She drew away and searched for answers in Kelly's beautiful face, not daring to ask. They were both breathing hard, and before Josie could speak, Kelly pulled away but kept her hands resting on Josie's shoulders.

"Wow."

"Yeah." She inhaled to settle her pounding heart. "I'm not going to apologize, even though it probably wasn't the wisest decision I've ever made." She placed her hands on Kelly's hips and tugged until the fronts of their bodies molded together. She fit perfectly.

"I don't want you to apologize. I know how you feel about long-term relationships, and I don't want you to think I'm pushing you. I believe we're attracted to each other, and I wanted the kiss, too. But...I guess that's all it should be." Kelly backed out of her embrace, leaving behind an empty space she feared could never be filled. She watched from the doorway as Kelly gave her a small smile before she walked away with a piece of the armor protecting Josie's heart.

Josie took a few settling breaths before going back to sit with Nooko. Kelly had asked her if she ever got lonely. Of all the women she'd kissed, she'd never felt one reach in and soothe her soul. Was loneliness what Kelly touched with her kiss? She went in to find Nooko alone. "I don't know about you, but I'm bushed. It's been a long day. A fun one, but long."

"Oh yes, dear. I'm ready to call it a day. Kelly said good-bye, and she'd see us tomorrow." Nooko rose and swayed a moment before steadying herself with her cane. "I might have done a few too many dances today."

Josie helped Nooko settle into bed and then headed to her studio. She carefully placed the finished dream catcher in a cardboard box and wrapped it in foiled paper. She'd never given away anything she'd crafted. She didn't try to figure out why she was doing so now, or why thoughts of Kelly had become a nightly event. Tonight's, as she drifted into sleep, were of the feel of Kelly's warm soft lips on hers.

Chapter Fourteen

You have a date? With a conservation officer? When did this happen?" Debby pulled Kelly aside from the group seated on their cabin's deck. They had congregated to share pasties for lunch and talk about the powwow.

"It's not a secret, Deb. She asked me out at the powwow yesterday, and I accepted." Kelly leaned back against the deck rail and sipped her iced tea. "We're just going out to dinner."

"What about Josie?"

"What about her?"

Debby stood next to her and tilted her head. "I thought maybe you two would…I don't know. Maybe work out your differences? She's keen on you."

"Josie isn't keen on me, Deb. She's not interested in dating. Well, she's not interested in an actual relationship, anyway." Kelly sighed. Did she hope otherwise? "I won't deny Josie is way sexy, and strong, and kind, and intelligent, but she's also totally unavailable. I'm ready for something real, not a fling. So I'm going out with Barb to see where it goes."

"I get it, Kelly. I was only looking for a date to take to a wedding when I met Alex. You go out with Barb and enjoy her company. I really believe things happen for a reason and there's someone out there meant for you. If it's not Barb, someone else will come along. Have fun."

"Thanks, Deb. That's the plan." Kelly hugged Debby and went into the cabin. She was looking forward to her date with Barb despite the fact she couldn't get Josie's kiss out of her mind. She wondered if Josie had seen the two of them together, and why she cared if she had. Desire heated her to the core when she remembered the feel of Josie's body pressed against hers, her lips claiming her, and her own need reflected in her obsidian eyes. She wondered if Josie was going to mention the man she'd been staring down at the powwow, but it was none of her business, and she questioned when she'd started to feel like part of her family, and if it was wise. *Geez. It's only been a week. It's not like we've spent months together. What am I thinking?* She shook off her musings and carried a tray of pasties out to the group. "I'm sure glad we got extra of these. I may go back to the restaurant tonight. I love them."

"I'll go with you. I love these, too. I'm planning to talk them into giving me the recipe," Alex said.

"Great. I'd get the recipe, too, but I know I'd never use it. I could pass it along to my sister. She'd be happy to give it a try." Kelly took a bite of her pasty.

"We'll enjoy them while on vacation." Kristen spoke from her spot in one of the deck chairs.

"I'll second that," Jaylin said.

"Is this like, what we eat on vacation, stays on vacation, thing?" Kelly laughed, enjoying the light banter with her friends.

"Oh, I like it. Let's get some ice cream, donuts, chocolate, and wine to go with it all." Debby stood and held up her car keys.

"I'll go help carry everything." Alex jumped to her feet and raised her arms, flexing her biceps.

"Okay. I'll see you all later, then." Kelly waved to her friends and retreated to her cabin. She had a new romance novel she'd started and looked forward to getting back to it.

Kelly watched the police cruiser inch past the cabin as she sat with her feet propped on the front deck railing. She wondered if the police presence had anything to do with the man she saw Josie talking to at the powwow. More likely it was a routine service the police provided to property owners. She made a mental note to ask Josie about it and went back to reading. She was so engrossed in her book she didn't hear anyone approach and was startled when the shadow fell over her book.

"Kelly. Hello." Barb leaned on the step railing, arms folded. She smiled and pushed off toward her.

"Barb? Hi. I didn't expect to see you until Friday. Where'd you come from?" Kelly stood to look for another vehicle but stepped back when Barb sprang up the steps.

"I could lie and say I couldn't wait until Friday to see you again, but I'm here to see Josie. This is just a welcome surprise and I thought

I'd pop over and say hey. But I've got to run. I'll see you Friday." She bounced off the deck and headed to the lodge.

Kelly sat back in her chair bemused. *This date will be interesting.*

"Who is she?" Alex asked as she climbed the steps to her porch.

"Her name's Barb. I met her a few days ago when I went into town. We're going out to dinner on Friday."

"Ah. I hope she's as nice as she is hot in her uniform. You ready to go?"

"Sure. Did you get everyone's order?" Kelly set her book inside her cabin and followed Alex to her car, wondering what business Barb had with Josie and why she cared.

It was nearly dark by the time Kelly and Alex returned from picking up more pasties, and Kelly presumed the car parked next to the lodge belonged to Barb. She had no reason to go to the lodge but scrambled for an excuse as she walked toward it. If Alex's raised eyebrow was any indication, she didn't buy it, but she waved her off as she went to take the food to the rest of the group. Kelly entered the large room and saw Ruth sitting in her usual spot on the couch. "Hey, Ruth. How're you doing today?"

"Kelly! I'm so glad you came by." Ruth patted the seat next to her on the couch. "Please sit."

"Is everything okay?"

"I think so, dear. Barb and Joslyn have been in the office for a while now. I'm not sure what's going on." Ruth looked nervous.

"Is it about the man I saw talking to Josie at the powwow?"

"I don't know. It could be. He was scary." Ruth wrung her hands in her lap and clutched the emergency button pendant hanging from her neck.

Kelly took Ruth's hands in hers. "I'm sure Josie's doing whatever is necessary to keep us safe."

"I know she is. I just wish there was something I could do to help. This guy wants to buy the cabins and we don't know why."

"Huh. I'm sure Josie will figure it all out. Don't worry. Have you had dinner? I picked up a bunch of pasties today. Can I bring you one?"

"Thank you, but Josie's made stew tonight. I'll just have a bowl later."

"I can get some for you now, if you like? We don't know how long Josie will be."

"I can get it, dear. I'm sure you have other things to do than wait on me." Ruth stood and stepped toward the kitchen, but looked unsteady on her feet.

"You relax. I'm going to the hot tub shortly and the kitchen is on the way. I'll bring you a bowl, and you can eat while you wait for Josie to finish her business."

"Thank you, Kelly. You're a sweetie." Ruth sat with a groan, looking tired.

Kelly filled a bowl with stew from a covered pot. She left a note for Josie so she'd know what was going on and took Ruth her dinner. "I'm going to be in the hot tub. If you need anything, just find me there."

"I'll be fine, you go. Josie'll be back soon." Ruth picked up her spoon and waved Kelly away.

She hurried to her cabin, changed quickly, and went straight to the hot tub. She enjoyed spending time with her friends, but the solitude was nice too. Kelly rested her head on the edge of the fiberglass tub and let the hot water from the bubbling jets flow around her. She closed her eyes and allowed herself a short fantasy of Josie's naked body sliding over her; the memory of her demanding kiss sent shivers of heat racing to her clit. She opened her eyes to quiet her overactive imagination and focus on the present. Ruth was obviously worried. Whatever was going on with whoever this man was had her and Josie concerned. She tried to convince herself she should mind her own business and let Josie take care of whatever was going on. Somehow, she'd allowed herself to become attached to Ruth and Josie. Being too close to either of them could be potentially painful. She'd be leaving in less than a week, and this vacation would be a fond memory. Even if she was working nearby, that didn't mean she'd continue to see them. She took a deep breath and released it, vowing to distance herself for the sake of self-protection but unsure if her heart was listening.

"Thanks for getting Nooko dinner, Kelly. I appreciate it." Josie stood at the entry to the hot tub room.

Kelly faced her as she spoke. "I didn't mind at all. I was headed past the kitchen anyway. Everything all right?" She winced, realizing she was overstepping her boundaries.

"Yeah. Everything's fine. I had a few questions for Barb about some guy who wants to buy my cabins, but it's all good. Enjoy the hot tub." There were tension lines around her eyes, and her smile was distant. She left before Kelly could say anything more.

She rolled over in the warm bubbling tub and concentrated on relaxing. She lost track of time as she stretched in the tub and slowly moved to the steps. The faint scent of smoke surprised her. The evenings had warmed nicely as the week had progressed, so she doubted Josie would have started a fire in the fireplace. As she stepped out of the tub and wrapped in a towel, she realized the smoke filtering into the area couldn't be coming from the fireplace chimney. She grabbed her bag containing her robe and cell phone and hurried to the lodge. There was no fire in the fireplace and the room was empty. She turned toward the back door just as Josie rushed in. "Is there a fire somewhere?"

"It's just a small can fire. Kids do it all the time around here. It's annoying and a pain in the ass, but it's contained." Josie ran her fingers through her hair while her gaze darted about the room. "I just wanted to make sure everything was okay back here."

"What's a can fire?"

"Someone, typically a kid, rolls a rusty old oil drum into the woods and fills it with brush and leaves, then starts the thing on fire to watch it burn. It happens a few times every year, and I'm sorry if it interrupted you. It usually only creates a lot of smoke and burns itself out quickly. I'm not sure how they got it so close to my building, but I've drowned it with the hose, so it's not dangerous. I'm going to call Barb to come back as soon as I check on Nooko." Josie turned and sped toward Ruth's room.

Kelly dried off and headed back to her cabin to relax some more. She'd been mellow, but Josie's worry had piqued her curiosity and she couldn't stop wondering what was going on. She sat on the rocker on the front porch of her cabin watching the red and gold streaks of the sunset spread across the sky. She'd changed into sweats after leaving the hot tub and decided to leave Josie alone with her fire issue, confident she'd let the group know if there was anything they needed to worry about. She propped her feet up on the rail and shifted her thoughts to her upcoming date with Barb.

"Hello again." Barb stood on the bottom step of her porch smiling up at her.

Kelly shook her head to shake off the surprise of the connection between her thoughts and seeing Barb standing before her. "You do get around, don't you?"

"I got a call from Josie complaining about hooligans, so I came to investigate. I better get to it."

Kelly watched her saunter away and decided to jump on the

opportunity. "Wait. I want to see this, too." She scurried off the porch after Barb.

"Thanks for coming, Barb. You…" Josie turned and stopped talking when she saw Kelly.

"I'm just nosy. I won't get in the way. But I'll leave if you want me to." Kelly turned away to go back to her cabin but Josie grabbed her arm.

"No. It's okay, Kelly. There's nothing to see, anyway."

Barb had moved to the edge of the woods to scrutinize the ground in the area of the now smoldering metal drum with a large flashlight. "Kids usually roll these. It's part of the fun, I guess, but I think this one was carried."

Kelly moved closer to look. "How can you tell?"

"See those boot prints?" She pointed the light toward a path in a small opening in the woods. "The footprints are deeper coming in as if they were carrying something heavy. See?" She pointed again and stepped to the side. "The ones going back out aren't as deep, so I'm presuming they weren't carrying anything. We lucked out that the area is low enough to have some soft ground." Barb took out a notebook and pen and made notes as she reviewed the area.

"She's very thorough, isn't she?" Josie leaned close, and Kelly caught the spicy scent of her shampoo.

"Yes, and she looks as though she knows what she's doing." Kelly responded, unsure why they were whispering but liking it. As though they shared something belonging only to them.

"I don't know if there's anything you can do about this unless you catch someone in the act. If you want to make a report with the police, I'll give them my opinion. Let me know." Barb put her notebook away and reached for Kelly's hand. "Shall I walk you back to your cabin?"

"Thanks for letting me butt in, Josie. I'll see you tomorrow." Kelly allowed herself to be led away. She resisted looking back at Josie as they walked away but couldn't shake the discomfort and admitted to herself that she'd rather be holding Josie's hand.

"I've said this before, but I'll say it again. I'll see you Friday." Barb squeezed her hand. "I'm looking forward to it."

"Me, too, Barb. I'll see you on Friday." Kelly grabbed her book and settled in for the evening, wondering whose touch she'd dream of that night.

CHAPTER FIFTEEN

Everything is fine, Nooko. We don't know who was responsible for the fire in the barrel. There's no way to prove it was Abe. I've got the police patrolling, and Barb's going to keep her eye out for anything suspicious. It's probably mischievous kids." Josie didn't want her nooko to worry, but she wasn't sure it had anything to do with kids. She couldn't figure out why the guy was so anxious to buy her property or why he thought notes and a little vandalism would convince her to sell. "Let's go get some ice cream."

Nooko didn't look convinced but let it go. "Good idea. Is Kelly coming with us?"

Josie had the same thought, although she knew it wasn't a good idea to keep including her in their plans. "Maybe the whole group will come along. We'll ask them on our way out." Josie stopped at each cabin on her way out of the parking lot. Kelly sat on her deck reading with her feet propped on the rail. She rose when she saw them. "We're headed to the Teepee for ice cream. We were going to ask you all to join us. Where is everyone?"

"They took the dogs to a little park by the water they found yesterday. I'll join you, though." She crawled into the back seat and Josie concentrated on driving instead of sneaking glances at Kelly in the rearview mirror.

Kelly settled Ruth at one of the picnic tables while Josie went to stand in line. The small teepee-style building was a popular stop for residents of the island as well as tourists. They sold sandwiches as well as ice cream. She was about to place their order when she felt a presence behind her. "Chocolate, please." Kelly's breath tickled her neck, and she fought the impulse to step back into her arms.

"Chocolate it is. Do you want a sandwich or anything?"

"No. Chocolate ice cream is a good start. Your grandmother wants vanilla."

"Great. I'll bring them to you if you want to go sit with her." Josie turned to look at Nooko and started. "What the hell?" Abe sat across from her at their table. She couldn't hear what he was saying, but she disliked him so close to her.

"What's the matter?" Kelly asked and looked toward Ruth. "Who's at our table? Is he the same guy who was at the powwow?"

"Come on." Josie stalked toward Abe.

"Good afternoon. I was just talkin' to your grandma here about how foolish you're bein' by not sellin' to me." Abe's leer did nothing to quell Josie's apprehension.

"You need to leave us alone. We're not selling." Josie stood behind Nooko with her hands on her shoulders.

Abe narrowed his eyes and stared at each of them. "You ought to be grateful I'm willin' to make a decent offer. I have rights to this place, so you decide how much you want 'cuz I ain't waiting much longer." He turned and walked away.

"Good riddance. Did he touch you, Nooko?"

"No. I'm fine, dear. Abe thinks he knows your father. He kept calling him Jack, though. He said he knew the owner before you, and his name was Jack. I told him the owner was your father, Johnathan Harlow, but he said he didn't care what we called him. He was here to buy Jack's land."

"Let's eat our ice cream. That's why we're here, right?" Josie went and got their ice cream, her hands trembling. The guy was becoming more than a nuisance, and it was beginning to scare her. But she couldn't let Nooko, or Kelly, know that. She didn't want her grandmother upset, and Kelly was a paying guest. The last thing she wanted was a bad review because of some weird guy who had nothing to do with her resort.

"I know it's none of my business, but sometimes Jack is a short form of John, isn't it? Maybe this guy only knew your dad as Jack." Kelly ate a spoonful of ice cream.

"I hadn't thought of that," Ruth said.

"No. I hadn't either." Josie didn't recall anyone ever calling her father Jack. But then, she hadn't known him very well at the end of his life. He'd been distant and different.

"It's the English short form of a name. Or a pet name such as Nooko for Nookomis. You couldn't pronounce it as a child so you shortened it." Kelly smiled.

"Whatever the reason, my property must be important to him. I can't believe Dad never said anything to me."

"John's death was sudden, honey. Maybe he never got the chance to tell you, or maybe Abe didn't want it back then." Nooko finished her ice cream and scraped the bottom of the bowl.

"He told me the day of the powwow that he didn't want it back then. Something sure makes him want it now, though, but he wouldn't tell me what. Do you want more ice cream? Maybe we ought to get a couple of burgers." Josie grinned at Nooko's look of excitement. "Their hamburgers are fantastic, Kelly."

"Yum. I'll help you carry them."

Kelly followed her to the window and Josie pushed thoughts of Abe and Jack aside as she enjoyed the feel of Kelly close behind her. Things would become clear eventually. Or he'd get fed up and go away. But she wouldn't give him any more time in her head right now.

When they finally got back after a leisurely lunch, Josie made sure Nooko was comfortable on the couch by the fireplace before heading to check on the buildings. Her encounter with Abe had her concerned, so she took extra time on her usual rounds on the property, stopping to check each cabin and the grounds. She took out the garbage and secured the locks before heading to her studio to unwind. The dream catcher she'd made for Kelly sat in its wrapped box on the corner of her worktable. She'd told herself it was a gift for Kelly's help with Nooko, but she recognized her self-deception. She liked Kelly more than she acknowledged, and their shared kiss threatened areas of her heart protected by fear. The more time they spent together, the more she found that she really liked her calm nature and quick wit. She was intelligent without conceit, caring but not smothering, honest and straightforward, with a sense of humor. When she really thought about it, the best thing about Kelly was the connection she felt to her. It was as if they could talk about anything and comfortably share quiet time together. She trusted her with her nooko, and that was the most important thing in her life.

She picked out several beads to make a rainbow colored line on her worktable and worked on her new design for a large Harlow's by the Bay dream catcher. An hour later, she stood to stretch and locked up the room. Before she could move away from the door, however, Nooko came hurrying out of the lodge.

"There you are, Joslyn. Kelly came looking for you." Nooko looked nervous.

"Did she go back to her cabin?" Josie scanned the room.

"No. I'm right here." Kelly came out of the hot tub room. "There's something you need to see."

Josie followed Kelly past the hot tub and into the woods behind the building. "What is it?"

Kelly pointed to the back of the woodshed. "I saw this when I returned from my walk this afternoon."

A message had been scrawled with red spray paint that dripped like blood below the letters.

I want what is mine!

"I'll bet Abe did this." Nooko had followed them out, unnoticed. She leaned on her cane looking alarmed.

Kelly put her arm around Nooko's waist. "Let's go back inside, Ruth. I'll make us a cup of tea."

Josie caught her eye and smiled a thank-you. "Good idea, I'm going to call the authorities to come out to see this before I clean it up. I'll be in shortly." She checked the outside of the lodge and the cabins before heading to her office. There was no envelope and nothing else was amiss, but she was certain it was Abe's doing.

It took longer than Josie anticipated to finish talking with the officer on duty, so she rushed to the lodge as soon as she hung up the phone, but didn't see Nooko and Kelly in their usual spots.

"We're in here, Joslyn."

Josie followed the sound of Nooko's voice to the hot tub where she was smiling and kicking with Kelly holding her afloat on her belly. "Ah. Exercising again?"

"I thought it might be a good distraction." Kelly spoke as she spun Ruth in a circle.

"Everything's taken care of, and the police will be out tomorrow." Josie smiled at Nooko in the tub. "How're you feeling?"

"I'm fine, dear. Why don't you join us? The water temperature is perfect."

Josie deliberated Nooko's request. The thought of sharing the tub with Kelly, their bare legs brushing, the jets pulsing against her body caused her breath to catch. She could use Nooko as a buffer. *Right.* "Maybe I'll join you tomorrow. You can show me your new exercise routine."

"Sounds good. Shall we plan after breakfast? About eight thirty." Kelly released Nooko, who floated onto the seat, looking far more relaxed than she had earlier.

"I'll plan on it." Josie ignored her racing pulse as she watched Kelly's lithe body as she rose out of the tub and grabbed a towel. She stood mesmerized at the sight of her smooth skin and firm ass as she leaned to dry her legs. *Thank goodness she's wearing a bathing suit.* Her hands shook as she supported Nooko to help her out of the tub.

"See you tomorrow." Kelly waved as she left the room.

Josie waved back, shaking off an unusual sense of loss. "Tomorrow, you'll show me what to do, Nooko." Josie's throat tightened at the idea of Kelly not being around to spend time with Nooko in the hot tub. She'd gotten used to her smile and her self-confidence. She'd miss her terribly.

❖

"Is it eight thirty already?" Nooko looked up from her plate of scrambled eggs and hash browns.

"No. It's only eight, Nooko. Finish your breakfast and relax a while. I'm just filling the coffeepot, and I'll build a fire this morning to take the chill off." Josie had the fireplace blazing a few minutes before Kelly walked in.

"Good morning. Am I too early?"

"Not at all. I made some coffee and hot water for tea. Help yourself. Did you sleep well?"

"Yep. Like I said before, I love how quiet it is here. Peaceful." Kelly smiled and poured herself a cup of coffee. "Did you get some rest, Ruth?"

"Yes, dear, and I'm ready for my workout this morning. I'm glad you're here."

Josie settled into one of the leather chairs facing the fireplace. Everything was quiet, and the police were sending a patrol car this morning. There was nothing more she could do, so she relaxed and concentrated on Nooko. "After I get some practice with your exercises, we'll set up what I'll call a hot tub therapy schedule for you, Nooko. Every day or every other day, maybe."

"Thank you, dear. I'm ready whenever you two are."

Together they cleaned up the breakfast dishes, and Josie and Nooko got into their bathing suits. Josie wasn't altogether comfortable in her suit while Kelly stood by fully dressed, but she'd survive the self-consciousness if it meant helping her grandmother. Kelly said it would be good for her to practice without her there, so she could do it on her own. She gave instructions from the side of the hot tub while Josie put them into motion. It bothered her how frail her grandmother seemed. In the water, it was that much clearer, and it made Josie's heart ache.

"You're pretty good in there." Kelly grinned from outside the tub.

"Nooko's been practicing with an excellent teacher. She's pretty much doing it all herself. I'm just helping to support her, the way you told me to." Josie admitted it was a better learning experience for her to be alone in the tub with Nooko while Kelly supervised from outside, but she wished she'd been able to see Kelly in her swimsuit again. "It's not too complicated, is it?"

"Nope. Just make sure she's doing all the work. Kicking and moving her arms. You two are doing great. I can see I'm no longer needed. Unless you need me for anything, I'm heading to my cabin." Kelly smiled but lingered at the edge of the tub.

"Thanks, Kelly. We'll be fine." Josie helped Nooko out of the tub and wrapped her in a towel. She felt the growing, but necessary, distance between them. In a few days, Kelly would be returning to her work and life away from Harlow's by the Bay. She wondered if Barb would be pursuing Kelly while she was still on the island. The mental picture of her holding Kelly's hand at the powwow prickled her gut while the memory of their shared kiss soothed it. Just as she'd thought, relationships were far more complicated than she had time for. She just wished it hadn't needed proving quite this close to home.

CHAPTER SIXTEEN

B arb had said jeans and a T-shirt, but Kelly sighed with relief that she'd chosen the only nice outfit she'd brought, her blue silk blouse and black slacks. When they arrived at their dinner location, Barb opened the door to a rustic hotel as nice as any she'd ever seen. They followed the maître d' to a small table for two toward a private area in the back of the dining room. Barb pulled the chair out for her and waited for him to leave before stroking her hand and speaking. "You look beautiful, Kelly. I'm thrilled you agreed to go out with me."

"Thank you. I'm glad you asked, and you look pretty good yourself. I see you're not wearing jeans either." Many of the various patrons *were* wearing jeans while others were dressed for a night out on the town.

"No." Barb looked sheepish. "I couldn't very well show off my classy date if I didn't look presentable myself. I know the owner of this place, and the food's great. My favorite is the grilled fish. Would you care for a glass of wine?"

"Sounds nice. White?"

"White it is."

Kelly watched the interaction between the groups seated around the room. They talked, laughed, and waved to each other. She noted a few glances their way from several couples. She surmised most of them knew Barb since she said she was one of only a few conservation officers on the island. She wondered how many of these people she'd get to know herself in the next few months.

"So, Kelly Newton. You're a nurse, you like white wine, and you came to Drummond Island for a vacation. Anything else I should know about you?" Barb leaned back while the server poured their wine.

Kelly took a sip, willing herself to relax. She didn't know why she was nervous. This was what she wanted. A real date to explore the possibilities of a real relationship, but now that she was there with Barb, her thoughts involuntarily strayed to Josie. *Unavailable Josie.* She mentally shook herself. "Not much to tell. I'm a nurse supervisor at a nursing home in Novi, Michigan, and my friend and coworker told me about Josie's new lesbian resort. I decided I needed a vacation, so I joined her and her partner and two other couples for this trip. I have a horse I ride in gymkhana events, I love soft jazz, and I love to read."

"I love to read, too. Fiction or non?"

"Historical fiction. I love to read about real places or events with a romance woven in. I want to learn something from what I read. How about you?"

"Pure romance with happy endings. It has to have a happily ever after, or I don't bother. I've got a whole bookshelf full of them."

Their conversation was interrupted by the server taking their order.

Kelly's heart rate increased a notch. *She's a romantic.* "I agree with the happily-ever-after part. It's a must for me, too. How long have you been on Drummond Island?" Kelly refilled their wine glasses, unsure if the tension she felt earlier was relieved from the wine or from getting to know Barb. So far, she liked what she heard.

"I've only lived on the island for three years. I was born and raised in Detour. It's the little town you went through to get here. The ferry leaves from there."

"I remember. My group's planning to go there tomorrow and check it out."

"Cool. I'd offer myself as a tour guide, but I have to work all day tomorrow."

They spent the rest of the meal talking about the island and about Barb's work. She gave her tips on where to go in Detour, and they talked about Kelly's horse riding. It was fun, uncomplicated conversation, and Kelly enjoyed herself immensely. The food really was delicious, and she had to turn down dessert but definitely wanted to come back for it one day. It looked divine.

Barb took her hand as they left the restaurant and strolled on the sidewalk. "Why is someone as sexy as you still single?"

"I could ask the same of you." Kelly pulled Barb to sit on a bench set away from the walk. "I guess I just haven't met the right woman yet."

"Ah. I can use the same excuse, I suppose. I met a few women in my DNR conservation officer training academy, but most were married, and the rest of my classmates were male. I was twenty-eight before I met my first long-term lover. It lasted a few years until she decided I was too wrapped up in my work. She said I worked too many weekends and holidays. I've only dated since." Barb frowned and shifted. "Twelve years of holding out hope for 'the one.'"

"Hey. You okay?" Kelly put her hand on Barb's, feeling her sudden withdrawal.

"Yeah. I'm fine. Sorry. I've been told I get too pushy. I try too hard." Barb turned to face her. "Have I pushed you? Am I being too…I don't know…forward?"

Kelly searched Barb's face for a moment. "No, Barb. I don't think so. I can see how someone could, but I see you as romantic and physical. I suppose if someone felt uncomfortable with you, it would be up to them to tell you. I like you very much. I'm single. You're single. Let's get on with our date and see where it leads?"

"Sounds good to me."

Barb's huge grin pleased her as they resumed walking. They followed the sidewalk until it ended at a small grassy area with another bench where they sat again. Barb extended her arm behind her, and she automatically leaned into her embrace. They sat in comfortable silence for a while listening to the night sounds and the voices of a few couples strolling by, hand in hand. "This was nice. Thanks again for asking me out." She sat up and turned to face Barb, pleased by her huge grin.

"Believe me, it was my pleasure. I'll walk you to your car."

They took their time returning to their cars in the parking lot.

"Be careful driving back. Maybe we can do this again before you leave?" Barb looked hopeful.

"I think that'd be nice. I'll actually still be around working at the new nursing home, so give me a call."

"I will. Let me know when you get settled. Be safe."

Kelly appreciated that Barb waited until she'd started her car and began to drive away before moving to her own vehicle. She looked forward to seeing her again.

❖

It was dark when Kelly parked in front of her cabin. The security light lit the porch before she reached the first step and reminded her of Josie. She hadn't lied to Barb. She'd found her to be the most enjoyable date she'd been with in a long time, and she wanted to get to know her better. She hoped she could get her stray thoughts of Josie under control. She retrieved a bottle of water and settled on the chair on the porch. She thought back to the street corner where she and Barb had lingered to talk and enjoy the warm evening and nearly full moon. Their kiss began as a light good-night kiss but quickly grew in intensity until Kelly wanted more. She would have gone home with Barb and spent the night with her, but Barb hadn't asked, and now Kelly was grateful. They'd both felt the connection between them, but Kelly feared her wandering thoughts of Josie would follow her into Barb's bed, and that was unacceptable.

Barb's concern about being too forward showed they were in agreement in their desire to take things slow. She wanted a permanent, committed relationship, and Barb's disclosure about her ex-lover triggered her own memories. She'd also wrapped herself in her work when she'd first graduated from college. How many dates had she broken with Allyson due to her varying work schedules? How many times had she changed their plans at the last minute because one of the nurses called in sick, and she took over her shift? Was it the reason she'd held out hope for Kristen? They were both so busy with work and riding their horses they could connect when it was convenient, but that didn't make for a strong relationship. But was it what she was looking for? A convenient perfect fit? Her thoughts were interrupted by the sound of footsteps.

"Hey, Kelly. It's just me." The motion sensor light went on again as Josie stood at the bottom of the steps. "I hope I didn't startle you."

"Oh no. I like these security lights. They don't miss much." Kelly wondered if Josie was going to ask her where she was all evening. *Get over yourself.*

"I'm glad they're doing their job. I'm just making my rounds before turning in for the night. Debby told me you all are going into Detour tomorrow. I look forward to hearing how you like it."

"It seemed like a cool little town when I drove through it."

"It is. It has a rich Ojibwe history, so I suggest you stop at the museum. You'll learn about the Métis population and how they came to be, as well as the shipping history."

"Métis?"

Josie sat on the top step and turned to face her. "The Métis are people many used to call half-breeds. The English and French fur traders came here in the seventeenth century and hooked up with the

Native American women. Their offspring were mixed race and called Métis. It comes from the French meaning half of one thing and half of another. The museum has more detailed information, and you'll enjoy it."

"So, would you consider yourself Métis?" The information fascinated Kelly even beyond her desire to know Josie.

"I suppose technically I am, but the Métis people define themselves as a separate ethnic group. They're mainly in Canada with a culture of their own. I consider myself a woman who was fortunate enough to have had an Ojibwe mother and an honest white man for a father."

They sat in companionable silence for a few minutes while Kelly's thoughts strayed to a young Josie. "Ruth mentioned your mother's death. If you don't mind me asking, how did she die?" Kelly regretted her question when she saw the pain in Josie's face.

"It was a long time ago." She shifted to the chair next to Kelly. "It was a snowmobile accident when I was fifteen. For years, I blamed myself because I'd pleaded with her to join me and my dad on a ride. We'd ridden those trails for years, and it happened so fast I didn't even know anything was wrong. I stopped when I saw my dad turn around and head back the way we came." Josie stopped talking and tipped her head back. "One minute, we were laughing and enjoying a beautiful winter day, and the next she was gone. There were icy patches on the trail, and she hit one and lost control of the machine. She smashed into a tree, flipped over, and my father found her buried in the snow, pinned under the snowmobile."

"I'm sorry, Josie." Kelly rested her hand on her arm.

"Like I said, it was a long time ago. I take some comfort in knowing it was fast. Her neck was broken by the impact, and the paramedics believed she died instantly. I know it was nobody's fault. I only wish my father could have gotten over it. It was an accident for a reason only the Creator knows, but he never stopped blaming himself. Her death crushed him and left me feeling guilty for a long time." Josie stood and stretched before descending the steps. "See you tomorrow. Sleep well." Josie waved as she walked away.

Kelly leaned back in her chair and suppressed the craving to rush after her. To take away the pain of her loss. Why was she so drawn to her when she knew it was impossible? She pushed aside those desires and went inside and crawled into bed alone.

CHAPTER SEVENTEEN

Josie's thoughts wandered to the previous evening with Kelly as she swept the office floor and cleaned windows. She rarely spoke of her mother's death, preferring to keep her vibrant and alive in her memory. She wasn't totally truthful with Kelly when she'd told her she'd let go of the guilt she'd felt. She still struggled with regret for insisting her mother come on their ride with them, and guilt for being responsible for the event from which her father never recovered. The loving, caring father she remembered, the man who'd shared his life with her beautiful mother, had been transformed into a broken, angry shell of who he was. She pondered why she'd felt so comfortable divulging the memory of her mother's death to Kelly.

Her disclosure to Kelly had come from a place so natural it had taken her by surprise. Whatever it was she felt for Kelly could lead to nothing or it would end badly. Her trust in the permanency of love remained buried in the snow underneath a crushed snowmobile lying atop her mother's shattered body and her father's endless tears. That didn't mean she wasn't glad to see Kelly had come back from her date with Barb, and she wouldn't have admitted that she'd been listening for her return, wondering if she'd end up staying the night elsewhere.

She turned her attention back to her task. She wondered again why Abe was so insistent on buying her place, and she wished her father had said something about him. Even if he didn't want the property then, she didn't have any clues as to why Abe wanted it now. The officer had come out earlier in the week, taken photos, and said he'd add them to the file of complaints she'd started, just in case they caught anyone. There wasn't much more they could do, and it left her feeling frustratingly helpless. She locked up her office and headed inside the lodge.

Nooko sat in her usual spot on the end of the couch with a cup of tea and a plate of cheese and crackers. "Is Kelly with you?"

"No, Nooko. She's going into Detour today with the group." Josie sat in one of the chairs. "Were you expecting her?"

"No. I just thought she might be going to the hot tub this afternoon."

"She might when they get back later. Did you want to do some exercise today? I'll help you now if you want." Josie pushed aside resentment at Nooko's first choice of Kelly's help.

"Maybe later, dear." She moved the plate to the coffee table closer to Josie. "She's leaving tomorrow, isn't she?"

"They all are."

"I'm going to miss her."

Nooko looked so sad Josie moved to sit next her and put her arm around her shoulders. "She's still going to be on the island for a while. She'll be working at the new nursing home, remember?"

Her grin lessened some of Josie's concern. "Will we still be able to see her sometimes?"

"I would imagine so. I'll ask her." Josie smiled and hugged her, hoping her words would make it happen. "I'll be back in a bit. I need to go get some work done. Do you want something more for lunch before I go?"

"I'm fine, dear. I'm going stay here and read the paper. I'll get another cup of tea in a bit."

Josie settled into her work chair in her studio but hesitated to reopen the box she'd carefully wrapped. She'd remembered she hadn't added the intended note. She wanted to explain the significance of a dream catcher, so she retrieved her calligraphy pen and paper and began writing.

> *The dream catcher originated with the Ojibwe and begins with a willow hoop which symbolizes the circle of life. It is woven with a web with an open center. Good dreams flow through the center and gently glide down the feathers to the sleeping person. Bad dreams are caught in the web and disappear when the sun rises.*
>
> *May all your dreams be good ones you'll remember for a lifetime.*
> *Josie*

She tucked the note in the box, repositioned the dream catcher next to it, and rewrapped the gift. She planned to give it to Kelly when she checked out on Sunday but considered asking her to dinner for the occasion. *As a friend.* She repeated it to herself several times as she returned to the lodge where Nooko lay sound asleep with her head on the armrest. Josie covered her with a light blanket, grabbed a book, and settled on the couch with Nooko's feet on her lap.

"Hello. Anyone home?"

Josie opened her eyes and winced at the crick in her neck as she sat up and blinked a few times to get her bearings. She'd obviously fallen asleep next to Nooko, and someone was here. "Hello." She checked on Nooko, still sound asleep, before standing.

"Josie? It's Kelly. Sorry to take you by surprise, but I wanted to thank you for the suggestion of the museum in Detour. It was fabulous." Kelly plopped into one of the chairs. "I'm pooped."

"You're welcome. I'm glad you enjoyed it." She gently squeezed Nooko's leg. "Kelly's back, Nooko."

"You don't have to wake her."

"I'm afraid she wouldn't forgive me if I didn't. She asked about you hours ago, so I told her you'd gone sightseeing in Detour. She missed you today." Josie didn't add she'd missed her, too. Her smile, her gentleness, her sexiness.

"Kelly." Nooko sat up and straightened her hair. "How was your trip to Detour?"

"It was great, Ruth. We saw the museum, walked around town and by the water, and finished by going to the Ship Wreck Grill for dinner. Josie was right about the museum. I loved it."

She smiled at Josie and butterflies came alive in her belly.

"I'm glad you had a good time, dear. Are your friends—" She was interrupted by a commotion at the door.

Kelly's group entered singing their version of "For He's a Jolly Good Fellow" and carrying white paper bags. Kelly stood and joined them. "We brought you both a little parting gift." She set the bags on one of the tables. "They're homemade pasties. We hope you'll think of us when you eat them. We've all had a wonderful time and we wanted to thank you."

Ruth stood and opened her arms wide. The whole group, one by one, took turns hugging her.

"This is great, you guys. Thank you." Josie struggled to hold back tears as she watched Nooko beam and give each woman her advice for their life. She caught Kelly's eye and the earlier butterflies took flight. "You have been a fantastic group for our first ever at Harlow's by the Bay, and Nooko and I feel blessed to have met you all." Josie hoped the next group would be as welcoming. Fulfilling her dream was going smoothly, so far. Now she had to figure out what to do about Abe and decipher her feelings for Kelly. The overwhelming disappointment she felt at her leaving the next day contrasted with the pleasure at knowing she'd still be on the island. She'd decided not to intrude by asking Kelly for a final meal before she left. She'd want that time with her friends, and Josie knew she'd made the right decision. Hopefully, the plan she had in mind would work just as well.

The group sat chatting and laughing for a while, talking about their trip to Detour, as well as about the other things they'd spent the week doing. Josie hadn't gotten to know the others as well as she had Kelly, but she liked them very much and enjoyed the final evening of banter. She made sure to remind them they'd be welcome back anytime. Nooko began to yawn, and Josie called it a night. The others said they had to pack, and everyone filed out.

After Josie had gotten Nooko settled, she went back outside and found Kelly waiting for her. Unprompted, she fell in beside her and walked her to her cabin. The night held the promise of the warmer days to come, and she breathed deeply.

"Nooko hasn't stopped smiling. Thanks for being so kind to her." Josie stood at the foot of the stairs leading to Kelly's cabin. She shuffled her feet and took a deep breath before continuing. "I wanted to ask you something." She paused.

"We all think this place is great, and Ruth is fantastic. You didn't have to walk me to my cabin, you know. I've been here two weeks." She grinned. "I know the way."

"I guess I just wanted an extra minute to say good-bye."

"Come on up on the porch and sit." Kelly reached for her hand and tugged her up the stairs. "Now ask."

"I know you're going to still be on the island, so I wondered if you'd go to lunch or dinner with me one day. Whenever is good for you." Kelly sat quietly for so long Josie almost began to speak again.

"Are you asking me for a date? Because—"

"No. Not a date. I know how you feel. I just thought we could share a friendly meal while you're around." She willed herself not to hold her breath.

"It sounds nice, Josie. I'd love to."

"Great. Let me know when you get settled in, and we'll pick a place." Josie fought the urge to skip back to her room, but didn't bother to suppress her huge grin. It hurt a little less knowing Kelly was leaving tomorrow now that she knew she'd get to see her again.

CHAPTER EIGHTEEN

Kelly rolled over and groped for her phone. She canceled the alarm and groaned. Her relaxing two-week vacation lingered in her memory as she stretched and rose to get her bearings in her short-term apartment. She'd spent a couple of days unpacking the few pairs of scrubs she'd brought, using the compact-sized washer and dryer, and stocking her cupboards and refrigerator. She was as ready as she could be to begin her new assignment. Thoughts of Josie and her invitation followed her throughout breakfast and on her drive to the nursing facility where she'd spend the next few months. She enjoyed the anticipation of seeing Josie again. She missed their easy connection, and she missed Ruth's enthusiasm for life. She took the longer route to enjoy the beautiful morning. She parked in front of the building and prepared to focus on her new responsibilities.

"Good morning. You must be Kelly." A tall dark-haired man in green scrubs greeted her at the entrance with an outstretched hand. "My name's Jim. I'm one of the aides, and I'm glad to have you on board."

Kelly returned his firm grip, encouraged by his eagerness. "Good morning, Jim. I'm glad to be here. I look forward to helping to get this facility up and running."

"You and me both." Jim sighed. "The company began advertising availability throughout the state last week, but we've hesitated to begin the screening process until you arrived. From all the calls we've been getting, we'll be at full capacity sooner than later."

Kelly wasn't surprised by the information. Based on the state of the healthcare system and aging population, she figured the new facility would fill quickly. "I guess we better get busy." She followed Jim to the main nurses' station to meet the nursing staff.

It was lunchtime before Kelly stopped to take a break and decided a more thorough tour of the building was in order. She accompanied a young nurse from room to room until they took a break in the cafeteria. "I'm glad you're here, Kelly. I feel like we've made a lot of progress already."

"Thanks, Rona. We have made good progress. The protocols may have to be adapted a bit once all the patients move in, but I know they've worked for me in the past. We need to be ready by next week when they start arriving." Kelly's thoughts drifted to the hot tub only a few miles away. Would Josie mind if she stopped by to use it?

She spent the afternoon getting to know the rest of the staff and preparing for her meeting with the administrator the next day. She shut down the company computer after copying files to her own laptop. She didn't want to take a chance of losing a day's work to a power failure. "See you tomorrow, Rona. Thanks for your help today."

"You're welcome. See you tomorrow." Rona waved and went back to her station.

"How'd your first day go?"

Kelly recognized Barb's voice, but it took a moment for her brain to register she was standing next to her car. "Barb? What are you doing here?"

"Sorry. I didn't mean to startle you. I knew you were here today, and I was working nearby, so I thought I'd stop and see if you'd go get a burger with me."

"You didn't startle me. I just wasn't expecting you. It's a nice surprise." Kelly realized she meant it. She liked Barb and hoped they'd see each other often while she was on the island. "Are we talking the Teepee?"

"The one and only."

"I'm ready." Kelly followed Barb to her car and nestled her laptop bag on the floor in the back seat. "Don't let me forget my laptop. I've got all my work backed up on it."

"No problem." Barb leaned over and kissed her as soon as she settled in the passenger seat. "You look amazing in those scrubs, by the way."

Barb made it sound as if she was the most beautiful woman who'd ever donned a pair. She swallowed around the lump in her throat. "I'm not sure I agree, but thank you." She slid a hand behind her neck, drew her toward her until their lips were a breath apart, and pressed her lips to hers. Barb pulled her close and she shifted to lean over the center column. Their tongues moved to the beat of their hearts, and Kelly lost herself in the velvet of her lips sliding across hers, demanding, and unsheathing a passion she welcomed. This woman wanted her. Was it enough? Could she take this further without getting hurt? Or worse, hurting Barb? She gently pulled away, uncharacteristically unsure. Still, thoughts of Josie continued to haunt her, and until she could put that behind her, she needed to slow down. "Whew. This is probably not the best place for such public display of affection. Especially given that it's my first day and all."

"Let's go get those burgers." Barb's touch was gentle as she cupped Kelly's face, her eyes dark with desire.

Kelly took her hand as they drove the short distance to get their dinner. Her thoughts bounced between inviting Barb to her apartment for the night and not moving too quickly. She didn't need to remind herself of her vow to find someone who shared her desire for a long-term relationship, but could she clarify her feelings as pillow talk, or did she need to speak beforehand? She ate her hamburger and decided to relax, enjoy Barb's company, and see where it led. Her resolve to keep Josie out of her thoughts turned out to be more difficult, and worrisome.

Kelly woke to dream memories of soft kisses and gentle caresses. The fogginess of her sleep cleared and flooded her with longing. The star of her dream troubled her. *Josie.* Granted, their date had finished without the kind of make-out session that had started it, and they'd mostly just walked and talked, getting to know one another, but surely she should be dreaming about the woman she'd been with that night, not the one she hadn't.

She shook off the nighttime fantasies and concentrated on preparing for her day. The text she'd received from the administrator after midnight notified her of three occupants who'd arrived in the late evening. By the time she pulled into the parking lot and parked, she'd settled into work mode.

"Good morning, Jim." Kelly stowed her laptop under the nurse's desk and turned her attention to the office computer. "How'd our first few residents do last night? I know their arrival was earlier than we anticipated."

"Hey, Kelly. My shift last night was quiet. Everyone's comfortable, and the night nurse, Jen, made extra notes since we hadn't expected them until next week." Jim leaned on the counter and pointed to the screen.

"Great. I'll review them this morning. I understand we'll be getting two new patients tomorrow."

"We'll be ready. You've done an excellent job with the preliminary schedules and procedures. Thanks again, by the way, for letting me take the later shift. It's wonderful to be able to spend time with my wife again."

"No problem. I'm glad it works for you. It's hard to find people to work the night shift sometimes. So, no problem with Mrs. Robins? It looks like they brought her in directly from the hospital."

"None I'm aware of."

"Thanks, Jim. You go home and get some rest. I'll get Jen's take on things." Kelly scrolled through the nurse's notes. Kelly wasn't certain the latest patient was stable enough to be away from her doctor, but it wasn't her call. The downside of her job was she had little control over who was admitted or when. Medicaid, the housing company, and the administration made those decisions. All she could do was make sure the residents received the best nursing care possible. The buzzing of her phone startled her.

She smiled when she read the screen. "Hi, Deb."

"Hey, stranger. How're things going up there?"

Kelly pinched the bridge of her nose. She hadn't even checked to make sure her friends had made it home safely, she'd been so busy moving and getting settled in. "They're going well. The facility is filling quickly already. How're things there? You all got home okay?"

"We did. It's not too bad here. Megan's doing a great job working with the nurses, and I've been catching up, but I miss our lunches together. Have you seen Josie?"

"No, but we're planning to get together for lunch."

"Cool. How about the hot conservation officer? Barb?"

"Yeah. Barb. She's great. I'll probably see her often while I'm still here. I'm not sure if it's going anywhere serious, but I like her a lot."

"I'm happy for you, Kel. Take care of yourself, and keep in touch, okay?"

"I will, Deb. My cell phone works better here than from Josie's place, so I'll give you a call during the day."

She disconnected the call and took a settling breath. She hadn't told Debby how much she was looking forward to seeing Josie. Her time with Barb was nice. But did she want to settle for *nice*? Was this another of her temporary connections? It definitely didn't hold the same…whatever the feeling was when she'd kissed Josie. She pushed aside her ponderings and concentrated on work.

By the end of the day, she was exhausted but proud of the amount of work they'd done. "I'm heading home, Rona. Call me if you have any questions." Kelly walked through the occupied wing of the building to look in on the residents before heading to her car. Barb had called to let her know she'd be working at a ranger's station on the opposite side of the island until late, so she was on her own for dinner. She hesitated for only a moment before turning onto the highway toward Harlow's by the Bay.

Josie's Jeep was parked in its usual spot when she arrived. The cabins all appeared to be empty, and she wondered when the next group was due to arrive. "Hello? Anyone home?" She knocked on the door as she let herself into the lodge.

"Kelly?" Ruth peeked out the partially open door to the kitchen.

"It's me, Ruth. I stopped by to say hello." She opened her arms and met Ruth halfway to wrap her in a hug. "I missed you."

"And I missed you, dear. How's work going? Do you like it? Can you stay for dinner tonight?"

"Whoa. Let's sit, and I'll tell you all about it." Ruth's warm welcome dispelled her awkwardness at her hasty decision to stop by unannounced.

"Josie's getting the cabins ready for our next group, so would you mind helping me with my hot tub exercises tonight?"

"Of course, Ruth. I don't have my swimsuit with me, but I have a pair of shorts and a T-shirt in the car. Do you think Josie would mind if I wore them?" She made a mental note to toss her suit in her trunk for the next time, unsure of why she knew there'd be a next time.

"I'm sure she wouldn't."

"Okay. Let's go exercise." Kelly helped Ruth into the tub and relaxed into their routine, feeling like she'd never left.

Chapter Nineteen

Josie chuckled at the sounds coming from the hot tub. "Hey, you two." She leaned in the doorway watching Nooko splash and giggle like a little kid. Her breath caught at the unexpected pleasure of seeing Kelly again.

"Hi, honey. Look who came by to say hello." Nooko kept her gentle kicking as she spoke while Kelly held her up.

"I hope you don't mind. I just wanted to see how Ruth was doing." Kelly looked nervous.

"Not at all. It's good to see you. I'd offer to help, but you've got things under control here. I've made vegetarian lasagna for dinner. Can you stay?"

"I didn't mean to invite myself over for dinner."

"I didn't think you did. I'm…we're glad you're here. Please stay." Josie mentally rolled her eyes. The last thing she wanted to do was sound desperate.

"Thank you. Lasagna sounds great." Kelly and Nooko stepped out of the tub and changed into dry clothes.

Josie retreated to the kitchen to prepare a salad to go with the lasagna, unable to suppress her excitement at Kelly's unexpected visit. She automatically set the table they'd used while Kelly was a guest and filled three water glasses after setting the bowl of salad on the table. She arranged, and then rearranged, the napkins. She wanted it to look inviting.

"Dinner smells great, Josie." Kelly spoke from across the room as she followed Nooko to the table. She pulled out Nooko's chair and made sure she was seated before turning to her. "Can I help with anything?"

"We're good. I just need to bring out the lasagna." She retrieved dinner from the kitchen and settled at their table in the lodge.

"How's your job going at the new place?" Nooko asked as Josie served up dinner.

"It's going well. We're filling up already and expect more residents next week. When are your next lodgers arriving?"

"They'll be here in July. More Canadian lesbians. I'm looking forward to meeting them." Josie set the pan of lasagna on the table and concentrated on her food instead of Kelly.

"So am I." Nooko beamed and raised her water glass in a toast. "They'll have to be great to beat your group." She sipped her water and continued. "I was planning to go home next week, but Josie convinced me to stay awhile longer."

"I don't think I ever knew you had specific plans to leave." Kelly looked back and forth between them.

"I told you she fell, and I worry about her being alone, so we'll have to negotiate." Josie squeezed Nooko's hand.

"Right. You mentioned it at the powwow. There was so much going on, I forgot."

"It was nothing. Just an accident," Nooko said.

"An accident isn't nothing." Kelly set her fork down and looked at Nooko. "What happened?"

"It was in my bathroom. I just reached a little too far and fell. I wasn't hurt."

Kelly rested her hand on Nooko's and leaned toward her. "You know, Ruth, after we reach sixty, we begin to lose muscle, and our ability to balance decreases. It's the reason I'm happy you're doing those exercises in the hot tub."

"Sixty?" Nooko looked perplexed and sighed. "I passed sixty a long time ago."

"I'm glad you're staying with Josie longer. We've got a great occupational therapist at work, and I'll bring her list of exercises to you. It'll help you stay strong."

"That would be wonderful. But I have to get back to my house before winter." Nooko sat up straight with a determined look on her face.

Josie tried not to groan. "Winter won't be here for a while. You'll have plenty of time for more exercise." She'd managed to convince Nooko to stay past their planned date, and now she had to figure out how she was going to let her be independent and still keep her safe. "We're having fruit for dessert, Kelly. Can I bring you a bowl?" She picked up Nooko's empty plate and her own and started for the kitchen.

"I'll help." Kelly followed her carrying her plate and the empty salad bowl.

"Thanks." Josie put the dishes in the sink and turned to face Kelly. "Can I ask you something?"

"Sure." Kelly leaned back on the counter with her arms at her side.

"You saw Nooko at the powwow. Do you think she's strong enough to live alone?"

"I'm afraid I'm not qualified to judge. From what I've seen of her, she's in pretty good shape for her age. Falling is serious, though, if she lived alone. I'm glad she has an emergency fall pendant."

"Yeah. It's the first thing I got for her after I witnessed her fall. I have my doubts the fall I saw her take was the only one. I sense she didn't want to worry me, but I can tell when she's holding something back. When I went to see her in March, she'd been treated by her doctor for a respiratory infection. Her neighbor told me she hadn't been out of bed for three days. If it hadn't been for her, I don't know what would've happened." Josie filled three small bowls with mixed fruit. "Let's have some dessert."

Kelly stopped her from leaving by gently resting her hand on her arm. "Do you want me to bring the occupational therapist by next week? She can give us her opinion of Ruth's possible falling tendencies."

Josie supposed the relief she felt showed on her face, since Kelly smiled sympathetically. She wrapped Kelly in a hug and spoke softly. "Fantastic, Kelly. Thank you, so much."

"Consider it done. I'll let you know when she's available." Kelly stepped out of her arms but not before she caught her slight hesitation.

"Let's finish dinner. I have something I want to give you. I was going to wait until our lunch next week, but since you're here, I'll give it to you tonight."

"I'm intrigued."

The sparkle in Kelly's eyes set off fireworks in her belly. She served the dessert and Kelly told them all about her new job, and Josie noticed that when the subject of her apartment came up, she became more subdued and changed the topic. They moved to continue talking in front of the fireplace, and Josie watched Nooko nod off in her seat on the couch. The temperature outside had dropped, and she covered Nooko with a blanket. She sat in comfortable silence with Kelly in the chair next to her. "This is nice. Thanks for coming over tonight."

"Thank you. Dinner was great." Kelly stretched her legs out in front of her and rested her head on the back of the chair.

"I'll be right back." Josie hurried to her studio before she gave in to the urge to straddle Kelly's lap and explore her full lips. Her breath hitched as the memory of their kiss flooded her senses. Kelly had her eyes closed and appeared to be sleeping when she returned. She rested the gift box on her lap and traced her jawline with her fingers. Her skin was soft and warm. Her eyes fluttered open and flashed an intense longing before she looked away.

"Sorry. I dozed off for a minute." Kelly sat up and cradled the foil wrapped package in both hands. "This is lovely." She carefully unwrapped and opened the package. "Oh, Josie." She dangled the dream catcher in front of her and watched the reflected rainbow colored patterns dance on the wall. "Thank you. It's beautiful, and I'll treasure it always."

"I'm glad you like it. Hang it above your bed and have sweet dreams." Josie sighed in relief at Kelly's positive reaction. She smiled as she watched her read the note and carefully place everything back in the box.

"I've really enjoyed this evening, but I've got to be at work at seven tomorrow, so I'm going to say good night." She patted sleeping Nooko's leg before moving toward the door.

Josie followed her out to the porch. "Thanks again for being so kind to Nooko. She thinks you're pretty special, and so do I."

Kelly stepped closer and rested her arms on her shoulders while carefully holding her gift. "You're both special to me, too. I don't how or when it happened, but I've come to feel like part of your family." She leaned forward, whispered a kiss on her lips, and quickly moved down the steps.

Josie watched her drive away, fearing she carried a piece of her heart with her. She checked on Nooko before checking the grounds and cabins for the night. Everything looked in order until she unlocked her office and found a note stuffed under the door.

Are you tired of cleaning up yet? Don't think a few lights and the police are going to keep me from getting what's mine. I'll be there in one week with my checkbook. Have the deed ready to sign or there will be consequences.

Josie checked her safe and found nothing out of the ordinary. She locked the note away and rushed back to the lodge to check on Nooko.

"It's time to go to bed." Josie gently stroked Nooko's arm to wake her. She wanted her tucked up in bed before she called the police yet again. At least this time they could be there when the bastard showed up.

"Sorry, dear. I fell asleep, didn't I?"

"You did. Kelly said to say good-bye, and she'll see you again soon."

"She's so nice." Nooko balanced with her cane as they walked to her room. "She's single, isn't she?"

"Yes. She's single." Josie pushed Abe's note out of her mind to concentrate on Nooko. She laid out her nightgown and helped her remove her slippers.

"I was thinking. Those other nice lesbian couples were so happy together. They probably dated first, don't you think?"

"They probably did. Yes." Josie anticipated where this conversation was going as she pulled the comforter down.

"Maybe you and Kelly could date. Maybe it would lead to something extraordinary for you. You need someone special in your life, dear."

"You're special, Nooko. You're all I need right now. Get some rest tonight. I'm making pancakes for breakfast."

"I saw the lovely dream catcher you made her. Your mother would be proud." Nooko's voice drifted quietly across the room as Josie turned out the light.

CHAPTER TWENTY

"Is this necessary, Joslyn? I've never had a lock on my bedroom door. I'm not sure I'm happy about it." Nooko spoke from her seat on the side of her bed.

Josie finished installing a deadbolt and a new lockable doorknob. "I don't trust this Abe guy. I don't want to scare you, but I'll show you the note he left. This makes me feel better." She tested the keys in the lock. "This key works in both the deadbolt and door lock. Whenever you're here alone, I want you to lock yourself in. Just until we get this dealt with, okay?"

"Fine, dear. If it'll make you happy."

"It will. Please don't forget. I've put your key on this wristband so you can wear it along with your emergency button. All the time."

Nooko held out her arm so Josie could put the wristband on. "Am I allowed to leave my room now?"

"Nooko, don't be like that. I'm sorry, but this is only until I can clear up this Abe thing. I'm going to try to talk to him and find out why he wants this place so badly. But until we know he's really gone away, I just need to know you're safe. Okay?" She chastised herself for not insisting he give her a phone number to reach him. It might have given her a little control over the situation, but that was probably what he wanted to avoid.

"Fine, honey. Can we have breakfast now?"

"Sounds good."

Josie scrambled eggs while Nooko sat at the kitchen table stirring the pancake mix. Her thoughts strayed to Kelly. Nooko's suggestion they might have something special between them prompted memories of her mother standing at the stove stirring a pot of corn soup while her father snuck up behind her to nuzzle her neck. It never failed to make her giggle and turn in his arms for a kiss. She fought to keep those happy memories of her parents' love and affection for each other forefront before the oppressive memory of loss, her mother ripped from their lives forever, took over. She'd seen how one day had changed her carefree energetic father into a bitter, miserable shell of his former self as if part of his soul had died along with the love of his life. She wouldn't take a chance of that happening to her, and it wouldn't be fair to Kelly. She was better off alone. She served the eggs and pancakes and concentrated on breakfast with Nooko.

Late that afternoon, Josie put Abe's note in her office safe and marked the date on the calendar before calling Barb. Abe hadn't threatened anything in particular and there hadn't been any more incidents of damage to her property lately. She hoped this would be resolved when he showed up in a week. She sat and dialed Barb's number, ignoring the slight twist of jealousy that surged when she thought of the time that she and Kelly might be spending together. She and Barb had been friends for a while now, and she didn't want an irrational emotional thing to come between them. That didn't kill off the little green monster, though.

"Hello, Barb. It's Josie."

"Hey, Josie. How're things at the new Harlow's by the Bay?"

"They're good, but I have a question for you. I got another note from Abe, and he's coming here in a week with a check, intending to buy the place. I'm not selling, but I'm a little worried. The note says there will be consequences if I don't sell, which doesn't make it sound like a friendly visit. He also said something about getting what's his. I don't know what he's talking about. Would you be able to plan to be here with me when he comes over?"

"We're looking at next Wednesday?"

"I believe so. His note says one week, and I got the note yesterday." Josie heard rustling of papers and figured Barb was consulting her calendar.

"Okay. I'll plan on it, and we'll do a search on him in the Secretary of State's driver's license database. That will, hopefully, give us a picture of the guy."

"He hasn't done anything, but his tone is sort of threatening. Would it be possible to, I don't know, maybe pick him up for questioning? I worry that would piss him off, though. What do you think?"

"I'll plan to be over early morning Wednesday. I'd like to see the message before he gets there. But I think it might be worth having an officer there, too, since they've already got a file on him."

"Thanks, come anytime, Barb. I don't plan to go anywhere this week. I sure wouldn't mind if the police came, too." Josie disconnected the call and phoned Kelly. She got her voice mail and left a message.

"Hi, Kelly. It's Josie. I'm calling about our lunch date this week. I've got a situation here, and I'm not comfortable leaving Nooko alone, so could we make it for Tuesday? And can you come by here and I'll fix us something? Thanks."

She hung up and went to find Nooko.

"Joslyn. Look who's here!"

"Kelly? Hey. I just left you a voice mail."

"Yeah. I just got it. I was on my way out of work and wanted to stop by to let you know about Caitlin, the occupational therapist. She can come by tomorrow, Ruth. Just to check on your balance and reflexes, okay? That will give her a better idea of what exercises to give you." Kelly took Nooko's hand but looked at Josie. "Next Tuesday sounds good for lunch. Is everything okay? You said something about a situation."

"Yes. Everything's fine."

"Tell her about the note, honey."

Nooko looked worried, and Josie wished she hadn't shown it to her.

"Note?" Kelly tipped her head and furrowed her brow.

"Abe left a note. He's coming next week with a check to try to convince me to sell to him."

"Would there be an offer high enough you'd consider selling?" Kelly asked.

"I grew up on Drummond Island, and I know for sure city living is not for me. I have a chance to create a safe relaxing space for lesbians and make a living doing it. I plan to have groomed cross-country ski trails available this winter. I can't imagine doing anything else, and I don't want to." She saw the spark in Nooko's eyes and knew she supported her in her decision. "There's nothing to do now but wait, so shall we relax with a cup of tea?"

"Tell me about your family, Kelly?" Nooko asked after they'd settled in their usual places on the couch.

Josie rose to check on a group of three women quietly playing cards at one of the tables before retaking the seat next to Kelly. She was happy Nooko had forgotten about Abe.

Kelly whispered to Josie, "When did they get here?"

"This morning. They called on short notice asking if they could stay until the weekend."

Kelly turned back to Nooko. "I have a younger sister who's staying in my house while I'm here, and she'll be going to Michigan State University in the fall. My parents live near Tampa in Florida, and I have an aunt and uncle in Ohio I see a couple of times a year." Kelly sipped her tea and glanced at her watch.

"I'm glad you stopped by tonight, dear." Nooko patted Kelly's leg. "I've made a pot of corn soup, can you stay for a bowl?"

"Thank you for offering, but I've got dinner plans tonight. I'm glad I stopped by, too." Kelly finished her tea and stood.

"Thanks again. I'll see you on Tuesday." Josie pushed away her desire to know if Kelly's dinner plan was a date with Barb, but she had a harder time pushing away her anticipation at seeing Kelly again soon.

"Call me if you need anything," Kelly said in her ear as she hugged her good-bye.

Josie watched from the porch as Kelly pulled away. Her jealous reaction to Kelly's dinner date puzzled her. Kelly wanted love and permanency. She did not. Why should it matter to her who Kelly dated? She went inside with a heaviness in her gut she couldn't identify.

❖

Kelly pulled into the Teepee's parking lot five minutes behind their agreed-upon time. She didn't see Barb's SUV in its usual spot, so she waited for a few minutes before going to the window to place their order. They'd been meeting there for dinner often enough in the two weeks she'd been in her apartment that they were comfortable ordering for each other. Kelly liked that aspect of their growing relationship. She liked most things about Barb, and her punctuality was one of them, so this tardiness was unusual. She knew Barb would have a good excuse, but she wondered how much time she wanted to invest in something that might not go anywhere, reminding herself she wanted someone available. She tipped her head back on the seat and considered her definition of available. Certainly, she had to be single, but what good was trying to build a life with someone who was rarely around?

Barb's one relationship had failed because of her intense, unpredictable work schedule. Was that something Kelly could live with? She pushed aside her brooding, certain she still wanted to see where their connection would take them. She checked her phone for messages and sent a text. She started to worry after half an hour. Barb's job wasn't dangerous, but she'd told her stories of poachers and angry landowners getting into shoot-outs. She sent another text but remembered how spotty the reception could be if Barb was on the other side of the island. She finished eating her burger and tried calling. The call disconnected before she could leave a message, so she gave up. Her phone pinged before she had time to start her car.

Sorry I'm late, but I'm on the way.

Barb pulled into the lot a few minutes later.

"Sorry, Kelly." Barb hopped out of her vehicle and rushed to her car. She settled into the passenger seat and grabbed the bag of food. "Thanks for ordering for me. I'm starved."

"Problems today?" Kelly sipped her drink and watched Barb bite into her burger.

She swallowed before speaking. "It's been a weird day, for sure. I got a call this morning from a resident on the north side of the island about someone trespassing. I went to check it out, and before I finished with him, I got a call about a trespasser on another property. I finished with that call and received two more from neighboring residents. They were pretty close to Josie's place, so I'll stop by and check on her tomorrow. It's odd to have so many similar calls in one day. We get the usual kids on their ATVs and hunters infringing, but not just someone walking about someone's property. And with the problems Josie's been having…well, seems like I should give her a call." Barb finished her burger and leaned to kiss her. "Sorry. I'm all wound up tonight. How was your day?"

"Quieter than yours. We're still waiting for the last few patients to move in, so I was able to leave a little early today. Things will be ramping up next week. We'll be nearly full, and I have three new nurses starting Monday." Kelly enjoyed their easy conversation and the feeling of familiarity between them. It was what she wanted in a relationship. Sharing her day with her lover over dinner and sitting in comfortable silence. But something she was having a hard time identifying was missing with Barb. They enjoyed each other's company, but where was the passion? Why didn't she long to kiss Barb and hold her throughout the night? To wake up with her and share breakfast in bed? She hadn't thought of her all day except when she realized the time at Josie's. *Josie*. Thoughts of her had drifted through her mind all day. She'd taken a coffee break and wondered what she was doing. At lunchtime, she'd wondered what she and Ruth were eating. The afternoon break had her speculating what Josie was planning for dinner and if they would have a fire in the fireplace. She started, realizing Barb had spoken. "Sorry, I drifted for a moment. What did you say?"

"I asked if you wanted anything else to eat or drink."

"Oh. No, thank you. I'm good. Are you getting anything more?" Kelly stuffed their empty cups into the empty bags.

"No. I'm sorry to cut our evening short, but I actually have to get back to my office tonight to file reports and try to make some sense of today's events."

Kelly leaned over and kissed her, hard, willing herself to feel more than a dull spark. She laced her fingers through her hair and pulled her closer while exploring her mouth with her tongue. Barb responded by tugging her shirt out of her pants and cupping her breast through her bra. Her nipples tightened and her pussy clenched, but her thoughts drifted. She slowly pulled away and stroked Barb's cheek.

Barb sat back and gathered her in her arms. "Whew. I'll have a hard time working after this." She kissed her and exited the vehicle. With a quick wave, she was gone.

Kelly took the long route back to her apartment. She sat in her car for a few minutes trying to sort out her feelings. Her final thought as she entered her kitchen was that Barb was special, but the woman she wanted was Josie, which meant Barb wasn't special enough. She tossed her keys on the counter and plopped onto her bed. She grappled with her feelings for sweet, romantic Barb compared to intense, caring, gentle, unavailable Josie. She gazed at her dream catcher hanging above her bed and willed it to bring her resolutions in her dreams.

Chapter Twenty-one

I hope you got my message. I'm looking forward to our meetin' and finally claiming what's mine. I don't have any idea why you ended up with the place. Jack never said nuthin' about having a lesbo daughter. It would be in your best interest to make sure the deed is ready to hand over. I hope you'll be smart about this.

Josie carefully put the letter in the safe and locked it. *Why in the world does this guy want this place? And how does he sneak around here without being seen?* Questions swirled in Josie's mind, so she went to talk to Nooko to look for answers.

"I don't know, Joslyn. Harold never said anything about knowing a Bernstein."

"Yeah. Dad never did either. Abe told me when he came in February he'd hunted with him. Even though he called him Jack. I know Dad went hunting often with a couple of his buddies, but he never told me their names. Did he ever say anything to you about any of his friends?"

"As you know, after your mom died he withdrew, and we had little contact with him. I do remember him mentioning his hunting trips, but he never said who he went with. Sorry, dear."

"I remember the list of chores he left for me on the days he was gone, but he never told me who he was with either. I looked at all the papers in his desk, and nothing had the name Abe Bernstein on it. Or anyone else's name, for that matter. I guess I'll have to wait until next week and see what Abe offers. His letters are just scary enough to worry me, but not threatening enough for the police to do anything.

Barb is searching for his driver's license picture. That way they'll at least be able to recognize him."

"That's a good idea, dear."

Josie pushed aside her worries to concentrate on Nooko's exercises. "Let's do some work in the tub. Caitlin told me you were doing great and to keep up the good work."

They finished doing the therapist's suggested movements and settled in the lodge before dinner. "Thank you for helping me, honey. I feel stronger since we've been doing those workouts. I might be able to get rid of my cane." Nooko looked so hopeful that Josie nodded and smiled.

"How does pizza sound for dinner?" Josie asked.

"Great. Is Kelly coming over?"

Josie took a deep breath, choosing her words carefully. She knew her grandmother was holding out hopes for something more between them, but that wasn't to happen. "Kelly's working, Nooko. She'll be here for lunch on Tuesday, but I don't think we're on her way home, so she might not come by anymore."

"Oh, she will." Nooko patted her hand and spoke with such conviction, Josie allowed herself to believe it would happen.

"Well, she won't be here today, so I'm going to put the pizza in the oven."

Josie attached the final two eagle feathers on the lodge's dream catcher before holding it up to review the finished product. The multicolored beads reflected the light from the setting sun, casting shimmering lines of colored beams across the floor. She rethought her original intention of hanging it above the fireplace. It would be perfect in a window. She carefully situated it in a drawer and went to finish her evening walk about the grounds.

Barb's vehicle pulled up just as she reached her office door.

"Hey, Josie. I left a message on your voice mail I was coming over. I wanted to see how everything was going."

"Thanks, Barb. Sorry, I was going to check my messages now. I talked to my grandmother, and neither of us can remember ever hearing of this Abe guy. Is there any way you could do some sort of search or a background check on him?"

"Yeah. I can go to our main office in Sault Saint Marie tomorrow and do a computer search. They have software to find anything on anybody, assuming they've committed some kind of crime or are on the database for some other reason. I'll print out a few pictures when I look him up so you can verify we've got the right guy, assuming anything pops on him. I'll also run that Secretary of State search for a driver's license. Maybe we'll get a hit on that. So, has everything been quiet here otherwise?"

"It has. Other than his notes, I haven't had any incidents since the spray painting, and I'm sure it was Abe. I just can't figure out why he's pushing so hard to buy my property."

"Other than the issues you've told me about, have you or any of your guests noticed anyone creeping around the property?"

"No. But my lights only have a limited range. Why?"

"It's weird, but the other day I got several calls from residents on either side of you. They reported seeing someone wandering on their property."

"My lights are only close to the buildings. I wouldn't know if someone was lurking farther away than maybe thirty feet, and he seems to know when I'm not around when he drops off his little love notes. Would you like to walk with me on my rounds now?"

"I will, thanks. It could be kids looking for private places or potential poachers, but I'll keep my eye out for you."

Josie and Barb followed her usual route through the woods, past the cabins, and back to the lodge. "All is quiet tonight." Josie didn't believe the kids or poachers explanation. Abe's notes convinced her he was most likely behind everything, but she wasn't sure what she could do about it.

"I'm glad you're doing so well with this place, my friend. I know your dad had it mortgaged to the hilt. Congratulations on bringing it around. You've made it into a comfortable space."

"Thanks, Barb. I can't imagine doing anything else. I love it."

"I have to thank you, too."

"For what?"

"For bringing Kelly into my life. We've been seeing each other, and I have to say, I'm smitten."

Barb's faraway look and blissful smile stifled any response. Josie led the way toward the lodge in silence. Her assumption that Kelly's dinner plans had been a date with Barb were true. The knot in her stomach tightened, and she swallowed hard to relieve the tightness in her throat. She reminded herself again that it was none of her business who Kelly dated.

"Hi, Ruth. It's good to see you again." Barb leaned to hug Nooko.

"Hi, Barb. Are you here to help us figure out who Abe is?"

"I'm going to make some inquiries tomorrow. You and Josie just call me if you need anything before we sort this out."

"Thank you, dear. We will."

"Thanks, Barb. Hopefully, I won't need to call you before Wednesday." Josie walked her to the door, coaxing herself to sound cheerful. She wouldn't let on how the idea of her with Kelly made her want to curl into a ball.

"I'll let you know what I find on this guy. Take care."

"Ready for some popcorn?" Josie sat next to Nooko after Barb left and rested her arm over her shoulders.

"You're worried. I can feel it." Nooko leaned into her and sighed. "It'll all work out as the Creator wills, and popcorn sounds good."

Josie leaned against the kitchen counter, listening to the popcorn crackling and wondered if her heart might make the same sound if Barb and Kelly became an official item. She tried to push the thoughts away. There wasn't any point in thinking about what couldn't be or what could happen. There was only today.

A couple who'd been playing Scrabble was gone when she returned with two full bowls of popcorn. "I see we're alone tonight." She passed Nooko a bowl and took a handful from hers.

"I miss our first group. They were so friendly." Nooko spoke between bites. "Have you heard from any of them besides Kelly?"

"No. I don't expect to unless they come back to stay someday. It's sort of the way it works. Not all our guests will be as engaging as they were."

"Do you have anyone coming for the Fourth?"

"No. The July couple canceled, so unless someone calls, we'll be empty until the snow flies."

"I never knew what it was like for your father, being responsible for caring for the place to make sure the lodgers were comfortable. I see it's quite a bit of work. Have you considered selling to Abe? Maybe he'll make a big enough offer to make it worth selling."

Josie tipped her head back on the couch and considered Nooko's question. He had said he'd make a hefty offer. "I want to keep it. I've finally paid off the high-interest loan Dad took out, and I'm sure I can make a profit. I do need to get rid of this Abe guy, though. I worry he might start messing with my guests."

"You keep working as hard as you are, and I know you'll make it. I'll bet Barb'll be able to help get rid of Abe."

Nooko squeezed her hand, and Josie wondered who was taking care of whom.

❖

Josie rolled over and checked her clock. Six thirty. She noted the soft glow of the sunrise filtering into her room and the faint scent of bacon cooking. *Bacon?* She quickly slipped into shorts and a T-shirt before rushing to Nooko's room. It was empty, the door wide open. The aroma drew her to the kitchen, where Nooko stood over a pan of sizzling bacon with fork in one hand and her cane in the other.

"Good morning, dear. I thought I'd make breakfast this morning. You can get the bread out for toast if you don't mind. And would you scramble the eggs for me, please?"

"No problem. It's six thirty already. Half the day's gone." Josie grinned, pleased to see the smile spread on Nooko's face.

"I told you I wanted to help, and I'm grateful for you and Kelly helping me to get stronger, so I'm making breakfast today." She deftly lifted the strips of bacon out of the pan and onto a plate lined with paper towels. "Now bring me those eggs."

They sat at the tiny kitchen table sipping coffee after eating. "I'm glad those exercises are helping. The therapist will be back tomorrow to check on you, remember?"

"I hope Kelly comes with her."

"Yeah, Nooko. Me, too."

"Have you given any thought to my suggestion that you and Kelly go out on dates? You're a grown woman, and I don't mean to be nosy, but everything I've seen about Kelly seems to be wonderful. Is there something about her I don't know? That you don't like?"

"No, Nooko." Josie opened up, knowing if she was going to trust anyone with her real fears, it could be her grandmother. "I'm afraid. I'm afraid to fall for anyone because I don't want to go through what Dad did. I couldn't live through loving someone and losing them." Josie shuddered as she took a breath. "Can you understand? You saw what

Dad went through. He was never the same after Mom died. It's just too painful to even think about, much less live through."

"What about all the amazing years they had together? What about the beautiful child, you, they bore and raised together? The opportunity to share a life and love with someone is the greatest gift the Creator gave us humans. Kelly and her group are the only lesbians I've ever met." Nooko looked pensive. "At least that I know of, and they are an excellent example of love. I could see how much they cared about each other, how tender they were with their partners. What I see is that you and Kelly care about each other. Awful, senseless accidents happen all the time. Do you think those women would give up one minute of time together for something that might happen? It might never happen and they'll grow old together." Nooko sighed. "Maybe you could consider that, honey. I love you, and I want to see you happy."

Josie choked back tears as she hugged her nooko. She didn't understand, but that was okay. It was enough to know how deeply she was loved, even if she couldn't love someone else the same way.

CHAPTER TWENTY-TWO

Kelly finished the last of her daily reports and closed her laptop. "I'm ready to go home for the day." She spoke to the three nurses standing at their stations recording patient information. She was pleased with the progress they'd made since the facility opened and figured she'd be able to cut her stay short by a full month at the rate they were going. "You all have my cell number if you need anything." She acknowledged a few waves and mumbled good-byes as she exited the building. She didn't hesitate when she reached the end of the parking lot and turned toward Harlow's by the Bay.

"Hello. Anyone home?" Kelly scanned the empty room. The seat on the couch she'd grown to think of as Ruth's was empty, as was the rest of the lodge. She checked the hot tub room and noted the wet towels hanging on the racks. She went through the kitchen to the back door and followed the path toward the water's edge, aware she was technically trespassing. She turned and started back to the lodge when she heard Ruth's exclamation.

"I've got one!"

She followed the sound and grinned when Ruth came into view sitting on a folding chair at the end of the dock, dangling a tiny fish on the end of her fishing pole. She watched Josie clap and remove the fish from her line before attaching a night crawler on the hook and tossing it into the water. "I think you two are having fun."

They both turned toward her, and her stomach rolled at the welcome in Josie's eyes.

Ruth waved her over. "We are. Come join us. Are you staying for dinner?"

Kelly laughed and worked her way toward them through the bush. "From the looks of what you're catching, I should've brought you dinner." She sat on the same bench she and Josie had shared on one of the first days she'd been there. It felt like long ago, and at the same time, like only yesterday. "You go ahead and do all the work. I'll watch from here." Just as she spoke, Ruth's pole bent, and she squealed, obviously thrilled.

"I've got another one." She lifted the rod and reel at the same time as the teeny bluegill flailed until it flipped off the hook. "Oh." Ruth looked dejected enough to believe she'd lost a forty-pound bluefin tuna.

"It's okay, Ruth. Keep trying. You'll get a keeper." Kelly watched Ruth lean to Josie and murmur something. Josie smiled and nodded. She put another worm on Ruth's line and left the dock to join Kelly on the bench.

"Hi there. I'm glad you came by. Nooko's enjoying herself and wants me to thank you again for sending Caitlin over. The exercises have done wonders to boost her confidence, and I can see her stability improving."

"Oh, you're welcome. Caitlin's a sweetie. She has all the residents clamoring for her attention at work, so I'm not sure she'll be able to get away anymore. We're nearly full now, and she's needed full-time." Kelly relaxed back on the bench, feeling as if there was nowhere else she'd rather be. "I didn't mean to intrude, Josie. I only stopped by to see how she was doing and let you know about Caitlin."

"You're never intruding." Josie had turned to face her and their knees touched. "You're welcome anytime, Kelly." She gently cupped her face with one hand and Kelly watched her eyes darken before she dropped her hand to her lap.

Kelly willed her breathing back to normal. Josie's hand was warm and gentle and smelled lightly of fish. She felt so close to being kissed, and Kelly wanted her kiss more than anything she'd wanted in a long time.

"Are you guys planning to cook those teeny-weeny fish you're catching?" Kelly asked, shaking off the inappropriate longing.

Josie laughed. "Heck no. I thought Nooko needed a little something different to do today. I've got a pot roast with vegetables, potatoes, and corn cooking, and we thought we'd go to the Teepee for ice cream later. Can you join us?"

"I'd love to. Thanks."

They sat in silence, enjoying the breeze off the bay, watching the sunlight sparkle on the water, and Kelly relaxed into the moment, pushing aside her confusion. She was dating Barb, and Josie hadn't indicated that she'd changed her mind about being open to a relationship. What was she doing putting herself back into situations that made Josie so tempting? She mentally shook herself, her serenity shattered.

Kelly stood abruptly, willing a solution into her jumbled thoughts. Her desire for Josie had only grown in the time they'd spent together, and she could tell Josie desired her, too.

"You okay?"

Josie's brow furrowed, and Kelly knew she needed to offer an explanation.

"Yeah. I'm fine." She debated whether to disclose how unsettled she was. "I'm just not sure I'm being honest with myself, or you, about why I'm here." She sat back onto the bench. "I don't want to send you mixed messages, but I miss you, and I don't know what to do about it."

Josie was quiet and Kelly covered her hand with hers, allowing herself that small connection, fearing it wasn't enough.

They were silent for a while, until Josie squeezed her hand softly. "I'm not sure what to say to that. You know where I stand, but I also can't get enough time with you. I don't want to send you mixed messages either." She stood, pulling Kelly up with her. "So maybe we should call it a night?"

Kelly knew her smile probably wasn't convincing, given the look of sadness in Josie's eyes, but she couldn't fake being happy. "That sounds like a good idea."

The trip home from the Teepee was quiet. Kelly appeared lost in thought and Josie struggled to find words to respond to her claim of missing her. She missed Kelly when she was gone, too, but she refused to acknowledge it meant more than missing a friend. She parked in front of the lodge and helped Nooko out of the vehicle.

"Thanks for inviting me along. I'm going to end up twenty pounds heavier by the time I get home if I keep eating so much ice cream." Kelly placed her hand on her belly and grinned.

"I'm glad you came with us. Would you like to come in for a cup of tea or coffee before you leave?" Josie helped Nooko up the steps and waited for Kelly's response, unsure of what else to say.

"Thank you, but I think I'll head home. Take care and you keep up the good work, Ruth. I'll tell Caitlin how well you're doing."

Nooko looked content after she hugged Kelly good-bye and sat to peruse the local newspaper. Josie understood Nooko's desire to go back to her house, her home, where she'd spent so many years with her husband. She thought of her mother happily cooking, or sweeping the floor, always smiling and positive, always loving her and her father. "Do you think love just happens, Nooko?"

Nooko set her paper aside but didn't immediately answer. "No, honey. The Creator gave us the ability to love, but we have to be brave enough to embrace it. We all are part of nature, of the world around us, of the great plan of the Creator. Think about how many people we have the opportunity to meet in our lifetime. All of our relationships have meaning and purpose and are offered to us as gifts. Lessons to learn." Nooko sat back quietly and looked at her, clearly waiting for her to continue.

"How did you know Grandpa was the person you wanted to love and spend the rest of your life with? And weren't you afraid of losing him?"

"I spent many months getting to know Harold. Times were different. There wasn't dating the way you kids do it now, but we spent time together and learned what was in each other's heart. The body, mind, and spirit of another are what show their ability to give themselves in love. Harold's love called to me. Our spiritual interaction joined us, and I believe the Creator was pleased with my choice. As to fearing I'd lose him, I can only say if I worried about loss all the time, it would have kept me from enjoying the wonderful years we had together. None of us knows how much time we've been given. All we can do is appreciate the time we have."

Josie quietly contemplated her nooko's words for a few minutes before standing and tossing the book she'd only glanced at on the table. "I'm going to make my final walk around for the night."

"I'll be here, dear. I want to finish reading this article about the library."

Josie followed her usual route around the cabins and back to her office. She double-checked the safe and the locks on the doors. Everything was quiet. She took a path through the woods on her way back, needing to process what Nooko had said about love. She remembered, as a child, her mother talking about the Creator, and her father, God. Her own beliefs had fallen somewhere in between until her mother's death. What kind of God or Creator would allow such tragedy? Why give a person someone to love and snatch them away? She hadn't been able to make sense of it before, and she still couldn't.

But…maybe Nooko was right about making the best of the time you had and not worrying about what might happen. For the first time in years, she felt a spark of hope that the lonely emptiness she'd defined as solitude could be filled. Memories of Kelly's face, her touch, her kiss arose. But Kelly was with Barb. She lumbered back to the lodge. *Maybe Kelly isn't the one. Maybe she's just the one to show me that I want more.* It didn't seem likely at the moment, but for the first time, she was open to the idea.

"Everything looks good." She sat next to Nooko on the couch.

"I miss…never mind. I've already told you." Nooko stood and took two steps without using her cane. "Look, Joslyn! I'm getting steadier."

"Great. Just be careful."

Nooko used her cane for the rest of the trip to her bedroom, wearing a huge grin.

Josie made herself a cup of tea and took it to the front porch. She sat on one of the rockers to appreciate the summer evening, and her thoughts strayed first to Kelly, then to Nooko's words. Her emotions tumbled about inside her like loose marbles. She worked to make sense of her feelings, but the irrational fear of loss kept creeping to the forefront, and she didn't know how to change that.

Chapter Twenty-three

I'm sorry, Josie. I didn't find anything criminal on this guy. No arrests, no nothing. We searched the Secretary of State database and found this picture, though. Is this the guy?" She held up the driver's license picture she'd found online for the only Abe Bernstein living in the Upper Peninsula.

"Yeah. That's him." Josie cringed at the sneer on his face. "Creepy guy."

"His son, Joe, has been picked up twice for drunk driving, but Abe appears to be clean." Barb leaned on the front desk reviewing the paperwork she'd brought.

"Just because he doesn't have a record doesn't mean he's trustworthy." Josie allowed her disappointment to show about the information Barb had found on Abe.

"You're right. He could be a sneaky one. I did find an Abe Bernstein who was a member of the Purple Gang out of Detroit in the nineteen twenties, but he died almost fifty years ago. Maybe this Abe is related somehow."

"Thanks for trying, Barb. I hope to find out more about his motives on Wednesday. Are you still planning on being here?"

"Oh, yes. We'll probably post his picture around the island if necessary. Did he give you a time?"

"No. I guess I'll just be ready all day."

"Okay. I'll plan to be in the area and you can text me when he gets here. I've got to get back to work."

"Thanks, Barb. I appreciate your help." Josie collected her cleaning supplies and headed to the vacated cabins. She pushed aside thoughts of whether Barb and Kelly were going out later as she finished her chores and went to find Nooko. It was none of her business, and Barb had been a friend for a long time. She should just be happy for them. *Sure. I can do that.*

"Any news, dear?" Nooko asked from her seat on the couch.

"Barb didn't find anything significant about Abe, but she did find his driver's license picture. I guess we'll just wait and see what happens Wednesday."

"Maybe he'll offer you ten million dollars for the place." Nooko chuckled.

Josie laughed. "I'll admit I might consider ten million, but only for a second. I don't want to sell. I love it here, and I love what I've accomplished so far. I don't think the land value will decline, so I'm not worried about getting my money out of it. Do you understand?" Josie worried her nooko might prefer she sell the place and move to her house.

"I'm teasing you, honey. Of course you should stay and do what you love. You have a wonderful opportunity here, and happiness and contentment mean more than all the money in the world."

Josie had concealed her anxiety at the thought of seeing and talking to Abe all week, but knowing she had Nooko's support helped quiet her nerves. She held back tears and pulled Nooko into her arms. "Thank you. I love you, Nooko."

"I love you, too. Everything will work out."

Josie supported Nooko under her stomach as she kicked and waved her arms against the resistance of the water. "You're doing great." She counted the number of turns as she circled. "Just two more." She rounded the last turn and started at the sight of Kelly standing in the doorway clapping.

"Good job, you two." She entered the room and sat on one of the plastic chairs.

"Kelly!" Nooko called out, then whispered, "I told you she'd be back."

"Hi, Ruth. You're doing a super job. Do you feel stronger?"

"I do. Wait. Joslyn, help me out of here." Nooko kicked and turned until she was standing.

"Whoa, Nooko." Josie supported her as she stepped out of the hot tub and followed her out.

"I don't mean to intrude. I just stopped by to see how Ruth was doing without Caitlin."

"As you can see, she's doing quite well." Josie wrapped a towel around Nooko's body and then her own. She curbed her pleasure at Kelly's unexpected visit. "Can you stay for dinner?" She smiled inwardly at her covert intent to find out if Kelly had a date with Barb.

Kelly stood and held up one finger in a "be right back gesture" and left the room.

"Did she leave?" Nooko asked.

Kelly reappeared in the doorway before Josie could answer.

"I told you it was my turn to bring food." She held up two bags from the homemade pasties restaurant.

Nooko led the way to a table in the lodge, barely leaning on her cane at all.

Kelly spoke softly. "She really is feeling better, isn't she?"

Josie nodded. "I'll get the plates while she shows off for you." Josie hurried to the kitchen to take a moment to settle her nerves. Kelly's unexpected visit thrilled her, but the confusing questions about her own feelings dulled her enthusiasm. She took a deep breath and returned with plates and silverware. "Here we go. Let's eat."

"How's your job going, Kelly?" Nooko asked between bites.

"It's going well. I'll be able to go home earlier than originally planned. The nurses and staff are catching on quickly, and the patients are being well cared for."

Josie took a bite of her pasty and scrambled for something to say to ease the blow to her gut. She knew Kelly was only on the island temporarily, but she didn't figure on the hollowness the reality caused. "You'll be here for our lunch tomorrow, won't you?" she asked.

"Of course. I'm looking forward it."

She smiled and the now familiar butterflies fluttered in Josie's belly. "Good. I'm looking forward to it, too. So, Nooko, how's ice cream at the Teepee sound?"

"I'm ready," Nooko said.

"I can drive, if you want," Kelly said. "It'll make me feel like I'm burning some calories." She smirked and pulled out her keys.

The restaurant was more crowded than Josie had ever seen it. "Wow. It must be the beautiful evening. I've never seen it so crowded. You guys relax. I'll go stand in line." Josie climbed out of the car.

"Kelly will go with you." Nooko waved her hand, shooing her away. "I'll be fine here."

Josie continued to the end of the line and waited for Kelly.

"I'd say Ruth is trying to prove her independence." Kelly stood close as the line grew and a group of kids milled about them.

Josie suspected Nooko had ulterior motives by staying in the car and sending Kelly out. She surveyed the crowd and took a step back to allow a kid to cut through the line. The heat from Kelly's body against hers enveloped her as if she were in her arms. "Yes, I think she is. She wants to go back home, and I guess I hope she can, although I'll miss her. I've gotten used to having her here. And I think having so many people around has been good for her, too." Josie moved forward to place their order and handed Kelly her ice cream.

"Thanks. This might sound odd, but I'd miss her, too. I enjoy spending time with her." She paused and licked her ice cream. "And you."

"I like spending time with you, too." She stood unmoving, tethered by their connection, until her cold fingers reminded her Nooko was waiting. "I guess we better get this to Nooko before it melts." She held up the bowl of melting vanilla ice cream.

"I thought you'd forgotten about me." Nooko grabbed her ice cream and scooped a spoonful into her mouth.

Josie watched Kelly taste the top of her scoop with the tip of her tongue before sliding the spoon into her mouth. She hummed as she swallowed, and Josie whimpered inside.

"Thanks for coming by tonight and bringing dinner. You made Nooko's day." Josie and Kelly sat on the porch and watched fireflies flicker in the fading evening light.

"My pleasure. It seems I'm having a hard time staying away." Kelly shifted in her seat and leaned forward with her elbows on her knees. "I should go and let you get to bed."

Josie checked her watch. "It's still early. Nooko's reading the paper, and I need to make my final walk around the cabins."

"Could I walk with you?"

Josie stood and reflexively reached for her hand. "Let's go." The rightness of their connection took her by surprise, but the dullness of the usual gnawing fear stunned her for a moment. She pushed aside the unfamiliar feeling and glanced at Kelly. Her eyes were lowered, and she walked slowly next to her. She wanted to raise their joined hands to her lips and murmur the words against her warm skin, words she knew Kelly wanted to hear. Instead, she breathed in the warm evening air, knowing Kelly deserved her honesty. She released her hand. "I'm glad your work at the facility is going smoothly, although we'll miss you when you leave the island."

Kelly looked surprised by the release for a moment and slid her hands into her pockets. "I've had a wonderful time here. Your resort is perfect, Josie. I think you'll do really well with it."

They continued at a slow pace and Josie's gut roiled at the feeling of distance between them.

They checked every cabin and returned to the lodge so Kelly could say good-bye to Nooko. "Good night, Ruth."

"Good night, dear. Thank you for dinner. I'll see you tomorrow for lunch, won't I?"

"Definitely."

"Good. You two run along. I'm going to finish the paper before I go to bed." Nooko lifted the newspaper in front of her face.

Josie shrugged and shook her head. "I guess we've been dismissed. I'll walk you out."

Josie leaned back on the porch post. "Drive safely. I'll see you tomorrow."

"I will." Kelly didn't move off the porch. "I'll be here about noon tomorrow." She still didn't move.

"I'll be here." Josie held her breath as Kelly moved closer, stood with her legs on either side of her thighs, and rested her hands on her waist. Josie stiffened, knowing this was a bad idea, but surrendered to her simmering need to feel Kelly in her arms, pulled her against her, and claimed her lips. Kelly pressed against her and, as the first time they'd kissed, she marveled at how perfectly they fit together, how right it felt. She cradled Kelly's face in her hands and pulled away slightly to place soft kisses on the side of her mouth. Kelly tipped her head back, and Josie trailed gentle nuzzles down her throat to the velvety skin above her chest. She craved to continue, to tear off her shirt and nibble the smooth skin of her breasts, circle her nipples with her tongue, and watch her excitement build until the explosion of release overtook her. She craved all of it and more. The something more frightened her to death. She wrapped her in her arms, drew her close, and held her as their heartbeats returned to normal.

"I feel safe in your arms. It feels...I don't know. As if I belong here."

Kelly looked so vulnerable, Josie's heart ached.

"You feel amazing." Josie kissed her temple and stepped away. "I'm looking forward to seeing you again tomorrow."

"Me, too. I'm not sure what's going on with me, Josie. I don't mean to lead you on or push you toward something you don't want, but it feels so right to be in your arms that I can't seem to stay away."

Josie watched Kelly take a shaky breath. "I probably don't need to tell you I want you. I want you in my arms." She swallowed the emotion that tore at her heart when she realized she wanted to feel Kelly everywhere. "I'm just not sure I can offer more than that."

"Thank you for being honest with me." Kelly gently stroked her cheek. "I'll see you tomorrow for lunch." She gave her a weak smile before stepping off the porch and getting into her car.

Josie leaned against the post, searching for serenity in the quiet night. Questions popped into her mind like a field of prairie dogs, each searching for an answer before ducking back into their burrow. She admitted she wanted Kelly in her life, but in what capacity? Could they have a friendship hundreds of miles apart? She blew out a sigh and went inside.

CHAPTER TWENTY-FOUR

K elly entered information for the latest patient into the computer. She was one of two residents she would have denied if it were up to her. Their facility wasn't equipped to care for dementia patients, so they were supposed to refer them to another nursing home off the island. She suppressed her frustration at the administration but scrambled to figure out a way to handle care for them. She made notes to the staff and, grateful for the new cable internet, sent an email to the administrator expressing her concerns. She worked until just before noon and closed her laptop. "I might be a little late coming back from lunch today," she said to the staff in the lunch room as she hurried out the door.

She didn't want to think too hard about the kiss she'd shared with Josie the night before as she drove the short distance to her place. This lunch wasn't supposed to be a date, but she was having a hard time convincing herself it wasn't and even a harder time convincing herself she didn't want it to be. There was more to their kiss than sparks, and she knew Josie felt it, too. Now all she had to do was figure out what to do about it. She pulled into her usual parking spot and turned off her car engine. She took a minute to compose herself, determined to refrain from grabbing Josie as soon as she saw her. She opened her car door, and Josie's appearance on the porch dissolved her willpower like sugar in water. She looked sexy and dangerous as she looked Kelly over, passion radiating in her gaze.

"Hey there."

"Hi. Lunch is ready." Josie reached for her hand as she slowly took the steps one at a time. "Nooko's waiting impatiently, I'm afraid."

"I'm not late, am I?" Kelly checked her watch.

"Not at all. She's just looking forward to seeing you."

"We better get in there." Kelly walked past Josie but stopped when she wrapped her arms around her from behind and pulled her up against her. She nuzzled her neck and tickled the smooth skin behind her ear with her tongue. Kelly swayed and allowed Josie's support. She'd never wanted anyone as much as she did Josie at that moment. "Isn't Ruth waiting?" Her voice sounded far away to her.

"Hmm." Josie released her and stepped back. "Sorry. You're irresistible. Let's go have lunch."

Kelly followed her on shaky legs.

"There you are. I was just going to look for you two." Ruth sat at one of the tables set with plates and silverware.

"Sorry, Ruth. We had something to discuss." Kelly hugged Ruth before offering to help Josie.

"You sit. I'll get the food." Josie returned from the kitchen with a huge bowl of spaghetti and meatballs. "Let's eat."

Kelly did have things to discuss with Josie. Her feelings for her had grown into more than friendship, and based on their mutual attraction, they were going to end up in bed together. She couldn't allow it to happen without some sort of commitment from Josie. Her heart was too vulnerable, and she had Barb to think of. She didn't know where they were headed, but she didn't want to hurt her. But she knew the spark she felt with Josie was far more intense than anything she'd shared with Barb, and that meant something. Her appetite fled as she felt the heaviness of her dilemma settle in her belly. A dilemma of her own making. She'd welcomed and returned Josie's kisses. She'd allowed herself to get involved with a woman who didn't want a relationship. Again. They'd have to talk. *At least I haven't slept with her.* She finished the spaghetti on her plate.

"You're quiet today, Kelly," Ruth said. "Are you okay?"

"I'm enjoying the meal. And I have a lot on my mind. Sorry if I'm being rude. A new patient came in today with dementia. I'm a little worried about her."

"I'm sure you'll do your best," Ruth said.

Kelly hoped Ruth was right. About everything in her life. "I suppose everything will work out as it's supposed to. Sometimes I wish I could control more than I'm able to." Kelly sighed, not expecting a reply from Ruth.

"We can only control how we react to each other based on what we want, or need, or perceive. That's what's so difficult. We can't know what's in another's mind unless they speak it. Fear is a powerful force, dear. The only way I know of to overcome it is with trust."

Kelly sat dumbfounded. Was she making more of what Ruth said or was she really that perceptive?

"Nooko doesn't hold back with her unsolicited wisdom." Josie shrugged one shoulder.

"I'm going to put my feet up and let my lunch digest." Ruth stood. "You two go do whatever you need to." She gripped her cane and moved to her spot on the couch.

"I believe we've been dismissed." Kelly smiled. Ruth was special.

"Let's go sit outside." Josie stood and took Kelly's hand to pull her out of her seat.

Kelly sat next to Josie on the porch. "I do need us to talk, Josie."

"Yeah. I thought maybe you would."

"I feel a connection between us, but I haven't changed my mind about wanting a long-term relationship. I can't get involved any further with you without knowing you feel the same way."

Josie stood and Kelly thought she was going to kiss her again. She scrambled to decide what to do, but Josie only took her hand and pulled her out of her seat. "I know. I'm not sure I'll ever be able to love the way you need me to. I'm just not brave enough to take a chance of losing it. I saw how much in love my parents were. They laughed together, shared work, cared for me, and cared for each other, and in an instant, it was all gone. I can't convince myself I could survive such a severe loss. It's safer to never try."

"Oh, Josie." Kelly stroked her cheek. "I'm so sorry it happened, and I understand that fear. I do. But I believe even if love is taken away by forces I can't control, at least I've experienced it. To me, it's worth taking a chance."

Josie stared at the ground, scuffing the dirt with her boot. "Thank you for thinking I'm worth taking a chance on. I wish I could believe it too. But I'm just not in a place to give you, or anyone, that kind of commitment." She sighed and her shoulders slumped. "If I had it to give, I'd jump at this chance. I hope you know that."

Kelly could see the truth in Josie's eyes, and her heart broke at the idea of someone so beautiful choosing to stay alone out of fear. Ruth's words about the power of fear came back to her, and she understood. "I think I should head back to work."

Josie nodded, her smile sad, and Kelly took Josie's hand as they walked to her car. "Emotional talks don't make for a lot of laughs, do they?"

"Not especially. But I love spending time with you, for whatever reason. You be careful driving. And come by anytime." Josie grinned. "I promise to be good."

Kelly was certain she would be better than good. "I will, and I'll let you know how everything's going at the facility." Kelly drove slowly on her way back to work, the conflict regarding her growing feelings for Josie weighing heavily on her mind. She couldn't allow herself to fall for Josie. She appreciated her sincerity but prayed it would be enough to convince herself to keep her distance. If Ruth was right about trust, could she ever earn Josie's? She'd be leaving soon to go back to her life. Was there even enough time? She turned her thoughts to Barb and their scheduled dinner date. More heavy conversation felt exhausting, but necessary. She parked her car and cleared her mind for work mode.

Kelly spent the afternoon coordinating schedules for the newly hired aides and nurses. They were fully staffed and the home was at ninety percent capacity. She calculated she'd be able to leave within a few weeks if things continued as they were. She checked the time, closed her laptop, and let the night staff know she was leaving.

Memories of her lunch date with Josie lingered while she drove to the Teepee. Barb stood in line, looking relaxed and sexy. Kelly remembered the first time she'd seen her at the convenience store and her immediate attraction. She was kind and attentive and cared about her, and they'd grown comfortable with each other. But was comfort what she wanted? Was it enough?

"There you are. I was just going to order for you. The usual?" Barb kissed her lightly on the lips.

Barb didn't care who saw or knew who she was with, one of the things Kelly liked about her. "Yep. The usual. Sorry I'm a little late. I got held up at work."

"No problem. You're worth waiting for." Barb kissed her hand.

Kelly waited until they were settled with their meals in Barb's car before speaking. She wasn't entirely sure what she wanted to say but knew she needed to start the conversation. "Remember on our first date, how we talked about reading and we agreed we want a happily-ever-after story?"

"Sure." Barb tilted her head and waited.

"I want you to know it's what I'm looking for in a lover, too. I want someone who wants a permanent long-term relationship. It's why I'm still single."

"Are you asking me to marry you?" Barb chuckled and winked at her.

"No. I just wanted to be completely clear on where I stand, because you've become special to me, Barb, and I don't want either one of us to get hurt."

"I appreciate your honesty, and I'm glad you feel comfortable talking to me." Barb hesitated. "I feel the same way, but I'm pretty sure I'm not ready for a commitment in my life yet. I've been working on Drummond Island for three years, and I love it here. I plan to stay on the island and obtain my CO Thirteen classification. It'll mean more responsibility but also higher income." She shrugged. "It's a lot of hours, and my job comes first right now. So a long engagement might be the only thing I can offer for a while."

"I'm not certain how much longer I'll be working here, which is another reason I wanted to talk." Kelly figured she only had a few weeks left working on the island, and she knew she didn't want a long-distance relationship.

"What if we just continue to see each other until you leave? We don't have to make any promises. We can see where we're at when it comes time for you to go." Barb finished her dinner and gathered the empty bags.

"That sounds good." She kissed Barb lightly. "No promises." Was that what she wanted? If not, whose promise did she want?

"I'm catching the next ferry to Detour tonight, so I can't stay long. I've got a meeting with Josie tomorrow, and I want to talk to my brother at the state police post about his availability, if necessary."

"Is it the meeting with the guy who wants Josie's property?"

"Yes. I'm not sure if it's a problem. She just asked me if I'd be there when she meets with him."

"Is your brother a state trooper?"

"Yeah. He told me he'd do some research on Abe."

"I know about Abe, but do you think he's dangerous?"

"I doubt it. He just insists on buying her property, and Josie doesn't want to sell. She's a little nervous about the notes he left. It's not cool that he's creeping around the way he is, and those notes aren't exactly asking to be buddies."

"I'm glad you're going to be there for her. The couple of times I've seen him he looked seedy."

Kelly deliberately turned away from Josie's direction as she left the parking lot. She couldn't fabricate a good excuse to go back, except she wanted to see her again, and she wasn't sure she was in an emotional state to do that yet.

CHAPTER TWENTY-FIVE

Josie paced in her office. She'd begun the nervous striding upon waking and decided she might be able to settle herself by keeping busy in her office. She retrieved the deed from the safe, read it, put it back, and pulled out her financial ledgers. The bank had appraised the property when she'd refinanced, so she had a figure in the back of her mind. *Maybe I should sell. No. I won't allow him to force me out.*

She continued her pacing until she heard a car in the parking lot. She forced in a deep breath and prepared herself for Abe's assault.

"Josie? It's me, Barb."

Josie's apprehension eased when she noted Barb in full uniform and her service weapon on her hip. She looked official, which was perfect. The police officer with her carried an envelope she presumed contained the information they'd found on Abe. "Thanks for stopping by. I'm Josie." She shook his hand as she introduced herself. "I haven't heard from Abe yet."

"I won't be far away today, and I've got Rob, my brother, on alert in case we need to call in the state troopers," Barb said. "I doubt you'll have any trouble. Abe's only been a nuisance so far."

"A big nuisance and he's creepy." Josie shivered at the thought of his sneer.

"You give me a call or text, but dial nine-one-one first if you feel threatened at all. Got it?"

"I will. Thanks, Barb."

Josie reviewed the driver's license picture the officer showed her, and Nooko confirmed it matched her remembrance of him. "I'm going to get breakfast for Nooko now. Can you stay?" She looked to Barb and the officer to be sure he knew he was welcome.

"Thanks, but I've got a call about some sick birds on the shore. I'll be within cell phone range."

"Thank you, ma'am, but I need to get this picture and information out." The young officer smiled and touched the brim of his cap in a semi-salute.

"Okay. See you later." Josie retreated to the kitchen and started a few bacon strips sizzling. She was scrambling eggs when Nooko entered the kitchen.

"Can I help with anything? It sure smells good."

"You can sit and relax. I poured you a cup of coffee, and the bacon will be done soon."

"Abe's coming today, isn't he?"

"Yes, he is. Barb's on call today in case we need her." Josie tried to keep her voice steady and sound unconcerned.

"It'll all work out, honey. They have his picture." Nooko sipped her coffee, looking relaxed. "Trust and believe."

Trust and believe. When had she forgotten the dictum both her mother and her nooko had repeated whenever she needed support? Nooko had tried to remind her to trust the will of the Creator and believe in the strength to continue when her mother died. She hadn't wanted to hear it at the time, but today she appreciated the encouragement. "Thanks, Nooko." She filled plates with their breakfast and quietly repeated the mantra.

Josie's day dragged as she waited. She checked the lobby several times before lunch, and she admonished herself again for not getting Abe's contact information. By late afternoon, she became concerned and wondered if she had the wrong day. He'd only said "in one week" in his note, and she'd taken that literally. Maybe he hadn't meant it that way. She began fidgeting and checked the locks on her office and safe for the sixth time. She texted Barb and let her know she was still waiting. Her thoughts drifted to Kelly and she hoped she'd come over before dinner as she had been doing lately. But she'd undoubtedly scared her away with their kiss, and what about Barb? Kelly hadn't mentioned their dating, so maybe she wasn't as taken with Barb as Barb was with her. She certainly could understand why Barb would be, but what did it mean for her, and what did she want?

By six o'clock. she gave up waiting, left the front door unlocked and a note for Abe on the desk, and went to make dinner.

"What happened? Did Abe show up yet?" Nooko asked.

"Not yet. I left him a note to look for me here. Let's have dinner. I'll check again later."

It was after dark when Josie locked the front door, tossed the note she'd left in the trash, and called Barb.

"He never showed up, Barb."

"Huh. And he didn't leave a letter or note?"

"Nothing. I'm kicking myself for not pushing him harder for his phone number. I have no way of contacting him and no way of knowing when or if he'll be back. I don't like this feeling of being on edge, just waiting."

"I'm pretty sure he'll contact you again because he's been so adamant about buying your place."

"Yeah. More than likely. I'll let you know if he does, and thanks again for being on call today." Josie flipped on the night-lights and headed to the lodge.

"He never showed up, Nooko." Josie secretly hoped he'd given up and moved on to someone else's property.

"I suppose he'll either contact you again, or not. Can we do some exercises in the hot tub before bed tonight?"

"Sure." Josie followed Nooko to the tub, trying to shake the uneasy feeling in the pit of her stomach.

Josie gently lifted her specially designed dream catcher from the drawer and laid it on the table in her studio. She hoped concentrating on the final touches of her latest creation would take her mind off Abe. She couldn't figure out why he hadn't shown up. She straightened feathers and attached a hanger before carrying it to the main room of the lodge where Nooko waited for her.

"Oh, it's beautiful, Joslyn. It'll look lovely over the fireplace."

"Yeah. I thought so, too." Josie suspended the dream catcher on a screw on the fireplace and stepped back to admire her work. "It does look nice, doesn't it? This is the first thing I've made for display out here."

"You have your mother's talent. She would be proud of you, and I don't mean only because of your artistic abilities. What made you do it now?"

Josie thought for a moment, struggling to put her feelings into words. "I guess I'm ready to add myself to Mom's living memory. I'll never forget her, but I think I wanted to put something of mine next to hers to help remind me of her alive. I think I'm finally letting go of some of the pain of her loss."

"I'm glad, honey. I'm positive she wouldn't want you grieving for her so long and hard that you couldn't move on with your life. It really is special."

"Thanks, Nooko. I used a few of the last of her collection of eagle feathers. She taught me so much, and there isn't a day goes by I don't miss her." Josie relaxed on the couch and rested her head on Nooko's shoulder, the heat of her body a healing balm. "I guess I'll try one more trip to the office and do my walk around the buildings. Do you want help getting to your room?"

"You go, dear. I can get myself to bed. I feel completely steady with my cane now."

Josie watched Nooko stride out of the room. She was much more secure than she had been a few weeks ago. She sat for a few minutes lost in the memories Nooko had triggered. Her mother had loved to spend time working on her crafts, or cooking, or enjoying the outdoors. Mostly, she remembered how much she loved her father and how balanced her life had been. She was happy. Grateful. Maybe there were still things she needed to learn from her. She headed to the office. The door was still locked, but when she opened it an envelope lay on the floor.

I'm sorry I missed you, but that's not important. I'm willing to offer you $30,000.00 cash for your property. It would be in your best interest to accept it. I'll be in touch soon.

Josie secured the letter in her safe and considered what Abe meant by "soon." She resolved not to miss him the next time, because she wasn't selling, especially for that price. Her Realtor would laugh him out of her office. She locked the door behind her and turned toward the lodge when she heard his voice.

"There you are. Are you gonna accept my offer?" Abe stood just outside the range of the motion sensor light.

"No, Abe. The property is worth way more than thirty grand. That's just absurd. If you give me your phone number, I'll let you know if I ever do want to sell, and I know the Mulligans' cabins and land are still available. Why do you want my property, anyway? There are much better waterfront pieces of land for sale. Talk to any local Realtor, and they'll show you land that's actually for sale. Although there's nothing around here for thirty grand."

"I told you, I want this property. My reason is my business, but I got plenty of reasons. I've been patient, but I don't wanna wait no more, and I ain't goin' through no Realtor. We'll settle this, just you an' me. You obviously haven't been shown how difficult it could be to stay yet." Abe turned and retreated toward the woods.

Josie called after him hoping he'd give her his contact information, but he'd disappeared into the darkness. She trudged back to her bedroom wondering when she'd hear from him again, and just what "reasons" he had for wanting her property so badly.

The next morning, Josie finished sketching her design for the outbuilding she wanted to build to house her ski equipment. The old toolshed her father had used for his workshop was close to collapsing. Besides being dangerous, it was in the perfect spot to begin her proposed ski trails. She took her plans to the kitchen table where Nooko was seated drinking coffee.

"Good morning, Nooko." She poured herself a cup of coffee and sat across from her.

"Good morning. The oatmeal is still hot. Help yourself." Nooko leaned over to see the papers. "What've you got there?"

"It's the shed I plan to build for the ski equipment. Remember I told you I was planning groomed cross-country ski trails this winter? I need a place to keep the equipment. Dad's old toolshed is falling apart. I'm going to take advantage of not having any lodgers and tear it down, then replace it."

Nooko sat back in her chair. "I thought maybe it was something from Abe. Did you hear from him?"

"I did. You were already asleep, and I was out locking up for the night when he showed up. He offered thirty thousand dollars, cash. I turned him down, and he left without giving me his phone number. I'm not sure if or when I'll hear from him again, but it doesn't sound like it's over."

"Did he say why he wanted the property so badly?" Nooko leaned forward in her seat.

"I asked him, but he basically said it was none of my business. I'll let Barb and the police know what happened."

"I sure hope he goes away."

"He couldn't have checked with a Realtor if he thought thirty thousand was enough." Josie took a sip of coffee.

"I'm going to finish the paper and let my food settle before my hot tub exercises. The authorities will take care of Abe, honey." Nooko rested her hand on her shoulder before leaving.

"I'm going out to do some measurements after I eat. Then I'll be back to help you." Josie's unsettled feeling after her meeting with Abe hadn't subsided, and her anxiety sat like a lead ball in her belly at his insinuation at how *difficult* things could be. She checked every cabin and the grounds before starting work on the shed. She removed the caution tape from the shed and began separating pieces of rotted wood from salvageable ones. She planned to replace the original wooden floor with cement, so she concentrated on clearing a space for the footings.

"It's getting hot out here, and Ruth wants to know if you're ever coming back inside?"

Josie turned toward the voice and set her shovel aside when she saw Kelly standing a few feet away holding out a bottle of water. She looked at her watch and realized she'd been working nonstop for two hours. She shook off her disorientation and took the bottle. "Thanks. I guess I lost track of time. I was only going to measure. Damn. I'm supposed to be helping Nooko." Kelly looked sexy in a pair of khaki cargo shorts and a T-shirt, but then, she'd look sexy in anything. *Or nothing.* She erased the image from her brain and followed her inside.

"I'm sorry I left you so long."

Nooko shrugged and waved as if to say it was no big deal.

"I'll get cleaned up a bit and we can do your tub exercises."

"Kelly helped me with them already, dear. She arrived just as I was on my way to find you, and we decided to get them done while you were working."

"I hope you don't mind. I stopped by to see how it went with Abe yesterday." Kelly settled into the seat next to Nooko on the couch.

"No problem." She didn't want to talk about his threats in front of her nooko. There was no reason to upset her. "Thanks for coming by, but aren't you supposed to be working?"

"I took off early. Things are starting to run smoothly, so I'm playing hooky. Was one of your lodgers watching you work out there?"

"I didn't see anyone." Josie felt her uneasiness settle back into her gut. "The last group checked out long ago."

"Strange. I thought I saw someone rustling in the brush." She shrugged. "Maybe I was mistaken. Or it could've been a deer. Can I take you two to lunch?"

"You know, it could've been a deer. I've seen several out there lately. Lunch sounds good to me if Nooko's willing. I have to clean up and put the caution tape back, and I want to let Barb and the police know that Abe showed up." The tightness in her chest told her she didn't believe a deer was watching her. *Damn it, Abe. Get out of my life!*

Josie took a quick shower, changed into shorts and a T-shirt, and phoned Barb from her bedroom. A niggle of concern prompted her to check her office and safe before going to join Kelly and Nooko. Abe wouldn't run her off, but he was starting to scare her.

CHAPTER TWENTY-SIX

I suppose you think I'm boring, but do homemade pasties sound good to you?" Kelly had decided against the Teepee since she had come to think of it as her and Barb's place. Except for the ice cream trips.

"I'm fine with wherever you want to go. And you could never be boring, dear." Ruth stood by the door waiting.

"I agree," Josie said.

The small family restaurant had a few people waiting to be seated when they arrived, so Nooko sat on a wooden chair to wait their turn. The young attendant led them to a table by the window, and Kelly smiled at the owner when they passed her. She'd wondered if she was going to get to know people on the island and now she greeted many of them by name. She'd miss that when she left. "Hi, Claudia. I brought a couple of friends today."

"Hey, Kelly. I know Josie, but who's the lovely lady with her?"

Kelly introduced Ruth, grateful Josie allowed her the honor.

"I'm privileged to have you in my establishment. Please order anything on the menu, on the house." Claudia went back to her kitchen with a wave.

"Tell me about Abe, Josie." Kelly sipped the water Claudia had set in front of her.

Josie flicked a quick glance at Ruth before answering. "He showed up late last night, made a lowball offer which I refused, and left. I'm not sure if or when he'll be back, but I expect he'll keep trying."

"Are you worried about him? Being dangerous, I mean."

Ruth was looking at her menu and missed Josie's slight shake of her head. "He makes me nervous for sure, but he hasn't threatened me."

Kelly decided to drop the subject. Clearly, Josie was concerned it would worry Ruth. They ate their lunch and discussed Kelly's job and Josie's plans for the resort. "So, what were you working on so diligently this morning?"

Josie swallowed a sip of water before replying. "I'm replacing an old shed my father used for tools with one I can store cross-country ski equipment and snow shoes in. I'm hoping it'll be a draw for guests to have ski trails available, but not everyone has skis, so I plan to keep a few pair available for rental."

"Sounds good. Maybe I'll have to come back this winter and give it a try."

"You come back anytime you want to." Josie blushed slightly and kept her focus on her plate.

Kelly watched Josie's reaction closely. She was sure Josie would want her to return, but was it for the same reason she wanted to?

The trip back to the lodge was quiet. Ruth's head bobbed as she nodded off in the passenger seat, and Josie appeared lost in thought. She parked in front of the lodge in a handicapped space she hadn't noticed before. "When did you add this?"

"The other day. It's a good idea to have at least one," Josie said. "I've got a ramp ordered for the porch, too, and I'm renovating cabin five."

Kelly appreciated Josie's attention to the potential of a disabled lodger. It was easy for property owners to inadvertently disregard that aspect. She helped Ruth out of the vehicle and into the building, aware of Josie following behind her. She was going to have to make a decision about what she wanted soon. Her required presence at the facility was ending, but she hadn't told Janis yet. Her schedule allowed her to stay through October, and she'd begun to think of it as a short time. She told herself it was because she was dating Barb but suspected it was due to her growing feelings for Josie. She got Ruth settled with a cup of tea in the kitchen before she headed back to the main room to say good night to Josie.

"Hello?" Barb said as she opened the front door. "Kelly. What a nice surprise." Barb kissed her lightly on the lips.

Kelly froze, feeling as if she were caught in a lie. She glanced at Josie standing motionless, watching the exchange.

"Hey, Barb. Come on in." Josie spoke without looking at her and turned away.

"How'd it go last night? You didn't elaborate in your phone call earlier." Barb wound her arm around Kelly's waist possessively.

"When he finally showed up, he made a super-low offer. Would you like a cup of coffee or something?"

"No, thanks. I've got to get back to work soon, but I worried a little when I didn't hear from you until this morning." Barb pulled Kelly closer. "A low offer, huh? Makes me wonder how much he wants the property. I would think he must've checked on the land values around here." Barb furrowed her brow. "Did he ever say why he wanted to buy you out?"

"He told me it was none of my business. I asked him for his phone number, and he said no to that, too. He said something about me not realizing how difficult it could be to stay, though."

"Makes me think he's behind all the vandalism you've experienced. I worry he may escalate, so I'll make sure the police are on alert. It sounds like they may have enough to pick him up for questioning."

"If they can find him." Josie looked frustrated.

Josie still hadn't even glanced at Kelly, who gently slipped out of Barb's embrace and retreated to the kitchen. She wished she'd mentioned she was seeing Barb to Josie and questioned her motives to keep it to herself. Was she holding out hope for Josie? *She knows now.* She felt as if she were in the middle of some kind of match where she was the prize, and she didn't like it. She plopped into the chair opposite Ruth at the kitchen table.

"Are you two dating?" Ruth asked.

Kelly sighed. "I guess we are."

"What's it mean if you have to guess?" Ruth looked at her with that wise, knowing smile she used when she already knew the answer.

"I don't know what it means, Ruth. Barb's special and she treats me well, but I don't know if it's going anywhere." Kelly relaxed in Ruth's presence, surprised at how easy it was to confide in her about something so personal.

"You're the only one who can figure it out. This is none of my business, but Joslyn means the world to me, and I don't want to see her hurt. We are all part of nature's plan. The Creator's plan. And when we find someone who fits that plan, I believe we need to respect it and explore what it means for us. You young folks call it dating. In my day, when someone touched us deeply, we just accepted the offering and gave thanks. I'm not saying it's not important to be treated with respect and caring. Never allow yourself to be discounted, but you must follow your heart. You must listen to its call. Don't settle for something your spirit doesn't feel."

Kelly hugged Ruth and slipped out the back door, unwilling to have another awkward moment. She thought about Ruth's words as she drove to her apartment. She poured herself a glass of iced tea and settled into her Adirondack chair to watch the birds. Did Ruth see or know something she couldn't? Was there a chance Josie wanted to commit? Whose touch was her heart feeling? Josie's or Barb's? She closed her eyes and willed answers to come.

❖

"I'll be out back working on the shed." Josie slipped out the back door, not waiting for an answer. She put on her leather gloves and began flinging pieces of wood into a pile away from the lodge. She stopped when she realized she'd run out of things to throw. She took a drink from her water bottle, grabbed her shovel, and began digging. She lost track of time as she used each thrust of the shovel as a release for pent-up anger. She scooped dirt until her arms ached and her legs shook from fatigue. She dug to blot out the sight of Barb's arm around Kelly's waist like it belonged there. She heaped soil into a pile to bury her frustration and confusion. Why did she care if Kelly and Barb were together? She wanted to be happy for Kelly. To feel relief she'd found someone willing to commit to her, but all she felt was regret. The hole she was digging in the ground felt tiny compared to the crater in her heart at the thought of Kelly leaving the island. Or, possibly worse, staying on the island and committing to Barb. She didn't know what she was going to do, so she kept digging.

"Joslyn! Are you going to work all night? Dinner's almost ready." Nooko stood in the doorway.

"I'm coming. I'm done for the night." Josie put away her shovel and dragged herself into the lodge. "I'm going to take a shower before dinner." She stood under the spray until the hot water ran out. No answers came and neither did peace. She dragged herself to the kitchen, the weight of unwanted emotions pushing at her.

"I reheated the leftovers. Are you all right, dear?"

"Thanks. I'm fine. Just a little tired."

"Let's eat. I have something to say to you."

Josie frowned. She knew from experience when Nooko had something to say, it was serious. She set out plates and silverware and helped serve dinner. "What do you have to say?" She poked at her food and sipped her water.

"It was hard for you to see Kelly and Barb together, wasn't it?"

Josie knew better than to try to lie to Nooko. "I suppose it was a little, but I'm happy for them." *Just a minor untruth.*

"Honey." Nooko patted her hand. "I can see you have strong feelings for Kelly, and I believe she does for you, too."

"I can't, Nooko. I'm terrified. Look what Mom and Dad had, and how quickly it was taken away. I can't bring myself to take that chance."

"Oh, honey. Life is full of chances. Where would we be if we never took a chance on anything? In my opinion, that's how we learn and grow." Nooko took a drink of water before pushing away from the table. "I'm going to read for a while before bed. Why don't you join me? We'll have a cup of tea, a fire in the fireplace, and you can relax and forget your problems for an evening."

"I'll be there in a minute. I want to make sure I put all my tools away." Josie checked the area for anything she might have left and walked the perimeter of the building. She placed a few boards over the useless holes she'd dug in her frenzy and headed back to the lodge. She'd nearly reached the door when she caught a figure in her peripheral vision scurrying out of range of the sensor lights. Certain it was Abe, she grabbed a flashlight and scanned the edge of the tree line, but he was gone. She retreated to her office to call Barb.

"Abe was here. I'm sure of it, Barb. I was cleaning up from the work I'm doing out back and I saw the shadow of a human figure."

"But you couldn't tell for sure it was him, huh?"

"No. But I'd be willing to bet it was him. He's really got me spooked."

"You try to relax. I'll keep an extra eye out for him, and I'll ask the police to add an extra patrol on your property."

"Thanks, Barb. Call me if you find anything. It doesn't matter if it's late." Josie went back to the lodge to try to unwind and take Nooko up on her offer. She found Nooko sipping tea with her feet up.

"Is everything all right, honey?"

"It's quiet." She didn't want to worry Nooko, but her concern must have shown on her face, because Nooko's eyes narrowed slightly as though she didn't believe her. "I cleaned up the mess I made and checked in with Barb about Abe. She's going to do extra patrols tomorrow." She sat next to Nooko, rested her head on the back of the couch, and willed the tension in her belly to settle.

CHAPTER TWENTY-SEVEN

How does an egg and Canadian bacon sandwich sound for breakfast?" Josie poured two cups of coffee and set one in front of Nooko.

"Sounds good, honey. Did you get some sleep last night?"

Josie put English muffins in the toaster and cracked two eggs into a pan. There wasn't any point in talking about the confused, dark dreams that had plagued her all night. Barb hadn't called, so she figured there was no news about Abe. "I did. I wore myself out this week."

"How much more do you have to do?"

"I have to finish digging the footings, and I want to put the shed on a cement slab, so I'll get Brian at the hardware store to help me. It shouldn't take long for me to assemble the kit I ordered. I decided to buy a kit instead of taking the time to design something. This will work well, and since it's only the beginning of July, it'll be done well before winter."

"That's a lot of work, but your skiing idea is a good one. There's not much else to do here in the winter." Nooko looked far away as she sat holding her coffee cup.

"I'm sure we'll get a few snowmobile and ice fishing enthusiasts."

There was a moment of silence before Nooko said quietly, "I love you, Joslyn, and I'm grateful to be here with you, but I miss my home."

Josie set their breakfast on the table and sat across from Nooko, searching for a reply. "I love you, too," was all she could manage. She didn't want her to leave, and she didn't want to have the conversation that would pin down the time she had to take her back.

Nooko seemed to accept that. "Are you going to work on the shed today?"

"I'll take a break today. Let's do your hot tub exercises and go for a boat ride."

Nooko's enthusiastic nod and smile convinced her she'd made the right decision. They finished eating and washed dishes before changing into their swimsuits.

"Keep kicking." Josie supported Nooko with both hands while encouraging her. "You're doing great. I can tell you're getting stronger. One more time around." Josie wondered at Nooko's quietness as she helped her out of the hot tub and wrapped her in a towel. "You're not dizzy, are you?" The closer she got to having to take Nooko home, the more worried she became about her health.

"Not at all. I feel fine, and I am getting stronger. Do you think we could invite Kelly to come with us today?"

Nooko's request didn't surprise her, but she paused before answering. "I'm sure she's working, and I hate to interrupt her."

"Maybe she could come over at lunchtime again. Could we call her?"

"Sure, Nooko. I'll give her a call later this morning." Josie squelched her excitement at the thought of seeing Kelly. She had no right to expect her to jump at the chance to join them when she kept pushing her away. She worried the whole situation would become awkward. She disregarded all of it and smiled inwardly. *She could always say no.*

"Thanks for inviting me today." Kelly leaned back and tilted her face to the sun as the rowboat bobbed in the water.

"I'm glad you could make it, dear. How's work going?" Nooko asked.

"Pretty good. Your call came at a perfect time." Kelly smiled. "I've been taking a few hours off every few days to let the staff get used to me being gone. Do you have any lodgers now?"

Josie's belly quivered at Kelly's beautiful smile. "No. I'm taking advantage of the lull to get some work done." Josie steered the boat, keeping it close to the shore. The breeze over the water had picked up, and she worried about Nooko getting chilled.

"And I'm working on my exercises and getting stronger," Nooko said.

"That's wonderful." Kelly patted Nooko's hand. "You look great."

"Can you come over more often now? Maybe for lunch or dinner? We could use the hot tub together." Nooko bubbled with enthusiasm.

Josie grinned and nodded when Kelly gave her look that seemed to ask if that was okay. She didn't think for a second that Nooko didn't have ulterior motives, not after their conversation at breakfast the other day.

"I'll plan on it, Ruth."

Josie noted a hesitancy in Kelly's voice that she longed to alleviate, but she couldn't push past her fear to try.

"If you two are ready, we'll head back now." Josie took her time rowing along the shore to enjoy the view of Kelly reposing.

Josie helped Nooko out of the boat, struck by how comfortably they worked together when Kelly held it steady. "Let's take the path along the back, and I'll show you where the new shed is going."

"Sounds good." Kelly walked next to Nooko.

Josie secured the boat to the dock and followed behind them. Her throat tightened as she saw Kelly rest her hand on Nooko's back to steady her along the path. *Nooko's right. She's great.*

Josie stopped when they reached the area she'd prepared for the new shed. "This is where it's going. I'll have help laying the cement floor, but the shed is a kit that shouldn't be too difficult to assemble."

"This is great, Josie." Kelly perused the area and nodded. "You do really good work."

Her smiled warmed Josie's heart and affirmed her own pride in her work. It also stirred a need for Kelly's approval that surprised her.

Kelly and Nooko settled in their usual seats on the couch when they got back to the lodge. "I'll be back in a minute. I want to check on the cabins." Josie took the wooded path behind the cabins and checked each one. She found nothing amiss and breathed a sigh of relief. Her edginess wouldn't subside until she resolved the issue with Abe. She confirmed there wasn't a note from him shoved under the office door and returned to the lodge. Kelly had her feet on the coffee table reading a book, and Nooko dozed next to her. The scene of tranquility stirred feelings she'd repressed, and memories of a time together with her parents, laughing and enjoying being together bubbled to the surface.

She sat across from them, and Kelly looked up and smiled. She realized how easily she could get used to having her there. *But at what cost?*

"Everything good?" Kelly asked.

"Yep. All's quiet."

"Have you heard anything more from Abe?"

"Not a word. I'm not sure what to expect from him, but I want it to be over. Thanks for coming over today. Nooko misses you."

"I miss her, too. And you."

Kelly's sad smile touched her in a place she struggled to ignore. Visions of her with Barb surfaced, but Kelly was here now. With her. She squirmed, unsure of a response. She wanted to tell her she missed her, too. She missed her touch, her smile, her kisses, her. She faked courage she didn't feel. "I miss you, too. You're special." She held Kelly's gaze a moment longer than she intended, and ripples of desire clouded her thoughts.

"Ruth and I are having tea. Would you care to join us?" Kelly grinned and lifted her cup.

Josie recognized and appreciated her effort to lighten the mood. "I believe I will." She made herself a cup and joined them on the couch. Nooko had awakened and looked disoriented for a moment.

"What else is on the agenda for today, Josie?" Kelly sipped her tea and shifted in her seat while resting her hand on Nooko's arm. She looked prepared to stay all day.

"I'm going to work on my shed project and spend some time cleaning the cabins in case I get any requests."

"Have you heard from Barb?" Nooko sat up straight, looking more awake.

"No. I expect she'll call if and when she finds out anything. I guess no news is good news." Josie hated that Nooko was worried about Abe. "Are you planning to go in to work today, Kelly?" She was certain Kelly hadn't planned to stay with them all day, but she admitted she hoped she would.

Kelly looked at her watch. "Yeah. I'll go check in with them pretty soon and make sure they don't need anything."

"Will you come back tomorrow?" Nooko looked excited.

"I'll try, Ruth." Kelly hugged her and stood. "Take care, Josie. Let me know how it goes with Abe." Kelly took her empty cup to the kitchen.

Josie followed, carrying her own cup. "I wanted to say good-bye and thank you again for coming over. Nooko always perks up when you're around." Josie scrambled to find the words she really wanted. "I do, too." She cringed as she blurted them, wishing she had something deeper, more intense. Something that matched what she was really feeling. But it would have to do.

"Thank you." Kelly smiled and gently stroked her cheek before leaving.

Josie checked on Nooko before going to finish moving the pile of wood from the old shed to a trailer she'd rented from the hardware store. She worried the area she'd cleared for the new structure could be dangerous, so she parked the trailer over the section she'd dug. She planned to work on preparations for the floor the next day. Kelly had gone to check in at work and they'd made no plans for her to return. *She's better off with Barb.* She collected cleaning supplies and went to clean the cabin her weekend lodgers had vacated and spruce up the cabins in case anyone called for reservations. She'd hoped to have them rented throughout the summer, but that hadn't panned out the way she'd hoped. She reminded herself she'd only been advertising since January, and many people already had their vacation plans made. It would take time to build the business, and she needed to accept that. She consoled herself knowing she had a few weeks already booked for the winter months. Anxiety returned when she thought of Nooko's intention to move back to her house. She strove to come up with a solution as she scrubbed and vacuumed.

She found Nooko still in her usual spot on the couch with a bag of popcorn. "Shall I start dinner?"

"I'm having a snack, dear. It's still early. Did you get everything done?"

"Yes. All ready for occupants. I was hoping someone would book for Labor Day weekend." Josie sat next to Nooko and grabbed a handful of popcorn. "It'll give me plenty of time to finish the shed, I suppose."

"It'll be all right. This is your first year. Wait until the word spreads about how great this place is. You'll be swamped next year." Nooko's confidence boosted her own.

"Thanks, Nooko. I'm sure you're right. This must be one of the times I need to trust and believe in myself."

Nooko chuckled. "You'll get there one day."

"How does the fish fry sound for dinner tonight? I saw it listed in the paper this week."

"I'd love to. I remember going to those with Harold, years ago." Nooko looked lost in memories, something that had been happening more often in the past few weeks.

"I'll go change out of my work clothes before we leave."

The Moose Lodge parking lot was full when Josie pulled into the handicapped spot. "They're having a good turnout today." She helped Nooko out of the vehicle and thanked the friendly woman who helped seat them. She recognized the back of Abe's head as soon as she glanced about the room. "That's Abe, at the table by the bar." She kept her voice low.

"I saw him, too." Nooko shrugged. "I guess he likes fish. Interesting that he's still local. I wonder if he's always on the island?"

"I don't think so. Barb and the police didn't find anyone with his name living here. The address on his license was from the west side of the U.P. I'd call her, but it's not like they have any reason to talk to him. Wanting to buy my place isn't a crime, and I can't prove he's done the other stuff." Josie hated feeling so helpless, especially when instinct told her something was out of place when it came to him.

They enjoyed the food and Josie listened to Nooko tell her about the people she'd known on the island over the years and how much it had changed. They were finishing their drinks when Abe stood and stopped at their table on his way out.

"Hello, ladies. I hope you've reconsidered sellin', Ms. Harlow. I'm almost out of patience." His backward politeness did nothing to improve his appearance or the menace of his words.

"Could I get your phone number? I'll call you if I do decide to sell." Josie hoped he'd relinquish his information.

"Ain't none of your business what my phone number is, just like my reasons. When you decide to sell, you'll tell me to my face. And that's gonna be soon. That property belongs to me." He glared at them before he muttered something unintelligible and left, slamming the door behind him.

"He's still creepy." Nooko finished her iced tea and stood. "Let's go home."

Nooko looked upset. Josie worked to find words to dispel her concerns as they settled in the car when Nooko surprised her with her question.

"What's going on with you and Kelly?" She'd turned in her seat and pinned her with her stare.

"What do you mean?" She gripped the steering wheel until her knuckles were white.

"You know what I mean. She's such a sweetie, and I can tell she cares about you very much. I love you, Joslyn, and you're old enough to make your own decisions, but I worry you'll allow your unfounded fear to stop you from having something extraordinary with her."

Nooko's words nudged away a small piece of the shield surrounding Josie's heart, allowing the quiet voice behind it to whisper possibilities. If she ignored it, Kelly could be gone forever and she'd never know what could've been, but if she listened, could she overcome the fear? "I'll think about it, Nooko. She's dating Barb, you know."

"At some point she's going to have to make a decision, and I'm betting on you, honey. If you're available. Fear isn't a good reason not to live."

"I suppose you're right, Nooko. I'm just so used to reacting with fear that I'm not sure I have the strength to break out of it."

Nooko just patted her hand without responding. They'd had this conversation about fear, so maybe she didn't have anything more to say on the issue. Or maybe she was hoping Josie would find her own way through it. Either way, her support and the fact that she seemed to know exactly when to say something and when not to, was much appreciated.

Josie made sure Nooko was settled when they returned to the lodge before making her rounds to check the cabins. She rounded the corner of the lodge and saw the trailer piled with boards had been moved away from the building. She retrieved a flashlight and inspected the whole area before moving the trailer back. There were some boot prints in the loose dirt, and she shivered at the sight of someone clearly messing with her stuff. The area still wasn't finished, and she wanted the hole to stay covered for safety's sake. Everything else was undisturbed. It was obviously Abe, but she couldn't imagine why he'd have moved it. She double-checked the area and found nothing amiss. She confirmed the range of her light sensors was at the maximum setting and added a nightly check of the area to her list of duties.

She reflected on Nooko's words as she went back to the lodge. She admitted that fear was keeping her from exploring anything serious with Kelly, but was she really so used to hiding behind it that she couldn't break out, as she'd said? Maybe it was time to test just how good living without fear could be.

Chapter Twenty-eight

No, Janis. We're not completely full yet, but I'm not sure we will be. Drummond Island is pretty remote, and the winters can be brutal. I sense most people choose to stay in the city on the mainland Upper Peninsula."

"I've been in touch with the administrator, and it sounds like they've hired as many staff as the budget allows. You could probably come back anytime now."

"But I'm scheduled to stay until October."

"We're pretty swamped here, Kelly. I could use you as soon as possible."

"I see. I'll do my best to get back there as soon as I can." Kelly disconnected the call and returned to her terminal. She reviewed the staff schedule and, satisfied everything was in order, closed down the computer. The recently hired nurse practitioners, physician assistants, and physical therapist completed the operating requirements, so her job there was nearly finished.

Her excuses to stay at the facility were beginning to sound weak, and Janis was pushing her to return. She wasn't sure how much longer she could find a reason to stay or put off making a decision about Josie. She and Barb had a standing date for dinner but still hadn't slept together or spent much time doing anything else, thanks to Barb's crazy work schedule. She could understand why Barb's previous lovers had issues with how wrapped up she was in her job. She packed her laptop and let the nurse on duty know she was leaving. It was time for her to make her feelings known and see what happened. She pulled out of the parking lot and headed for the lodge with butterflies in her stomach.

A trailer piled with old timbers took up four parking spots in front of the building. She parked alongside it and Josie poked her head up from behind it. "Hey there. Are you playing hooky again?"

"I sure am." Kelly got out of her car and leaned on the side of the trailer checking the contents. "Where'd all this come from?"

"It's the old shed. I'm getting ready to haul it to the dump. You're welcome to come along." Josie fastened the trailer to the hitch on her Jeep. "I just need to put a couple of bungee cords across this to secure the load and I'll be ready."

"I'll say hi to Ruth and be right out." Kelly found her seated at one of the tables with the newspaper spread across it. "Hey, Ruth."

"Kelly! I was hoping you'd stop over this week. Can you stay for dinner?"

Kelly smiled at Ruth's obsession with sharing meals. "I'm going to help Josie take a load to the dump, and I'll be back." She hugged Ruth and hurried out the door. She didn't want to get her hopes up if her talk with Josie didn't go well. Josie sat in her vehicle waiting. "What can I do to help?"

"You can keep me company." Josie tossed a pair of leather work gloves onto her lap. "And you can help unload when we get there."

The trip to the dump took less than fifteen minutes, and Kelly remained silent, watching the muscles in Josie's arm as she held the steering wheel. It seemed like the only things to talk about were the heavy things, and she wasn't ready to deal with those just yet. Besides, she wanted Josie's full attention. Josie turned in the seat and deftly backed the trailer to an area of the dump site designated for building materials. Kelly tried not to be obvious as she watched the material of Josie's T-shirt stretch across her breasts.

"Does all this get buried somewhere?" Kelly couldn't believe the state would allow this beautiful island to become a dumping ground.

"No. This all gets recycled. A company comes in and separates treated lumber from the pile and chips the rest."

They finished unloading the trailer, and she stole glances at Josie's firm backside as she lifted and tossed pieces of lumber. It took them less time than she would have liked to finish and head back. "Ruth looks good."

"Yeah. She's doing well. I'm still worried about her going home and being alone this winter, though."

"Could she hire a home care group to check on her daily?"

"I'm not sure she can afford it, but I'm planning on looking into it if she insists on moving back. I admit, I've been avoiding the conversation, but it isn't fair to her to put it off. She misses her home." Josie backed the trailer into a spot next to the building and turned off the engine.

"Can we take a walk? I want to talk to you." Kelly pushed away nerves, still unsure of what she would say.

"Sure. Let's check on Nooko first, and we'll go out back. You can see how much I've got done on the new building."

"Hi again, Ruth." Kelly retrieved two bottles of water from the refrigerator before following Josie out the back door.

Ruth waved from her seat on the couch. "You two be careful out there."

The afternoon sun radiated heat even in the shaded area of the bench as they sat sipping cold water. "Thanks for letting me help you today. The physical activity felt good."

"I'll bet you're looking forward to getting back to riding your horse."

"I am, but I've enjoyed my time here." Kelly chose her words carefully, wanting to convey her feelings and nudge Josie into revealing hers. "As I said before, I'm going to miss you and Ruth."

"And we'll miss you, too." Josie sat back on the bench and gazed at the water with her hands clasped in her lap.

Kelly covered them with one hand and gently gripped Josie's chin with the other. She turned her face to her and their gazes locked. "I'm going to miss you a lot." She kissed her, willing her feelings to transmit through her lips. She'd intended the kiss to show Josie how she felt, to spark feelings she couldn't, wouldn't, deny, but her passion flared, threatening to consume them both as the kiss deepened and Josie leaned over her. She stretched out underneath her as far as the bench allowed and pulled her on top of her. She squirmed as desire overtook reason. She dropped one leg to the ground, and Josie pressed her thigh to her center. Kelly writhed against her and tendrils of need crept through her.

Josie pulled away breathing hard. "Stay with me tonight?"

Kelly took a shuddering breath and nodded before pulling her in for another kiss. She groaned as Josie slid her hands under her T-shirt, gently exploring with her fingers. She arched into her touch, grabbed her hands, and pushed them against her breasts. Josie slid her hands under her bra, pinched her nipples, and she went limp in her arms.

Kelly pushed herself up, forcing Josie off her. "I'm going to explode right here and now if we continue, and that's not how I want our first time together to be." She straightened her clothing and waited for her breath to return to normal.

Josie kissed her lightly, stood, and pulled Kelly into her arms. "Let's go inside."

Josie held her hand as they walked toward the lodge, and Kelly nearly skipped at the wave of rightness.

Josie stole one more kiss before they opened the door to the lodge and found Ruth seated on the couch.

Kelly sat next to her and pulled Josie down beside her.

"I asked Kelly to stay tonight, Nooko."

"And I said yes." Kelly lifted their joined hands and kissed Josie's knuckles.

Ruth smiled, looking at each one of them in turn. "I think that's wonderful."

"So do I." She didn't add how much she was looking forward to being with Josie all night, good idea or not.

"I'm going to do my nightly check of the property." Josie lingered, looking adorably uncertain.

"We're going to the hot tub." Ruth stood and headed for the door.

"See you later, I guess." Kelly chuckled and rushed to kiss Josie before following Ruth. It was just a quick peck, but it fanned the flames of need already burning inside her.

"I'll put out a pair of shorts and a T-shirt for you on my bed." Josie's breath tickled her ear, and she shivered with anticipation of more.

Kelly sat with Ruth at one of the tables, content to watch her assemble a puzzle after their hot tub exercise. She'd seen many seniors enjoy the mental stimulation of puzzles and was glad to see her do so well at it. "You're pretty good." She picked up a piece and set it in place.

"It's supposed to be good for the mind, but you already know that, don't you?"

"Yes. It's a great mental exercise." Kelly wished Ruth would go to bed. She glanced at Josie seated next to her, grateful she was seated because she would have wilted from the heat of her gaze.

Josie rose to close the blinds in the kitchen, which must have reminded Ruth of the time. "I'm ready for bed." She stood and gripped her cane. "You two sleep well."

"Good night, Ruth. Pleasant dreams." Kelly hugged her and tried not to appear overeager to see her leave.

She carried their cups to the kitchen and jumped when Josie pinned her against the counter. She snuggled into her arms and tipped her head back.

"Ready for bed?" Josie spoke between nuzzles on her neck.

"Oh yes." She let her lead her to her bedroom.

Kelly's thoughts and concerns fled as they removed their shoes and Josie stripped off her T-shirt and sports bra in one motion, then reached for hers. She squirmed out of it and unhooked her bra just in time as Josie grabbed them and tossed them aside. She tried not to whine as their bare breasts met and her nipples tightened, triggering an aching need she feared could never be satisfied. She grasped Josie's head and claimed her mouth like a drowning person. Their tongues met with an urgency and need she'd never known. Her moans became pleas when Josie leaned away and placed her warm hands on her breasts, her gentle touch caressing her sensitive nipples. She unzipped Josie's jeans and yanked them down, but before she could reach for her own, Josie backed her to the bed. She fell onto her back, and Josie removed her jeans and panties, tossed them to the floor, and stepped out of her briefs.

Their sounds of passion echoed throughout the room. A warm breeze fluttered the curtains, and the silence was heavy with expectation.

With nothing between them but desire, Josie hesitated. Sweet, desirable, and lying beneath her naked, offering herself, her vulnerability, Kelly wanted love and commitment. What message was she sending her? *What does this mean?* She lost herself in exploring Kelly's gorgeous body with her tongue and all uncertainties fled when Kelly arched to meet her touch and cupped her sex. She moved her fingers and Josie's clitoris jerked. She pushed against the pressure and knew her wetness flooded Kelly's hand. A ripple of pleasure overtook her as Kelly lightly circled her clit and slipped a finger inside her. She pressed Kelly's hand against herself and turned slowly so they lay side by side. She matched her position by entering Kelly with her free hand.

"Oh, God."

Kelly's cry intensified her longing to please her. To satisfy her.

Only her. She pushed deeper inside her and massaged her clit with her thumb. Kelly rose to meet each stroke, clutched the sheets, and stiffened, overtaken by her orgasm. Josie held her as her shivers subsided, and kissed her lightly. *Oh, Kelly, what have I done?* She gasped when Kelly rolled on top of her and squeezed her clit between her fingers and massaged it. "Oh, yes." Her shout as she came reverberated through her soul, taking on a meaning she couldn't deny.

❖

The cool night air filtered into the room, cloaking them as they slept.

Kelly woke to the soothing sound of Josie's heartbeat under her ear. She shifted slightly to circle her waist with her arm. Her skin was warm and soft. She refused to consider the consequences of her decision to sleep with Josie. She wearied of denying her desires. If Josie didn't share the same feelings, at least she'd have memories of her kisses and her touch. She closed her eyes, and Josie's rhythmic breathing lulled her back to sleep.

It seemed only minutes before Josie's caress woke her again.

"Hey, sleepyhead." Josie kissed her forehead. She was fully dressed and looked as if she'd been up for hours.

"Hey. I guess I fell back asleep. Can you lie back down for a few minutes? I'd like to cuddle." Kelly's heart beat in her ears as she waited for Josie's answer.

"Sorry. Nooko's waiting for breakfast. I've started the omelets already." She lingered near the door, her hand resting on the door handle, her eyes anywhere but on Kelly.

Kelly reached for her T-shirt but kept herself covered with the bed sheets. Her greatest fear had materialized. What they'd shared the night before was less important to Josie than it was to her. She'd hoped for more, but she refused to deny what Josie had said with her touch, even if her words, her actions, didn't match. "I'll be right there. Let me know if there's anything I can do to help."

Josie slipped out and Kelly fell back onto the bed. Josie had never lied to her. She'd been completely honest about what she could give, and still, Kelly had run straight into that brick wall. Josie's expression had been that of an alert animal, waiting for danger, and there was no way Kelly could combat that kind of fear. If last night's passion hadn't broken through, she didn't know what would. She got ready slowly, putting off the inevitable moment she'd have to drive away and make a decision as to whether she'd ever come back.

Once in the kitchen, she put on a mask she hoped hid the turmoil and vulnerability flooding through her. She finished breakfast in silence except to answer Ruth's questions and to help her with her hot tub exercises before leaving. Josie went outside to work on her shed project, so she stopped to say good-bye. "I'm heading home now. Can we talk before I leave? Please?"

Josie set her shovel aside and shifted foot to foot. "Sure."

Not exactly a sit-down conversation, then. Kelly took Josie's hand and kissed it. "Last night was special to me, Josie. I hope it was for you, too. I can't leave without letting you know how much I care for you. And I'd really like to see what this thing between us could be."

Josie pulled her into her arms. "I care about you, too."

"I hear a *but* in there."

"Last night was special to me as well, but I'm sorry if I gave you false hope or led you on. I didn't mean to." She stepped back and rested her hands on Kelly's shoulders, but stared at the ground. "I'm afraid, Kelly. Too afraid. I thought I could move past my fear. I'm trying." Her voice was a whisper.

"When love calls to us, and we refuse to listen, I believe it leaves an empty place in our heart." She was certain in that moment that a hot poker in her heart wouldn't be as painful as what she was about to do. "I hope you get over your fear one day, lover. Take care of yourself." She kissed her with all the feelings she could muster before turning and walking away, perhaps for the last time.

CHAPTER TWENTY-NINE

Josie heaved a shovel full of dirt over her head and jammed the shovel into the ground. She continued her digging and flinging until her arms felt like rubber. She pushed away the memory of Kelly's touch, her impassioned kisses, the way her body shook when she came, but mostly she needed to forget her words. Her words of love and her endearment. She'd called her "lover." She'd never had anyone care enough about her to call her anything besides her name. As hard as she shoveled, she wasn't able to blot out the sounds as Kelly's orgasm overtook her. She tossed the shovel aside and went to make lunch for Nooko.

"I've made us some tuna sandwiches." Nooko had the kitchen table set and waiting for her when she arrived.

"Thanks for making lunch. I'm going to clean up a little before I eat." Josie washed her hands and cupped water to splash on her face. She hung her head over the sink and watched the water drip down her face like tears when she raised it to look in the mirror. What was she afraid of? Nooko's words came back to her. "If I worried about loss…" She blotted her face with a towel and trudged to the kitchen.

Nooko looked up from her newspaper and half-eaten sandwich. "Is it going well out there, honey? You're working hard."

Josie plopped into her chair and stared at the sandwich on the plate in front of her. "Do you have any regrets, Nooko?"

"Regrets? Oh, honey, when you get to my age, it's easy to look back and say I'd have done plenty of things differently, but I wouldn't call them regrets. The Creator's plan for our lives is one of love and happiness, but we can't know what the path is, so we do the best we can and make choices based on what we know at the time. The hard part can be living with those choices when they go against the Plan. This is about Kelly, isn't it?"

"I'm all mixed up about her. I feel myself wanting to draw her close but pushing her away. I'm afraid I hurt her, and I never meant to."

Nooko took her hand and squeezed. "It'll work out, honey. I know it will if it's meant to be."

"I really thought it would work. I thought I could move past the panic, but I froze. I wanted to try so badly with Kelly, but in the end, I wimped out."

"Kelly is a strong, loving woman, but you can't expect her to be rejected and keep coming back. You need to decide if she's worth giving your heart to, and if you do, you have to stick to that decision. I can't tell you what to do, honey, but if you love her, find her and tell her."

"I'm afraid it's too late, Nooko." She pulled her hand away, the need to get the emotions out building like a tidal wave inside her, propelling her away from the table. "I'm going out to work on the shed project." She grabbed a cold bottle of water before heading outside to begin shoveling.

A few physically exhausting hours later, Josie gulped her ice water and wiped the sweat from her face. The area planned for her new shed was nearly prepared. She only had one corner left to dig out, and she sighed with gratitude for the shaded area next to the building. She set the shovel aside and took a minute to sit on the porch with Nooko.

"I love sitting out here," Nooko said.

"Me, too. The water's beautiful with the sun sparkling off the gentle waves." Josie allowed the serenity to dispel some of her nervous energy. For the past couple of weeks, she hadn't stopped thinking about Kelly and where she was or what she might be doing. Was she still on the island or had she gone home without a word? She didn't think she'd leave without seeing Nooko one more time.

"Are you almost done with your project?"

"I am. I only have a little more preparation, and I'll be ready to assemble the shed I ordered. It'll be delivered to the hardware store next week."

"You did a good job with the cement. I peeked at it this morning. Oh, I almost forgot to mention, I think we have a critter running around out there. The light kept going on this morning."

"Yeah. I noticed it a couple of times, too. That's why I decided to put in a rat wall around the shed. I don't want to deal with a skunk making a home under it." Josie wasn't so sure it wasn't the human rat, Abe, that was crawling about. She couldn't figure out why he would be sneaking around, though. It seemed like he'd try to break in if he wanted to steal something. That seemed off, too. He'd already offered some money to buy her property. If the property had been his at one time, she would've known about it. And as far as all the documentation she had, her family had been the only owners since her great-grandfather, and she'd have some sort of proof it had changed hands. She sighed deeply. All she could do was wait and see if the authorities found anything out about him and keep a close watch on her property.

❖

"Hello? Anyone home?"

"Hey, Barb. I'm right here." Josie came out from her office.

"Everything quiet around here? I haven't heard from you lately. No more Abe sightings?"

"Not that I can be sure of. I've been trying to figure out what it is about my place that he thinks is his." *Have you seen Kelly? Have you slept with her? Has she called you "lover"?*

"Let me know if you hear from him again. We're sort of at a dead end, it seems." She looked thoughtful. "I'm on my way to the east side to check on some dead deer and thought I'd see how you were doing. No guests this month?"

Josie kept picturing Barb's arm around Kelly's waist. Did she know they'd slept together? *Probably not. Maybe it wasn't worth mentioning. Are they still dating?* The questions were going to drive her crazy. Barb was looking at her expectantly. She'd clearly taken too long to respond. She tried to be in the moment. "Nope. Not even for Labor Day. I doubt I'll get anyone now until the snow flies. But it gives me time to finish a couple of projects and spruce the place up a bit."

"Ah. You'll be busier next year after you have a year under your belt. Maybe we can get together for lunch one day. Call if you need anything." Barb got in her car and waved as she drove away.

"Was that Barbara?" Nooko asked from the doorway.

"Yes. She stopped to check on us." Nooko rarely ventured to the office area. "You're getting along well."

"I wanted to look at the pictures of Harold building this place. It's been years." Nooko walked slowly, stopping at each picture with a faraway look on her face. "He was a handsome man, wasn't he?" Her question was more of a statement. "It's funny. You're afraid of loving Kelly because you might lose her, and I was afraid of loving Harold because my parents didn't want me to marry a white man. They finally accepted him when they saw how miserable I was and how handy a carpenter he was. I guess both of our fears were based on factors we had no control over." Nooko continued looking at every picture as if she hadn't said a word.

Josie joined Nooko in the entry and studied the photos. "I suppose that's true. I'm glad your dad and mom finally accepted him. They must have loved you very much."

"They did. And I loved them, too." Nooko turned to face her and took both her hands in hers. "I know your parents loved you very much, too, and I believe with all my heart they'd want to see you happy. They'd welcome Kelly into the family with open arms. You just need to do the same." Nooko kissed her cheek and left the room.

Josie sat at her desk pondering Nooko's words. Her mother hadn't lived to meet the women she'd dated. Her feelings for her best friend had become confusing the summer before the accident, but she never had the chance to tell her mom she'd never marry a man. She'd never talked about it with her father. He'd been happy she was as handy with a hammer as a broom, so he never paid much attention to who she dated, as locked away in his own grief as he was. She checked the safe and locked the front door.

"I'm going to finish the shed prep. I'll be out back if you need anything," Josie checked on Nooko, who was stirring a pot of corn soup, then headed to the back door.

"Be careful, dear. I'll have lunch ready when you're done."

Josie began digging in an area next to the building. She removed several shovelfuls of dirt and struck something solid about two feet deep. She presumed it was a cinder block like the others she'd unearthed and kneeled to pull it out. She tugged on a corner and realized it wasn't a cinder block or a rock. She wedged the shovel under it and gently pushed it out of the ground. The dirt fell away to uncover a metal box. She extracted it from the dirt and set it on the ground to get a better look at it. The clasp had an aged lock, most of which was rusted away. She tugged on the top but it wouldn't budge. *Must be rusted or corroded closed.* She took it into her office and locked it away in the back of her wall safe, planning to deal with it later. She returned to her work site to put away her tools.

"I'm heading to the hardware store to pick up some things, Nooko. You want to ride along with me?"

"No. I'll finish the soup and read the paper until you get back. Who was out there with you?"

"No one. Why?"

"I thought I saw someone out by the edge of the woods. I figured maybe Barb came back to help you."

"Nope. Maybe it was a deer back again looking for handouts. I'll be back soon." Josie hooked her empty trailer to her Jeep and checked the area before she left. Nooko's words sparked her anxiety. She walked along the edge of the woods and searched for footprints, deer or human, and found nothing. She noted the time and headed to town.

Loading the odds and ends she needed didn't take as long as she anticipated, so she gave Barb a quick call and left her a message about the possible Abe sighting. She didn't say anything about the metal box but looked forward to examining the contents. It might be full of rocks. She didn't see anything unusual when she pulled up behind the lodge, backed her trailer close to the area she was putting the shed, and shut off the car engine. She'd unload the trailer in the morning. Right now, she wanted to see what was in the box. Intuition told her it was important, though she couldn't fathom why she'd feel that way.

She unlocked the outside door deadbolt and noted the scratches on the metal and the doorjamb. Apprehension constricted her throat as she entered the room. Everything looked in order until she reached the door to her office. The molding was ripped off, the wall deeply gouged, as if by a chainsaw, and the metal door had been thrown into a corner. She rushed to the wall safe to find it scratched and dented as if pounded on with a sledgehammer, but intact and unopened. She breathed a sigh of relief until she noticed Nooko's cane lying on the floor by her desk, and her GPS emergency button next to it smashed to pieces.

She raced to the lodge, running to Nooko's bedroom first. Empty. "Nooko? Are you here?" Her heart beat hard enough to restrict her breathing. She bent over and drew in air before rushing from one room to another. "Nooko!" she yelled as tears stung her eyes. Her grandmother was nowhere to be found.

Chapter Thirty

W e're going to miss you." The whole staff of Woodland Care
Center held coffee cups and bottled water in a toast to Kelly.

"Thank you all. I'm going to miss you, too. It's been an honor to work here and watch you all grow into your roles. I'm proud of each and every one of you." She raised her cup of tea and smiled. "I'll let you know when I get home." Platitudes and promises to keep in touch over, she packed her computer and left.

She resisted the pull to turn toward Josie's as she left the parking lot. She was sure a clean break was best for them both, but her heart still needed convincing. She wandered about the tiny apartment she'd grown used to over the few weeks she'd been there. She put all the dishes away, swept the floor, and straightened the bedding. She realized she was stalling. Hoping Josie would call and, what? Profess her undying love? Ask her not to leave? She considered contacting her, but cell connection was spotty from her apartment, and it was best if she got on with her life. Her only regret was Ruth. She'd miss her wisdom and tenacity. Memories of Josie's touch, her scent, her sounds, would undoubtedly plague her during sleepless nights for a long time. She left the key on the kitchen counter and put her suitcase in the back seat of her car.

She only had one stop to make before leaving the island and heading south. She'd tossed and turned most of the night, wrestling with what she was going to tell Barb. Sweet, romantic Barb, whom she grown to care about. But ultimately, she'd decided it was Josie who'd captured her heart. She sent Barb a text as she approached the main intersection of town. She pulled into the Teepee parking lot and saw her cruiser pull in within minutes. She took a deep breath for courage and smiled when Barb settled into her passenger seat.

"I'm glad you texted. I was hoping I'd get another chance to say good-bye, although I'm hoping it's *see you later* rather than an actual good-bye." Barb kissed her lightly on the lips.

"I couldn't leave without making sure things are clear between us. I care about you, Barb. You're a remarkable woman, and I hope we can remain friends, but I have to let you know that I'm totally in love with Josie." She took Barb's hands in hers, waiting for a response. Saying the words out loud made them real. That it made her feel sad instead of excited wasn't something she needed to admit to.

Barb squeezed her hands gently. "I kind of thought that might be happening. Josie's eyes light up when she looks at you, and I've sort of felt your distraction the last few times we've been together. I regret that I never dragged you into bed. This might surprise you after we talked about how *forward* I can be, but I've only slept with one woman. That was the lover I told you about. I can't jump into bed for the sake of it. I need to feel a connection that goes beyond desire. I need to feel love and commitment before I can offer the vulnerability of sex, and I didn't think that was happening between us, even though I really wanted it to." She let go of Kelly's hands and shrugged. "I don't know if we would've gotten to that point, but I think you and Josie make a great couple, and I hope it works out for you."

Kelly took a moment to process Barb's straightforward honesty before responding. "You are amazing and will make some lucky woman very happy." She kissed her one last time before watching her return to her vehicle and drive away. She backed out of the parking lot and turned her thoughts toward her life miles south of Drummond Island. She didn't need to tell Barb that she and Josie weren't a couple, and it didn't look like they ever would be. She'd acknowledged that her heart was taken, and that was enough truth to share. Now she just had to figure out how to accept that knowledge herself.

Kelly opened her garage door from the car, happy for the familiar sound. She'd stopped only once halfway home for gasoline. All she wanted was distance from the crazy emotional roller coaster she'd been on, and she couldn't get home fast enough. She tried to ignore the idea that her bed would feel extremely empty.

"Hi, sis. How was your trip?" Tory asked as she grabbed Kelly's bag after swinging the door open and giving her a big hug.

"A long ride home. But overall, it was good."

"Cool. I made roast chicken for dinner. Sit and tell me all about Drummond Island."

"Thanks, Tor." She sat in her favorite chair and Tory's little dog, MacIntosh, settled in her lap. "I see he's made himself at home." She hugged him, rubbed his belly, and reveled in the feeling of being home. "I had a relaxing vacation, and I feel good about what I accomplished at the new nursing home, but it's good to be home." She leaned her head on the back of her chair and wondered what Josie was doing.

"Are you back to work tomorrow?"

"No. I'll go back next week. I wasn't even scheduled to return until October, so I'm going to take a few days and ride Pogo." Kelly stroked MacIntosh's soft hair, wishing it were Josie's head resting in her lap. She shook off her lamentations and resolved to move on. There were plenty of women she could date. She just had to go out and find them.

"Sounds like a good plan. I know he's missed you. He's been off his feed for the past few days. I had Dr. Berglund take a look at him yesterday, and everything checked out fine. He told me to have you call him if he doesn't perk up after you get home."

"Thanks, Tory. I'm going to check on him before we eat, then I want to hear how school's going." Kelly went out to the barn to check on her horse, enjoying the feeling of familiarity. She'd missed her daily routine with Pogo, but the break had been a refreshing change. She worked to convince herself that she could settle back into her everyday life and forget Josie, but her heavy heart told her otherwise.

"Hey, boy. I missed you." Kelly grabbed a brush and spent the next hour brushing Pogo and telling him all about her trip. She tossed a fresh flake of hay into his stall and checked that his water bucket was full before heading back to the house. That little bit of routine helped settle her soul, and it was good to be home again.

"Everything good out there?" Tory asked as she set plates on the kitchen table.

"Yeah. I've missed my boy. He seems to be fine. Dug right into his grain and hay." Kelly retrieved silverware and water glasses before sitting at the table.

"Are you going to tell me what happened?" Tory sliced pieces of chicken and set them on the table before sitting across from Kelly.

"What do you mean?" Kelly avoided looking at her sister, knowing how observant she could be.

"You look genuinely happy to be home, but there's a sadness in your eyes that definitely wasn't there when you left."

Kelly considered her response for a moment. Even as a child, Tory had seemed to be able to read Kelly's feelings. Tory was twenty years younger than her, and Kelly was proud of the young woman she'd grown to be. Maybe talking about Josie would dispel some of the empty ache that had taken up residence in her gut. She took a bite of chicken and swallowed before speaking. "I met someone." She struggled to come up with words to describe her feelings. "I guess I should say I met someone and she became very important to me."

"Ah. This doesn't sound like a cheerful story, based on your despondent expression."

"No, it didn't end too well. I fell hard for the woman who owns the lesbian resort where I stayed, but the feeling wasn't reciprocated, or if it was, she was too scared to admit it." Kelly stabbed a cooked carrot, remembering all that Josie had spoken with her touch but denied with words.

"I'm sorry that happened, sis, but you are an incredible woman, and I have no doubt there's someone out there for you who'll appreciate and love you." Tory reached across the table to take her hand.

"Thanks, Tory. I'll be all right. I just need time to heal, I suppose." She hoped her heart was listening.

❖

Kelly spent the next day helping Tory pack for her trip back to her dorm and taking time to ride Pogo. She began to settle back into her life at home, hoping the memory of Josie's touch, her smile, her gentle way with her nooko, would begin to fade. By the end of the week, she gave up and decided to go back to work.

"Good morning, Megan. How're things around here?" Kelly leaned on the counter at the nurses' station.

Megan stood and hurried out of her seat to hug her. "I'm so glad you're back!"

"I'm glad to hear I was missed." Kelly grinned and stepped out of her embrace. "Fill me in on things before I head to Jan's office."

After listening to a quick rundown from Megan, she headed to Jan's office and listened to more. Then, finished with Janis, Kelly settled into her duties as if she'd never been gone. When her rumbling stomach reminded her it was nearly lunchtime, she went in search of

Debby. Debby stood with her back to the door so Kelly spoke quietly so as not to startle her. "Anyone home?"

"Hey, you're back! Janis didn't tell me you'd be in today." Debby closed the top of the pill bottle she'd been filling and set it aside.

"I just finished my rounds and thought I'd see if you wanted to meet for lunch?"

"Absolutely. I want to hear all about that sexy woman in uniform." She grinned.

"Not much to hear about. I'll meet you in the lunchroom." Kelly realized she hadn't thought about Barb for a couple of days, but there wasn't room since her thoughts were filled with Josie.

She sat at one of the tables waiting for Debby and wondering what Josie and Ruth were having for lunch. She allowed herself a moment of longing before pushing it aside. Josie had stated clearly she wasn't in the market for anything permanent, but Kelly'd allowed herself to hope, to take a chance she could convince her by sleeping with her and showing her the depth of her feelings. *Guess that didn't work.* Debby's arrival interrupted her reflections.

"Hey. You look a million miles away."

"I'm fine. Just remembering how nice it was to be on vacation." *And in bed with Josie.*

"It was great. Alex and I are planning to go back next year. So, tell me about Barb." Debby opened a bottle of Coke and looked at her expectantly.

"Barb and I decided we were better friends than lovers."

"That's it?"

"Yeah." When it came to Barb, that really *was* it. Aside from the issue with Josie, there simply hadn't been a real spark with Barb, which was easy enough to admit now that she had some distance.

"Why do I sense there's more going on here?"

Kelly sat back in her chair. She questioned her ability to talk about Josie without breaking down. She took a deep breath, supposing it might help to share her feelings with a close friend. "I slept with Josie." The words slipped out like a release of a pressure cooker and she felt the tears well in her eyes.

Debby reached for her hand. "I have a feeling this story isn't going to end well."

"I'm upset with myself for hoping for something she couldn't give. She was perfectly clear when she told me she didn't want a relationship, and I had to go and find out the hard way."

"Then she's a fool, and she doesn't deserve you. I've known you for years. You're a strong woman, and you'll get through this. Why don't you come over for dinner tonight? Alex is making shepherd's pie, and we're going to watch *The Wizard of Oz*."

Kelly smiled at her friend, grateful for her attempt to distract her. "What time should I be there?"

She walked back to her station feeling the heaviness in her chest lighten. An evening spent with friends would be a wonderful diversion.

Kelly and Megan finished reviewing the patients and revised the nursing schedule for the week. She closed her laptop with a sigh. "You've done an excellent job here, Megan."

"Thanks. I had a good teacher." She grinned and her eyes sparkled. "But I'm glad you're back. The corporation never came through with much help. We got a few new aides but no nurses, and certainly no one with your experience."

Kelly admitted it was good to be home and back to the familiar, but she couldn't shake the feeling of something missing. How could she have gotten so used to Josie and Ruth in only a couple of months? The ring of her cell phone interrupted her thoughts. *Josie's cell.* Her pulse raced and she answered quickly. "Hello. Josie?" Static scratched and buzzed before the call was disconnected. She quickly tried to return the call but was cut off after the first ring. She didn't have Josie's landline number with her, so she had to wait until she went home. She finished her shift with thoughts of Josie constantly present, and left with a hurried good-bye to Megan.

"Hello, Josie. It's Kelly. We got cut off earlier today. I hope everything is going well." Kelly left the message on her voice mail and disconnected the call quickly before she added she missed her. There wasn't much more she could do but wait for her to return her call.

❖

Kelly went to feed Pogo and set him up for the night before returning to change for her evening with friends. She covered the plate of cheese and crackers she planned to take and decided to try Josie's number again before she left. She'd waited all day for her to call back, but concern prompted her to try again. She got her voice mail again and left another short message letting her know she was concerned. She hoped it would push Josie to return the call sooner. She put the plate of hors d'oeuvres in the back seat and headed to Debby's.

Kelly plopped onto the couch and held her belly. "That was wonderful, Alex. Thank you."

"Yeah. The first time she made shepherd's pie, I fell in love all over again." Debby pulled Alex into her arms and kissed her.

"The movie starts in ten minutes. We can have our dessert while we watch." Alex took empty dishes to the kitchen.

"I think I'll wait for intermission. I'm stuffed." Kelly relaxed into the recliner next to the couch.

"Me, too, babe. I need to digest a while before adding tapioca pudding."

Debby and Alex sat next to each other on the end of the couch, and Kelly pushed away memories of her seat on the couch next to Ruth and Josie on the other side of her. She'd never stop missing them. The flying monkeys swooped to capture Dorothy and Toto when she heard her phone ping. She didn't want to interrupt the movie, so she waited until they took a break for dessert before checking it. Her disappointment sank in her belly like a lead ball. *Barb, not Josie.* She put her phone away and concentrated on enjoying the rest of the evening with her friends.

She punched in Barb's number as soon as she got home. "Hi, Barb. Sorry I missed your call. I was visiting some friends." Kelly took a sip of water and relaxed on her couch.

"Hey, Kelly. I miss you. How're things going?"

"Good. I'm settling back into a routine. How're things on Drummond Island?"

"I'm okay, but have you talked to Josie?"

Kelly sat up, unnerved by the emotion in Barb's voice. "No. She tried to call earlier, but we lost the cell signal. Is something wrong?"

"I'm not sure. I don't have many details yet, but her grandmother has disappeared. It sounds weird, but it's what happened. I'm on my way to help the police look for her."

"I know she wanted to go back to her house. Could she have found someone to take her? Never mind. She wouldn't do that to Josie. I have to come back and help you look." Kelly stood and paced in circles.

"Why don't you wait until we have some news? There's nothing you can do here. I'll let you know if anything develops."

"Would you have Josie call me, please? I've tried to call her back, but it keeps going to voice mail."

Barb's hesitation was momentary, but clear. "Sure. I'll be in touch."

Kelly decided to try Josie's cell before heading to bed but got her voice mail, so she left a message, concern roiling in her stomach.

She threw herself onto her bed knowing she wouldn't get any sleep.

CHAPTER THIRTY-ONE

Barb paced the length of the couch where Josie sat with her face in her hands. "The police are checking for fingerprints and the whole department is on alert to watch for her." Barb sat next to her and wrapped her arm around her shoulders. "We'll find her."

"I need to be looking. I can't just sit here and wait." Josie stood and scanned the room, unsure what to do. The police had told her to stay home in case they needed to get hold of her or an abductor contacted her. She suspected Abe, but she couldn't believe he would stoop low enough to kidnap an eighty-six-year-old defenseless woman. *Just to get my property?* "Do you think Abe would do this?"

Barb's deep sigh did nothing to ease the tension racing through her body. "We'll look at all options, Josie. If he's involved, we'll get him. You stay close to the telephone, and I'll be in touch."

"Wait, there's one more thing. I found a strongbox buried in a corner of the house out back. It might be what Abe is looking for. Nooko said she saw someone out there when I was working in that area. Maybe it was the jerk watching. Anyway, it's in the safe. Come on." Josie hurried to her office with Barb close behind.

She opened the safe and pulled out the metal box, determined to get it open. She pried it with a screwdriver and the top popped loose, revealing the contents. Several gold coins sparkled between Canadian fifty-dollar bills, and there were numerous gems in silver and gold settings. She examined one of the coins, unfamiliar with the twenty-dollar piece. She noted the 1925 date and the stamped Saint Gaudens symbol. It was beautiful and probably worth more than face value.

"Wow. I can see why he'd want this. Maybe it's what he referred to as his in his notes. Lock it back up in the safe and show it to the police before they leave. I'm going to file my report. Oh, by the way.

I talked to Kelly earlier and told her about Ruth. She said you'd called her and the call was dropped, so I didn't think you'd mind."

"Not at all, Barb. Thanks for letting her know. I know she'd gotten close to Nooko while she was here." Josie hesitated, at a loss for words. Kelly had been gone for a week. *Could she and Barb be carrying on long-distance? No. She called me "lover."* Memories of Kelly's kisses and her touch sparked a flood of longing tinged with regret.

"Okay. Good. I'll talk to you soon. Try to stay positive. We'll find her." Barb hurried out the door and hopped into her cruiser.

The police had finished processing the room and Josie brought them in to see the box of treasure. They made notes on it, but since it wasn't evidence and they couldn't be certain it was what Abe wanted, they left it with Josie, who put it back in the safe. She'd gladly trade it for Nooko, if the bastard had just left her a way to get in touch with him.

When Barb left, Josie began cleaning. She removed the broken molding, swept the debris, and reset the door on its hinges. She sat at her desk and reminded herself how brave her nooko was. She'd survive this. She had to. She closed the box and locked it in her safe. She began a list of items that needed replacement to keep her mind off Nooko. She jumped when the office phone rang and sprang to answer it.

"Hello. Josie? It's Kelly. Are you all right?"

"Hi, Kelly. Yeah, I'm fine but—"

"Barb told me. She said Ruth was gone. What happened?"

"We don't know yet, but the police and Barb are looking for her. I think Abe's involved, but there's no proof. I just know that someone has Nooko."

"Is there anything I can do?"

"You have just by calling." Josie took a deep breath, astounded how much she'd meant her words.

"Please, let me know if you need anything. And let me know when you find her?"

"I will. I'm going to get off the phone now in case someone's trying to call. Thanks for calling." Josie hung up the phone and sat back in her desk chair. *God, I miss her.* She wished Kelly was there beside her. Kelly grounded her, made her feel safe. Instead, she was alone by her own doing.

She walked out to the area where she'd found the buried box and gazed at the shed still in pieces. She checked the ground for any footprints or any other clues as to who would have taken Nooko. She knew the police would investigate everything, but her fear and feeling of uselessness nearly paralyzed her. She went back inside and wandered through the lodge.

Josie hesitated as she reached for Nooko's bedroom door handle. *A lot of good the lock did.* She wanted to look for clues, for something to indicate where she might be. She didn't expect to find anything, and invading her privacy wasn't Josie's intention. She entered the tidy room and broke down in tears. Nooko's robe hung on the clothes rack and her dream catcher on her bedpost. Her slippers were neatly positioned next to her nightstand. Nothing looked out of place, so Josie closed and locked the door, determined to leave the room untouched until her nooko was home again.

Josie went into the kitchen to make something to eat. In her worry about her nooko, she'd skipped both lunch and dinner. Nooko had been gone ten hours, and night had fallen. She lifted the phone receiver to make sure it worked and slammed it back on the cradle. She tramped to the front entrance intending to check the security light when she saw the manila envelope stuffed halfway under the door. She grabbed it and tore it open.

I warned you I was out of patience, and now you have somethin' that's mine. I want it back. You bring my strongbox to a location of my choosing, when I tell you to, and you'll get the old lady back. I'll let you know the time and place soon. A.

Josie put the note back in the envelope and briefly considered not involving the police. She could just give him the box, get Nooko back, and be done with this, but they were already out there searching, and Nooko was somewhere probably scared. No. He had to pay. She phoned Barb.

"It's Abe, Barb. He's got Nooko. He just left me a note." Josie gripped the phone, willing herself not to panic.

"Okay. Tell me what happened."

"I heard something out front while I was in the kitchen making something to eat. I found an envelope stuffed under the front door with a note in it from Abe."

"Did you touch the note?"

"I only opened the envelope and touched the edges." Josie relaxed slightly at the sound of Barb's composed voice.

"Good. I'm not far from you now, so I'll be there soon. You try and stay calm. We'll catch the bastard."

"Thanks, Barb. Please hurry."

Josie took a deep settling breath. Her first thought after talking to Barb was Kelly. She longed to feel her arms around her, the strength of her caring. She mentally shook herself. She could handle this. Her nooko was strong and brave and she'd be fine. She took some comfort in Abe's words claiming he'd bring her back, but she had no intention of letting him get away with this. She checked the safe again, grateful her father had spent the extra money on the most secure model made and had encased it in cement so it couldn't be stolen. Abe would have to knock down the whole wall and use a crane to get to it. The stuff in the strongbox must be valuable for him to want it so badly. Was that why he'd wanted to buy her property? Because of the box? She wondered if she could keep it since she found it on her land. The authorities would most likely take it, but it didn't matter. Nothing was worth more than the safety of her nooko. Too many questions raced through her mind.

She heard the siren two minutes before the cruiser pulled into her parking lot. Josie ran outside hoping they'd found Nooko and this nightmare would be over, but the trooper exited his vehicle with one hand on his weapon. She stood still with her arms at her side, her fingers spread, and her palm forward. *He must be new.*

"I'm Joslyn Harlow, the owner of these cabins." She didn't move.

He strode up and held out his hand. "I'm Trooper Brent Walker, ma'am. I understand you have a kidnapping situation here?"

"Yes." Josie released the tension in her shoulders. "Please call me Josie. It's my grandmother. She's been taken. Is Barb coming?" Josie looked past the trooper toward the road.

"Officer Donnelly is on her way, ma'am. We can wait for her if you're more comfortable."

Josie wondered when the state police had begun hiring sixteen-year-olds. The young trooper didn't look old enough to shave. "No, we don't have to wait, thank you, Trooper. I have the kidnapper's letter in my office."

Brent followed her to the office but rushed to open the door for her as she reached for it. She breathed a sigh of relief when she heard Barb's car pull in the lot behind them. An overeager rookie with old-fashioned chivalry ideas wasn't what she needed right now.

Josie opened the safe and pulled out all the notes she'd gotten from Abe, along with the strongbox. "This is the latest." She handed the ransom note to the trooper and greeted Barb, who stood reading over his shoulder.

"Let's show him the box," Barb said.

"Of course."

He watched as Josie opened the box. "This is some find." He inspected one of the gold coins. "This coin alone is worth some bucks." He replaced the coin and closed the box. "I'm going to report everything I find to the captain, ma'am. But I don't think we need to take this to the station." He was furiously making notes on a notepad.

Josie expected the young trooper to salute them both as he stood at attention. She looked at Barb, who rolled her eyes slightly.

"Relax, Brent. I'll stay here with Josie while you go make your report. I expect we'll have to revise our search plan now."

"Thank you, Officer Do—Barb." He grinned and turned to Josie to clumsily place a hand on her shoulder. "Don't you worry. We'll get this guy." He turned and left, his tires kicking up dust as he sped off.

"I missed being called ma'am again."

"Brent's a good cop. He's still the new kid, but my brother claims he's got potential. Let's review all of Abe's notes and see if we can find a clue to where he might've taken Ruth."

They spent time reading all the letters she'd gotten from Abe, and Josie answered Barb's questions the best she could. The uneasiness she'd felt knowing Kelly and Barb had dated eased as they discussed the situation and reviewed strategies. She trusted Barb to do her best to help her find Nooko, regardless of her relationship with Kelly. She needed a friend right now, and lucky for her, she had one who knew what she was doing.

CHAPTER THIRTY-TWO

Josie grabbed the phone on the second ring. "Hello."

"Hey, Josie. It's Kelly. Sorry to call so late. How're things going? Did you find Ruth?"

"Hi, Kelly. No. Nooko's been kidnapped by Abe. He left me a ransom note tonight, and Barb and I are reviewing options now." Josie took a breath, absorbing a sense of peace from hearing Kelly's voice.

"Oh, no. I'm so sorry, Josie. I remember how thorough Barb was, and she knows the island. If anyone can find them, it's Barb."

"I know. She's working with the police search team. When Abe lets me know his conditions, we'll make a more solid plan. I'm worried about Nooko, though." She bristled at Kelly's praise of Barb, then chastised herself. Kelly had called to support her even if she and Barb were an item.

"She's a strong lady. She'll be okay."

"I'll let you know as soon as I get any information. I appreciate your call." Josie hung up and repeated Kelly's words over in her mind. *She'll be okay.* She wished Kelly had offered to come, even though she knew she couldn't do anything. Just having her there would have been nice. *She's got her own life. It's nice she even bothered to call.*

"You said Abe told you he used to hunt with your father, right?" Barb sat back in a chair making notes.

Josie didn't miss that Barb didn't ask about Kelly. *She probably talks to her every day.* "Yes. He called him Jack, and we had no idea he ever went by Jack. After my mother died, Dad used to go hunting overnight sometimes. I'm not sure where, though. He'd just tell me to keep an eye on the place."

"I'll give all this information to the police, but I'm sure they'll send someone out to confirm it all. I'll tell you what I'm thinking. There are quite a few hunting shacks all over Drummond Island, and many are vacant this time of year. Hunters come for deer season and rarely use the cabins for anything else. I know of a cluster of deserted cottages in the middle of the island. It's remote, difficult to get to, and a perfect place to hide. I'll hike in there tomorrow morning and check it out."

"Hike in there? Nooko couldn't go hiking!" Josie stood and forced herself not to hyperventilate.

Barb stood and placed her hand on her back. "Josie. I'm sure he has an ATV. I doubt he wants to carry an old woman through the woods. We'll find her."

Josie lay on her bed willing sleep to come but doubting it would until Nooko was home safe. She padded barefoot to the couch where she'd last seen Nooko relaxed and happily reading the paper. She wandered into the kitchen and grabbed a bottled water to take to her studio in search of a moment of serenity. She ran her hand over her worktable. "I'll get her back safely, Mom." She spoke into the empty room, meandered to an open window, and listened to the quiet night. Nooko was out there somewhere, maybe scared, hungry, and cold. She crushed her empty water bottle and lobbed it into a wastebasket. *If you hurt her, you're dead.*

She plopped into one of the leather chairs in the main room and allowed memories of Kelly to surface. The three of them sitting talking, sharing a meal, or laughing in the hot tub. She hesitated for a second and then punched Kelly's number into her phone.

"Josie?" Kelly sounded alarmed.

"I'm still waiting for any word from the police or Abe. Sorry to bother you, but I guess I wanted to hear your voice." She wondered if she sounded as vulnerable as she felt.

"You're not bothering me. Your cell phone signal works better at night. How're you holding up? I can tell you're struggling."

"I keep thinking of Nooko alone with that idiot, scared, hungry, cold…I don't know what I'll do if he hurts her." Josie pinched the bridge of her nose, pushing away a headache underpinned by heartache.

"I can only imagine, but Ruth is a tough lady. Remember her determination in the hot tub?"

Josie smiled for the first time since Nooko disappeared. "Yeah. Once she sets her mind to something, she doesn't give up." It felt so good to talk to someone who knew Ruth, who knew how Josie felt about her.

"And the jingle dancing she did at the powwow?"

Josie laughed out loud. "Thanks, Kelly. I was beginning to think I'd never have anything to laugh about again."

"We'll get through this, Josie. Abe's a coward. Nabbing your grandmother to get you to sell to him isn't smart. They'll catch him. And thanks to all the exercise and good care you took of her, Ruth is healthy and strong. She'll be okay."

Josie realized she hadn't told Kelly about the strongbox. "He claims to own a metal box of jewels and money I found while digging out back. He wants to exchange it for Nooko."

"A box of money and jewels? Wow, that's crazy. What do the cops say?"

"I don't know yet. I expect to hear from them in the morning about the plan." Josie looked at the clock. "I'm sorry, Kelly. I just realized I called you at three o'clock in the morning."

"Don't worry about it. Call anytime you need to. Try and get some rest."

I wish you were here. I wish you'd offer to come. The thoughts were silly. Kelly had a life she couldn't just step away from. "Good night." Josie disconnected the call, leaned her head back, and fell into a restless sleep.

The next morning, Josie went about her morning routine hoping to calm her restlessness. She'd just finished her oatmeal when she heard two cruisers pull into the parking lot and hurried to the door. "Come in." Josie stepped aside as Barb and three state troopers entered her office.

"How're you doing?" Barb asked.

"I'll be better when we find Nooko."

"No word from Abe yet?"

"Not yet. I'm guessing he'll leave another note, but I doubt he'll show his face."

"We've got the state troopers and sheriff's department on alert for this guy, ma'am, and Officer Donnelly's volunteered to check a group of cabins on the island. We'll have a patrol coming around your place regularly to watch for him, just in case he comes to you. You just let us know when you hear from him, and we'll take it from there." Brent spoke so assuredly, Josie felt herself relax a little. She wasn't in this alone.

They reviewed all the evidence she had, including the contents of the strongbox, and gave her a copy of their report before leaving.

"Thanks, Barb. I appreciate the effort everyone's putting in to find Nooko." Josie regretted every uncharitable thought she'd had about Barb over the Kelly situation. She was a good friend, and a good officer.

"No problem. We're not letting anyone get away with kidnapping, especially an elder. He's going to pay for this. I'm going to check out that hunting area now. I'll have my cell phone, but I doubt there'll be a signal from there, so I'll call or stop by on my way back tonight."

"Be careful, Barb. Abe's probably armed."

Barb chuckled. "Yeah. So am I."

Josie locked the front door and checked the safe before going outside to finish her shed project. She'd finished assembling the sides and begun hanging the doors when she heard the faint sound of footsteps. She took a deep breath before peeking around the corner of the building. She caught a glimpse of someone slipping into the thick brush in the woods. Her anger urged her to follow, but her common sense took over, and she went to her office presuming she'd find a note.

There's a dumpster behind the middle school. You'll find a burlap bag under it. Put the strongbox in the bag and leave it there Tuesday at 10 a.m. No cops or the old lady's history. When I get the box, I'll leave Grandma at the back entrance of the school.

Josie stuffed the note in with the others in the safe. She didn't trust Abe at all, but it occurred to her that Nooko would be a burden to him once he got his strongbox. There was no reason for him to harm her or to keep her any longer, and kidnapping was bad enough. She doubted he'd want to add murder to his sentence. *No cops. He probably figures he's going to get away with this.* She stood and paced the length of the room trying to decide what to do. A part of her wanted to end this by following his instructions and moving on, but she didn't trust him and wouldn't let him get away with it. What if he'd already hurt Nooko? And why was he waiting three days? She sat at her desk and grabbed the phone.

"Hello, this is Josie Harlow. May I speak to Trooper Brent Walker, please?"

❖

Josie began to worry when Barb still hadn't returned by dark. She'd finished mounting the doors on her new shed and cleaned the area trying to keep her mind off Nooko. She put her tools away and went inside to wait. After ten minutes of reading, she tossed aside her book and seized her cell phone.

"Hello, Josie. I'm glad your cell call is coming through. Any news?"

"No. I needed to hear your voice again. I got another note with Abe's demands." Josie read the note to Kelly, calmed slightly from hearing Kelly's voice and her concern.

"At least he said he'd leave her, not hurt her."

"Yeah, I thought so, too. I doubt he'd bother keeping her, and he'd have no reason to hurt her, but I want him to pay for this." Josie rarely drank, but she fished out a beer from the back of the refrigerator and opened it.

"I have to wonder why he chose Tuesday."

"The police think he wants to have time to find a secure hiding place." She took a drink from the bottle and grimaced, remembering she hated beer.

"Do the cops have a plan to catch him?"

"They're coming tomorrow to review it all and discuss options. I'm waiting for Barb to get back from her search. I have to say, I'm a little worried." She dumped the beer in the sink and threw the bottle in the recycle bin. She heard a car pull into the parking lot. "I think Barb just got here. I'll let you know what happens."

"Okay. Take care."

"Oh, Kelly?"

"Yes?"

"Thanks for calling. It means a lot that you care."

"Of course I care, Josie. I hope you know how much I care for you and Ruth. I'm sorry I can't be there with you. Tell Barb I said hello."

So she hasn't talked to her. Josie ran out to meet Barb, alarmed by her significant limp. She rushed to help her inside. Barb sat on one of the chairs and Josie propped her foot on the coffee table.

"We've got thirty thousand acres of state land, and I think I trekked through half of them." She bent forward to stretch her back. "I'm sorry, Josie. I found the bugger, but he saw me and leveled his hunting rifle at me. I got away, but not before he nicked me with a shot."

Josie quickly inspected Barb's leg. "Damn, Barb. You're bleeding." She retrieved her first aid kit and secured a bandage on her wound. It wasn't deep, more of a long scratch, but it must have hurt like hell.

"I'm so sorry. I didn't see the exact building he went to, but I'm sure he's in that group I told you about. I was only a hundred yards away when he found me."

"He left another note today. What time did you see him?"

"It was late afternoon, why?"

"He was here earlier when he left the note." Josie showed Barb Abe's message.

"I'm sorry, I guess I've tipped him off about being on to him, but what a dope. I can't believe he thinks we won't be waiting for him. I let Brent know about my run-in with him right after it happened. Did you call the authorities?"

"I did. They'll be here tomorrow to let me know their plan."

"Good. We'll catch him." Barb grimaced as she spoke.

"Come on. We're going to get your leg looked at." Josie helped Barb into her Jeep and prayed their plan would work. Abe had said no cops, but he had to know they'd be waiting for him. She concentrated on getting Barb to the clinic and thought about calling Kelly back to let her know about Barb's injury. She decided she'd just ask.

"Do you want me to call Kelly and let her know about this?"

"It's not that bad. We don't have to worry her. I'm glad she called to support you." Barb shifted in her seat and looked pale.

"Yeah, me, too. Let's get you looked at." She parked in front of the clinic and helped Barb to the door. Things were out of control and she had no idea what to do next. She still didn't have an answer about things between Kelly and Barb, but right now, that needed to be the least of her worries.

CHAPTER THIRTY-THREE

Josie watched the clouds build as the temperature plummeted and lightning flashed. They'd had a fairly rain-free summer, but the front moving in threatened a change for several days. She cursed Nature's timing, thinking about Nooko getting soaked somewhere out in the woods, but sighed with resignation. She poured two cups of coffee and put a few cups out for the police officers who were due in an hour. Barb rested with her leg propped on the coffee table, her crutches leaning on the couch next to her.

"Thanks." Barb took her coffee and sipped. "And thanks for taking me to the ER last night."

"No problem. I'm glad you agreed to be checked out and to stay the night here." Josie sat next to Barb and drank her coffee. "What do you think the state police will suggest we do?"

"I don't know, but whatever it is, I'm sure they'll be careful."

"Yeah. I hope so." Josie wished Kelly were there. She hadn't been able to get her out of her thoughts since they spoke last. She considered calling her but decided to wait until she had some news. "We're in for a storm. I sure hope wherever Abe's keeping Nooko is dry."

The police arrived a few minutes later, and Josie led them to her office where they reviewed the latest note and discussed strategies. The rain had begun and the wind began to howl, so Josie left to check on the front door. She never would have noticed the envelope if she hadn't opened the door to close the storm window on the screen door. She took it into her office to open it. "I've got another one."

The group of officers stood close as she read the message.

I told you no cops! I won't miss next time if I see another one. You have one more chance and one more day. I want what's mine! I'm moving our day to Wednesday. 10 a.m. If the box isn't there, Grandma disappears.

She handed the letter to the trooper in charge and took a settling breath. The storm raged outside and, inside, her heart pounded.

"He must've seen Barb after he left the first message." Josie watched the raindrops run like tears down the window.

"Please, find her." Josie trembled as despair threatened to grip her heart. "Please."

Brent moved to wrap his arm around her shoulders. "We will, Josie. We will."

The police and Barb finished taking notes and writing reports before leaving. The intensity of the storm had lessened, but not the anguish in her heart.

The grumbling in her stomach reminded Josie that she needed to eat and Barb was probably hungry. "I'm putting a frozen pizza in the oven, Barb. Will you stay?"

"Thanks, Josie. I'll have a couple pieces before I head home. Let's go over my map."

"You're in no shape to trudge through the woods." Josie sat across from Barb.

"I will be soon, and I'll take it slow driving. Rob told me they could possibly get the aviation division involved. Here's where I spotted Abe."

Josie listened as Barb pointed out the wooded area on the map and described the conditions. Her heart pounded in her chest, imitating one of the powwow drums. "Nooko doesn't even have her cane. Some days, she can barely walk around the house without it, let alone through the woods."

"That may work in our favor. I doubt Abe wants to bother with her for long."

"I suppose." Josie's mental picture of Nooko helpless, tied to a chair or bed, unable to get up for the bathroom or food, triggered another round of hyperventilation. "Why do you think he's waiting until Wednesday?"

"I think Brent's correct. He knows the police are looking for him and he wants to be sure he's safely hidden. I bet he's got some getaway plan that includes getting off the island, which is why he's got such specific times and days. Maybe he's got someone meeting him off island as well. The guy is obviously stupid, what with offering you such a small amount of money for your land, making threats, and then kidnapping your grandmother. He's one of the dumber criminals I've come across, frankly. He may also think he can use his hideaway after the exchange, and he probably moved after I found him where I did, but we'll find him, and we will prosecute him."

"Barb, he has to know you'll be watching for him. It's as if he's taunting us by giving a specific time and place. And at such an open location."

"Guys like him aren't smart. They're narcissistic and self-centered, so they develop a sense of invincibility. My guess is he doesn't think he'll ever be caught. Or I suppose he may think we wouldn't bring weapons to a school."

"I just want Nooko back safe." Josie took a bite of pizza and put the rest away. Food soured in her stomach as soon as she ate it. Everything tasted like sawdust. If something happened to her grandmother, she'd never forgive herself.

Barb left with her map and a plan to get drones, helicopters, or planes involved in the search. Josie tried to ease her restlessness by washing windows and vacuuming. She left the vacuum sitting in the middle of the room and picked up her cell phone.

"Hey, Kelly. It's Josie."

"Hang on. I'm taking you to the break room." Kelly sounded far away. "Okay. Sorry I was at our nursing station."

"I'm sorry to bother you at work. I just needed to hear your voice." Josie's heartbeat slowed and the knot in her shoulders loosened slightly. She settled on the couch and cradled the phone to her ear.

"What's happening with Ruth?"

"Abe's pushed the exchange day to Wednesday. He saw Barb when she went looking for him and shot at her. I need this to be over."

"Shot at her? I'm not sure why, but until now I didn't think of him as very dangerous." Kelly sounded worried. "What the hell? Is she okay?"

"Yes. I took her to the doctor, and she has a few stitches and she's sore. But she's able to drive and walk. She'll take it easy for a few days."

"I'll give her a call later, but tell her I'm thinking of her, please."

"I will." *So they haven't talked.* "I don't know what to think about this idiot anymore. Barb is certain they'll catch him, but I'm scared to death."

"The police and Barb know what they're doing. We have to trust them."

Josie could tell Kelly was pacing as she spoke. She could picture that intense expression she wore when she was concentrating, and it made her heart skip. "Yes. We do."

Someone called Kelly's name in the background. "I have to get back to work. Let me know if anything changes, and, Josie?"

"Yes?"

"You take care of yourself."

Josie plugged her phone into its charger and stretched out on the couch. *Take care of myself?* That sounded...flat. She didn't want flat. She wanted words of care, of consideration...of love. *But I turned that down.* She dozed off, hoping Nooko was being taken care of. The landline phone interrupted her nap, and she jumped to answer it.

"Josie, this is Brent from the Michigan State Police post. I wanted to let you know our plan is in place and we're doing everything possible to find your grandmother. We'll be in touch with you daily."

"Thank you, Brent. I appreciate it. Is there anything you can tell me now? Did you find any clues as to where he is?"

"I'm sorry, but we don't know much. The fingerprints we retrieved don't match any in the system, but we're certain we're looking for the right guy. Just to be sure, I'll swing by this afternoon with a photo for you to verify for me."

"I'll be here. Thanks." Josie hung up and lay back with her arm over her forehead.

The rain had stopped and Josie sat on the porch, taking in the clean, fresh air and the view of the sun sparking off the water. It would be a perfect scene if Nooko were seated beside her. She took a settling breath and mentally reviewed the plan. The police would be waiting for Abe while hidden along the outskirts of the school grounds. As soon as they saw Nooko was safe, they'd grab him. It had sounded so easy when the captain laid it out for her. On this quiet Sunday morning, with the birds singing, and the leaves rustling in the breeze, it sounded too easy to believe, but too scary not to. She left the tranquility of the porch to do her daily walk around the area. She checked each empty cabin and the grounds, grateful now that she had no guests, before returning to walk through the lodge and stop in her office. She opened the safe and regarded the key to getting Nooko back. She relocked the safe and returned to the porch, astounded to see Kelly's car pull into the lot. She watched her step out of her car and hesitate before walking toward her, certain her stress had caused a mental breakdown. She blinked, but Kelly didn't disappear.

"Hey there."

Josie heard her voice and blinked again, but she was still there. "Hey, yourself." They were the only words that came to her.

"I hope you don't mind, but I couldn't stay away. I would've come sooner, but I had to make arrangements at work and for Pogo. Have you heard anything more?" Kelly stood on the first step facing her.

She shook off her shock and found her voice, thrilled to see her. "Come sit. Can I get you anything? Some water?"

"I'll get some in a bit, thanks. Tell me what's going on." Kelly climbed the steps and sat on one of the rockers.

"I told you Abe changed the exchange date, didn't I? He's doing it Wednesday." Josie sat on the edge of the rocker with her hands clasped in front of her to keep herself from reaching out to touch her. To make sure she was real.

"You told me yesterday." Kelly sat back and slowly rocked before leaning forward and matching Josie's pose. "Why do you think he chose Wednesday?"

"Barb and the police think he's dumb enough to believe he won't be caught, and he's securing his hideout."

"Are they planning to find him before Wednesday?"

"If they can. Barb knows approximately where he is, but not the exact cabin."

"I talked to her once for a minute while she was in her office, but she didn't have time to chat. How's she doing?"

"Good. She's back to work today doing as much as she can to help."

"It must be frustrating to have to wait here while they search."

"You have no idea." As Josie said the words, she wondered if they were true. Kelly came to be with her and help her get through this. She could have stayed home, worked, lived her life, and called occasionally. But she drove hours to support her. Maybe she'd found waiting frustrating too. "I'm going to get some water, and I've got leftover pizza. Want a piece?"

"Thanks. I'm starved." She followed her into the kitchen. "I left early, right after breakfast, but that was six hours ago." She pulled two water bottles out of the refrigerator. "Do you have a cabin available for a few days?"

"I have six. But if you're asking to stay, I have a better idea." She turned and pulled Kelly into her arms. "Stay with me?"

Kelly stood silently in her arms holding two cold bottles of water, searching her face. "I'd like that."

Josie placed a light kiss on her lips, unprepared for the need that exploded and wound through her body like ivy vines. She took a step back searching Kelly's gaze for rejection and saw emotions even scarier. She took a deep breath and vowed to attempt to face her fears. Kelly was worth it. "Thank you for coming. It helps having you here." She wrapped her in her arms, the warmth of her body a salve to her heartache.

Kelly kissed her back and then pulled away. "Let me get my bag and freshen up, okay? I'll be right back."

Josie watched the way she moved. She was so elegant, so light on her feet. So beautiful. She went inside and Josie stayed on the porch, determined to take it slow.

Barb pulled in behind Kelly's car. Josie squelched a wave of jealousy. Kelly was here to see her. To stay with her. Jealousy wasn't necessary. "Hey, Barb."

"Hi. Is that Kelly's car?" She climbed the steps with barely a limp.

"It is. She got here about an hour ago. Your leg feeling better?"

"Yes. Much. Thanks again for your help." She settled in the chair next to her. "Brent and I are taking an ATV out to the woods this afternoon. We can get to most of the cabins that way. I'll let you know what we find."

Kelly appeared in the doorway carrying slices of pizza, and Barb stood.

"Hi, Barb." She set the plate on the small porch table and they hugged. "Looks like you're moving okay."

"Yeah, I'm fine. I'm going back to work to find Ruth this afternoon. I'm glad you made it back. Josie can use the support."

Kelly placed a hand on Josie's shoulder. "Ruth became very special to me while I was here. I couldn't stay away. Would you like a piece of pizza?"

"Thanks, but Brent's waiting for me. You guys try to relax. We will find her." Barb looked between them and smiled.

Josie watched Kelly and Barb, sensing a comfortable, friendly distance between them. Barb hadn't kissed her and even the hug had seemed quick. She wrestled with her reaction. If she was still dating Barb, it was none of her business, but a small twinge of hope worked its way into her heart. Kelly saying she'd grown fond of Ruth was nice, but it made it sound like that was the only reason she was there. Was she softening it for Barb, or because she didn't want to give Josie the wrong idea?

"I'll be in touch." Barb waved as she took the stairs one at a time.

Josie didn't miss the fact that Barb left without another hug, and she didn't deny the elation it gave her. Maybe there was some hope after all.

CHAPTER THIRTY-FOUR

L et's go for a walk by the water." Kelly stood and held out her hand. They strolled to the bench where they'd shared a kiss weeks ago. Kelly relished the feel of Josie's hand in hers and in the way Josie seemed so glad to see her. It validated her fantasy, confirming Josie felt more for her than she'd admit.

"I'm glad you came back, Kelly. I missed you." Josie didn't look at her when she spoke.

"I missed you, too, and I couldn't stay away while Ruth is held hostage somewhere. It must be hard for you." She rested her head on her shoulder. She'd let Janis know she'd be gone for a few days because of a "family emergency." To her, this qualified.

"Yeah. It is. I keep wondering if he's treating her well. What she's eating, and if she's comfortable. She doesn't have her cane, you know. I found it on the office floor the day she went missing. I swear I'll kill him if he hurts her."

Kelly felt the tension in Josie's body and couldn't argue she didn't feel the same. "They'll find her, lover," she whispered.

They watched the few ducks propel through the water, their little feet paddling silently below the surface, and Kelly wondered what Josie was thinking. Her endearment had slipped out unexpectedly. She knew she couldn't keep her feelings for Josie quiet forever, but Josie had asked her to stay with her. She'd continue to support her and be patient. Keeping her expectations in check could prove to be more difficult.

"I need to get back to the building in case someone calls." Josie stood and pulled Kelly up with her.

Kelly took Josie's hand as they walked. She enjoyed the physical connection. It was enough for now.

Josie checked the voice mail when they got back to the lodge while

Kelly waited on the porch. "Nothing yet. Do you have any preference for dinner?"

Kelly laughed. "If I say pasties would you groan?"

"No. Actually, it sounds pretty good. Would you mind getting them? I want to stay by the phone. I'll make us a salad to go with them."

"Sounds good. I'll be back soon." Memories surfaced as Kelly drove the route to the restaurant. Her stay on the island had begun as a vacation and a new job and had ended in heartache. She vowed this return trip would bring either love or final closure on what might not be meant to be. She picked up the food and made another important stop before heading back to the lodge.

"Hello. I'm back." Kelly handed her the bag of food and turned to head back to her car.

"Where're you going?"

"I've got a surprise." She brought in a bag from the Teepee. "Chocolate for us, and vanilla for Ruth." She put the ice cream in the freezer, pleasantly surprised when she returned to see Josie had set an extra place at the table. "I'm glad you set a place for her. She'll get her ice cream when she gets home."

Josie pulled her into her arms, and Kelly relaxed against her chest, comforted by the feel of her heartbeat. "Thank you."

She wondered if the warm breath on her ear carried love or only gratitude.

❖

Josie stretched her legs out on the couch and leaned back into a corner. Kelly lay on the opposite end and intertwined their legs. They each had their individual books, but Josie had never felt so united. *And safe.* She sighed and Kelly looked up and smiled. She held her place in the book with her finger before speaking. "You know what I'm wondering? I guess, I mean, worrying about. What if there's a shoot-out with Abe? Nooko could get caught in the cross fire."

Kelly set her book on the end table and shifted to lie on top of her. "You need to quit worrying. The police know what they're doing, and they won't take chances with Ruth's life." She snuggled into her, and Josie kissed the top of her head.

"Yeah. You're right. I just need this to be over." She wiggled to adjust their position and softly pressed her lips to Kelly's. Their kiss deepened and their tongues met. She pulled Kelly's shirt out of her jeans and slipped her hands under it, desperate to feel the soft skin of her back. Kelly squirmed on top of her, pushing her thigh between her legs, kneading her center.

They slid off the couch with tangled legs and arms, and rolled on the floor with Josie on top. She nuzzled Kelly's neck. Her quiet whimpers shot waves of need throughout her body, to her groin, to her heart. She rolled to her side, pulled Kelly against her, and quietly held her. Kelly nestled against her and stilled in her arms.

"Bed?" Kelly mumbled against her shoulder.

"Yeah. This floor isn't too comfortable, is it?" Josie kissed her and slowly disentangled herself to stand and pull her up.

Josie sat on the side of her bed, captured both of Kelly's hands, and kissed her fingers. "I want this, Kelly. Are you sure you do?"

"Absolutely." Kelly pushed her back on the bed, straddled her hips, and leaned with her arms on either side of her.

Josie reached under Kelly's shirt, unclasped her bra, and pushed it up to cup her breasts. She squeezed her nipples between her fingers as Kelly leaned back, grabbed her hands, and pressed them against herself. She pulled off her own T-shirt and bra, and they crawled onto the bed and shed the rest of their clothes. Her reservations fled as she stroked the soft flesh of Kelly's belly and moved her hand lower to the curly patch of blond glistening with evidence of her desire. *Desire for me.* She slowly circled her clit with her fingers and stroked faster as it hardened. She increased the pressure and massaged, frantic to match the intensity of Kelly's whimpers. "Oh, yes. Don't stop." She stiffened and pushed against her hand as she clung to her and shuddered. Josie reveled in the feeling of Kelly's heart beating in sync with her own and rested her lips on the delicate skin covering the pulse in her neck. "You're beautiful."

Kelly shifted to rest her head on her chest and Josie ran her silky hair through her fingers, awed by the feeling of contentment. Angst for her nooko wasn't gone, but there was nowhere else she wanted to be that moment than right where she was.

She awoke with Kelly holding her immobile as her tongue flicked her nipple and her fingers worked to bring her to the edge of orgasm, then draw back. Kelly coated her clit with her juices and slowly teased her opening and pulled out. Josie bucked off the bed, fisting the sheets, her muscles taut. "Oh, yes, I'm coming." She didn't hear herself cry out as she came, but something she thought unmovable had moved. A part of her wall had fallen away and exposed a part of her heart that had opened to the possibility of love. She welcomed it as she drifted to sleep in Kelly's arms once more.

Josie woke with Kelly wrapped around her, and she never wanted to move. Her bladder convinced her she didn't have that choice, so she brushed her lips over Kelly's forehead and extricated herself. She returned to find Kelly grinning at her, leaning on one elbow with her head on her hand. She lifted the bedding so Josie could slide in, then covered her and wrapped her arms around her.

"Hmm. This is nice." Josie pushed back against Kelly, enjoying the feel of her embrace.

"Yes. It is."

Josie rolled onto her back and pressed Kelly's hand to her chest. "Why did you leave without saying good-bye?"

Kelly stiffened and a tear rolled down her cheek, but she didn't pull away. "Because I couldn't. I knew how you felt."

Josie waited. Scenarios raced through her mind. *Kelly is leaving again. She's sorry about last night.* She raised Kelly's hand to her lips and held it until she continued. She quieted the voices and listened to the one that mattered.

"I was scared because I already knew I was in love with you, and I couldn't put myself through seeing you, knowing you didn't feel the same way."

"Why are you here?" She still didn't release Kelly's hand.

"Because I don't care anymore."

Josie flinched as if she'd been punched in the gut. *I've done it. I've scared her away.* "I didn't mean to hurt you." Unexpected tears formed and spilled over her eyelashes.

"Oh, lover." Kelly framed her face with her hands and kissed her. "I mean I don't care anymore that I'm in love with you and you're not in love with me. I'll continue to love you anyway, and I want to spend as much time with you as you're willing to give me. If you never love me, at least I'll have had this."

Kelly's hand was warm where she placed it over her heart, and she felt it stir. Maybe she could try.

CHAPTER THIRTY-FIVE

Josie beat the eggs after she tossed vegetables into a pan to sauté.

"Something smells good." She caught the scent of Kelly's shampoo as she stepped behind her and kissed the back of her neck. "Can I help with anything?"

"You can set the table. The omelets will be done soon." Desire weakened her knees as she watched Kelly reach for the plates and coffee cups in the cupboard. Her hair was still damp from the shower and she wore a pair of worn jeans, a T-shirt, and no bra. She poured the eggs into the pan, trying to ignore how wet she was with arousal.

They sat at the table with Nooko's place setting, Kelly's words of love hanging heavy on her mind.

"Could I review all the information you have on Abe?" Kelly took a bite of her omelet. "Mm. This is wonderful. Thanks for making it."

"You're welcome. The police and Barb have reviewed all of it, but it couldn't hurt to have fresh eyes. It'll give me something to do, too." Josie longed to tell Kelly what she wanted to hear. To speak her own words of love. But they kept getting stuck in her throat. After breakfast, she held Kelly's hand as they went to her office. She wanted the constant physical connection, even if she couldn't say so out loud. Yet.

Josie emptied the envelope with all Abe's notes onto one of the round tables.

"He likes to write messages, doesn't he?" Kelly asked.

Josie shrugged. "I guess."

"The last one sure implicates him. He practically admits he shot at Barb and he's definitely threatening to hurt Ruth. What I can't figure out is how in the world he thinks he'll get away with it." Kelly shook her head and put the notes back in the envelope.

"I'm going to call Brent and see what's going on."

"Who's Brent?"

"He's one of the Michigan State troopers on the case. Come on." Josie put the strongbox on the desk for Kelly to look at.

Kelly sat at her desk looking through the strongbox when she finished her call. "There's some valuable things in here." She lifted the same coin Barb had examined. "I know in 1933 President Roosevelt issued an executive order recalling all gold. They needed to restock the treasury after the Great Depression. Obviously, whoever put this box together meant for it to be hidden a while. There's Canadian money in the bottom, and the stones in the jewelry appear to be precious gems. I think they're rubies and diamonds. I see why he wants this, but why does he think it's his?" Kelly closed the box and Josie locked it in the safe.

"I don't know. I need a distraction. How does the hot tub sound?" Josie gave her a tired smile. As much as she loved having Kelly there, she was still exhausted from worrying about her nooko.

Kelly grabbed her hand and led the way.

Josie pulled Kelly to her and kissed her as she unbuttoned her jeans. Kelly toed off her shoes, stepped out of her pants and panties, and pulled off her T-shirt. The desire simmering all morning burst into flames, and Josie sucked one nipple into her mouth and moved to the other. Kelly yanked at her pants, and Josie hopped on one foot, pulling off her sneakers and disrobing. Kelly climbed into the tub and Josie followed. Kelly leaned back, floating on the bubbling water. Her breasts swayed with the frothing movement and she waved her arms slowly and spread her legs, an invitation Josie couldn't resist. She glided over Kelly so their breasts met, their nipples touched, and she gasped. She cupped her sex and Kelly thrust against her hand. "Yes!" She grabbed Josie's hand with both of hers and bent forward, urging her to claim her. She wrapped her arm around Kelly's waist and entered her with one finger while compressing her clit with her palm. Kelly writhed, splashed water out of the tub, and collapsed into her arms. Feelings that were becoming familiar stirred as she wiped the water drops from her face and kissed her chin before moving to her lips. Kelly floated to her feet and rested her arms on her shoulders as their kiss deepened and their breasts, suspended in the frothing water, caressed and touched like leaves in a gentle breeze.

Josie wrapped her legs around Kelly's waist and leaned back to hold on to the side of the tub. Kelly supported herself with her legs on the tub floor and began her exploration. Kelly's touch was gently demanding, possessive, as she kneaded her thigh muscles and stroked the sensitive skin where her legs met her groin. She rested her head on the edge of the tub, and Kelly lifted her legs over her shoulders and took her clit in her mouth. All thoughts fled as she squirmed in time to Kelly's circling tongue. She clutched the side of the tub and raised her hips out of the water as her orgasm rippled through her, and she cried out.

Kelly's firm nipples tickled her back as she shifted to lean against her. The natural feel of her arms wrapped around her waist, lightly caressing her belly, surprised her. How could it feel so comfortable and right to be with someone you were afraid to love?

"I think this is the way a hot tub is supposed to be used," she said, pushing aside the words really trying to come out.

"It's certainly the best way I've ever experienced." Kelly kissed her shoulder. "Maybe we should get out and dry off. Feel like going out for a meal? Maybe a change of scenery would be a good distraction."

Josie drove, relishing the feel of Kelly's hand on her thigh. She felt the cold spot it left when they arrived at the restaurant, and when she moved her hand, the chill on her thigh was like an open coat in the middle of winter.

"This was a good idea." Kelly spoke as she sat at a window table in the diner.

"Yeah, you're right. I needed to get out for a bit. Thanks for reminding me I have remote access to my answering machine. I've never used it before. But I'm not sure how I feel about not being by the phone."

"The police are doing their job, and I'm sure they'd try your cell if they find anything important. And Abe doesn't call you, does he? He leaves letters, the coward."

They were almost finished with their meal when Josie saw Barb enter. She stiffened, her first thoughts of Nooko. When Barb paused at their table after stopping to greet several people on the way, Josie realized her attention was focused on Kelly. Her apprehension turned to jealousy that faded slightly when she only waved from the doorway.

"Hey, you two."

"Hi, Barb. Any news?" Josie forced a smile.

"Sorry. No. We've quit the search for the day because it was getting

hard to see in the thick woods. We'll be back at first light tomorrow."
Barb squeezed her shoulder. "We'll find her."

"Thanks, Barb." Josie was grateful to Barb for her help in the search for Nooko, so she focused on gratitude.

"I've ordered a carryout, so I'll talk to you sometime tomorrow. Good night, Kelly."

Barb nodded to Kelly again before she left, and Josie sighed in relief.

"Hey." Kelly placed her hand over hers. "You ready to get out of here?"

Josie didn't speak until she pulled into the parking lot and turned to face Kelly. "Is there something I should know about you and Barb?"

"I meant what I said about loving you, Josie. Barb and I are friends, and I hope that will always be the case, but that's all there is between us." Kelly cradled her face in one hand and kissed her. "Understand?"

Josie took her hand and kissed her palm before placing it over her heart. "Sure. Thanks for clarifying that. Barb and I've been friends for years. I hated feeling resentful toward her. She's a good friend. Let's start a fire in the fireplace and read for a while."

"Sounds perfect, as long as we can snuggle on the couch."

Kelly's request flooded her with memories of her mother reclining on their couch with her head in her father's lap, his feet propped on a footstool, both holding books, and him stroking her hair. A longing she was beginning to believe only Kelly could satisfy surfaced, and she didn't suppress it. Nothing was standing between them but Josie. Maybe it was time to get out of her own way.

Kelly stirred in her sleep and Josie pulled her close. She'd begun to realize how precious she'd become to her. Kelly was with her because she wanted to be. She loved her. She loved Nooko. Would she leave once Nooko was safe? That scared her almost as much as not getting Nooko back. She rolled over and kissed her shoulder.

"I can feel you thinking." Kelly snuggled her butt against Josie's belly. "Are you worried about Ruth?"

"I can't help it. I keep thinking about her alone and scared with that idiot." Josie pulled Kelly tighter against herself.

"We can hope the police find them today, wherever he's hiding."

"Yeah. We can hope. Tomorrow's Wednesday. Brent will be here later to review details. I'm not sure I can just sit here and wait for all of it to go down." Josie cradled Kelly's breast in her hand and idly stroked her nipple with her thumb. "You don't think he'd hurt an old lady, do you?"

"Lover, I can't think of much of anything while you're touching me. Either finish what you've started here, or let's get up and have breakfast."

Josie chuckled and lightly pinched her nipple before rolling away. "I'll make the coffee."

They finished breakfast and sat on the front porch rockers watching the sunlight sparkle on the waves of the bay.

"I should be doing something. I can't sit and wait much longer." Josie leaned forward and gripped her coffee cup. She hated feeling so horrendously helpless.

"I know what you mean, but I don't think there's anything you could do that the police and Barb aren't."

"Yeah, you're right. Barb called while you were in the shower. I guess some of our neighbors found out about her disappearance. They've formed a posse and are combing the island. I'm touched that so many care, but I worry they'll get hurt. Abe didn't hesitate to shoot at Barb, so I doubt he'd care about killing a civilian." Josie stood and clenched her fists. "If he hurts her, I swear…"

Kelly stood and embraced her. "I know. Come on. Let's go do some cleaning."

"What are you talking about?" Josie pulled away scrambling to figure out what Kelly meant.

"I think we need a distraction, so let's get obsessive about washing windows and scrubbing floors. Don't you have lodgers coming next month?"

"No. Not until January, and the cabins are pretty much ready." Josie paused, grateful for Kelly's intention. "But they could always use attention."

Josie led Kelly to the cleaning supply closet and laundry room, stopping once to kiss her soundly. They gathered mops, window cleaner, rags, and dusters and each took one cabin. An hour into their cleaning frenzy, Josie went in search of Kelly. "I'll be right back." Josie stuck her head into the cabin where Kelly was busy mopping the floor. "I'm going to check the answering machine."

As Josie rounded the corner, she heard a clatter coming from the lodge. She ran toward it and stopped when she saw the door to the office wide open. She rushed in and froze, her heart in her throat.

Abe stood with his arm around Nooko's neck and a handgun pointed at her head.

CHAPTER THIRTY-SIX

Y ou're not going to get away with this." Josie watched Nooko closely. She looked scared, but a spark in her eye showed her strength and determination as she held on to his arm restraining her.

"Shut up and give me my box, or she's dead!" Abe glanced around the room. He looked nervous.

"You let my grandmother go. Now." Josie stood still, hoping she looked braver than she felt.

"The box." He pushed the gun into Nooko's temple and glared at her.

Josie wanted nothing more than to stare him down and make him leave without Nooko, but she gave in to sense and turned to open her safe. She pulled out the box, still trying to figure out a way to get rid of Abe without harming Nooko. She wished Barb would fly into the parking lot to save the day. She set the box on the desk just out of Abe's reach. "Let her go, and I'll walk away from this desk. You can have the damn box. Just let her go." Josie took a step back and heard the scrape of the door behind her too late.

Kelly stepped into the room. "Hey, Josie, I wondered where—"

Josie dove in front of her and heard the discharge of the firearm, smelled the acrid odor of the gunpowder, and felt the heat of the bullet as it whizzed past her. She turned to see Kelly crumple to the floor. "No!" She rose and rushed toward Nooko as Abe shoved her, and they both tumbled to the ground. He grabbed the box from the desk and raced out the door.

Nooko lay unmoving on the tile floor. Her eyes fluttered open and closed once, and her chest barely rose and fell as she appeared to struggle to take a breath.

"Nooko. Don't try to talk. Lie still." Josie looked toward Kelly, who opened her eyes, groaned, and held a hand over the blood oozing from her arm. "Kelly. Are you all right?" She didn't want to leave Nooko, but she couldn't reach Kelly. The two people in her life she loved the most lay on the floor injured. Fear strangled her ability to take a breath, and inadequacy churned in her gut.

"I'm okay. I'm okay. How's Ruth?" Kelly crawled toward her with one arm, leaving a trail of blood.

"You're not okay. You're bleeding." She forced herself not to scream, and her voice echoed in her own ears.

"Listen to me." Kelly was breathing hard. "My med kit is in the bedroom. Go grab it and I'll stay with Ruth."

Kelly had managed to slide herself within reach, and Josie looked closely at her injured arm but couldn't see past the blood. She sped to her bedroom, willing her legs to keep moving even though they felt like Jell-O.

Kelly was holding Nooko's wrist, taking her pulse with fingers covered in blood when she returned. Josie opened Kelly's bag and pulled out a roll of gauze and a couple of sterile bandages.

"Give me your arm." The calmness in her voice surprised her. She found a pair of scissors in the kit and cut off the sleeve of her shirt, packed the wound with the bandages, and wrapped it tightly with gauze. Relief settled her roiling stomach as she saw the bleeding stop. Like Barb's wound, it didn't look as bad as it could have been.

"Thanks. I don't like Ruth's breathing or her pulse rate. Call nine-one-one."

Kelly pulled her stethoscope out of her kit and Josie called the paramedics. Her heart beat so loudly in her ears, she had to strain to hear the dispatcher. She finished the call and rushed to where Kelly sat on the floor leaning against the wall and holding Nooko's wrist. She forced back tears. It would do no good to fall apart. Nooko and Kelly needed her, and she'd do whatever it took to help them both.

"I'm riding along." Josie spoke to the young man wrapping a blood pressure cuff on Nooko's left arm.

"I'll take my car and meet you at the hospital," Kelly said.

"I don't think so." Josie turned to the paramedic's partner. "She's been shot. All I did was wrap it with gauze."

"It's stopped bleeding." She held her arm out for inspection. "I'm a nurse, and I feel stable enough to drive. I'm not in shock and I'm fully coherent. I can be treated when we get there. Please, just get Ruth out of here quickly."

"Can we take her to the medical center?" Josie asked.

"Yes. We called ahead and the doctor's waiting for us. We'll transport her to War Memorial Hospital if necessary after he looks at her."

"You stay close and follow the ambulance, Kelly, and we'll meet you there." Nooko could've been a rag doll, lying motionless and hooked to an IV and heart monitor. She lay quietly and her breathing had settled down, but she hadn't reopened her eyes yet. Josie held her hand with no intention of letting go.

She watched out the ambulance back window at Kelly's vehicle. She followed closely but at a safe distance, and Josie realized at that moment she appreciated Kelly's safe driving, but she no longer wanted her at a safe distance in her life. It was time she took a chance and let love bring her closer. She leaned over Nooko and whispered, "You were right. Wake up and let me tell you so." She didn't wipe away the tears that fell. "Please wake up."

Josie stepped out of the ambulance and winced. She hadn't thought of anything except Nooko and Kelly during the ordeal. Dried blood and a tear in the knee of her jeans reminded her she'd hit the floor hard. Twice. She'd have bruises, she supposed, but she strode next to the gurney transporting Nooko into the building with gratitude in her heart.

"I'm right behind you," Kelly said from the end of the sidewalk leading to the medical center. She moved slowly but caught up to them in the lobby and followed them to the examination room.

"I'm sorry. Only family is allowed with the patient." The nurse stood at the entryway like a sentry.

"She's definitely family," Josie said.

Kelly smiled and entered the room. "I think I'll need the doctor to take a look at my arm, but make sure Ruth is taken care of first. Oh, and please make sure he looks at Josie's knee." Kelly winked at her, gave the nurse all the vitals she'd taken at home, and kissed Nooko's forehead.

Josie shook her head. It was evident Kelly was used to being in charge, and the nurse fell into place instantly.

Nooko's eyes fluttered open and she reached for Kelly with a trembling hand as she strained her IV tube. "Thank you, dear."

"You concentrate on staying well. The doctor will be in soon." The doctor stepped into the room and nodded as Kelly was led to another exam room.

Josie watched him assess Nooko as she gave the nurse her medical history and the account of what happened.

"I'd like to take some X-rays, but she'll respond well to the fluids, I think. She's severely dehydrated but seems to be okay otherwise." He checked Nooko's monitors and reviewed the information Josie had given the nurse. "I presume there'll be a police report forthcoming." He looked to Josie expectantly.

"Most definitely."

"Good. I'll need a copy of it for my files." He turned back to Nooko. "It sounds like you've been through quite an experience, young lady." He held her hand as he spoke.

"I suppose I have." Nooko looked at her, unsmiling. "I'll be fine, though, won't I?"

"Yes, Ruth. I think you will, but I want an X-ray, blood work, and I want to keep you here overnight."

"I think it's a good idea, Nooko." Josie rested her hand on her shoulder.

"Is Kelly staying with you?"

"Yes."

"Good. I'll stay here tonight, then." Nooko lay back and closed her eyes.

"Thanks, Doctor. I'm going to check on Kelly and call the police." He nodded and she slipped past him to the nurses' station to find Kelly. "Would you please tell me what room Kelly Newton is in?"

"Are you family?" the nurse asked.

Josie only hesitated a second. "Yes."

The nurse looked at her warily but escorted her to Kelly's room.

"Hey there. How're you feeling?" Kelly's upper left arm was fully bandaged and she wore a sling to keep it immobile. She leaned down to kiss her but pulled back when the doctor entered the room.

"I'm okay. Right, Doc?" Kelly grinned.

"Yes. She was lucky. The bullet went through her arm superficially.

There's not much muscle damage, but take it easy for a few days. It'll be swollen and sore. I've written a prescription for some antibiotics and something for pain. I want to see you back here in a week for a recheck."

"I guess I'll be here for at least another week." Kelly ran her fingers lightly over the top of Josie's hand resting next to her on the exam table.

Josie beamed. "I guess so." She longed to tell her she wanted her to stay much longer than another week. She wanted her to stay for as long as their forevers lasted. But this wasn't the time or place. "I want to find out if Barb or Brent has any information yet and if they need us to hang around for them to come here. I'll be in the lobby trying my cell phone."

"You're welcome to use the clinic's phone," the doctor said on his way out of the room.

Josie made her call, giving Barb all the detail she could, before she returned to check on Nooko. "The state trooper is on his way here, Nooko. You can talk to him tomorrow when you're rested if you want to. Kelly and I will talk to him before we go." Josie watched Nooko's eyelids flutter closed several times as she tried to keep them open. "Am I right, Doc? She needs to rest tonight."

"Yes. I'll let the trooper know she's been sedated and I want to keep an eye on her tonight. He can come by tomorrow morning." The doctor listened to Nooko's heart and nodded to the nurse before leaving the room.

After Brent arrived, he offered to follow them back to Josie's place, where they could talk comfortably. An alert was already out on Abe. Josie followed Kelly to her car and helped her buckle her seat belt before hopping in to drive. "Are you comfortable?"

"I can't say it doesn't hurt, but it'll heal, and I can feel the pain pill they gave me kicking in."

"You close your eyes and try to relax. We'll be home soon. Brent's going to follow us. He has some questions he needs to ask while everything is fresh in our minds."

"What did Barb say about things?" Kelly shifted her position and winced.

"Not much. They've told all the neighbors to go home and lock their doors, and the police set up roadblocks and have officers posted at the ferry terminal and the airport. They're still out looking for him in the woods, too. I sure hope they catch the bastard." Josie gripped the steering wheel until her fingers hurt.

She parked in front of the lodge and helped Kelly into the building. Brent followed them in, holding the door open. "I'm sure glad to see you're safe. I'm here just to get some information. Who's this?"

"This is my friend Kelly Newton. Kelly, meet Trooper Brent from the state police."

Kelly mumbled a greeting with her eyelids fluttering closed.

"She was shot by Abe, and her pain meds are taking effect."

"I'm thinking there's quite a story here." Brent helped settle Kelly on the couch, took a seat at a table, and pulled out his notepad. "Do you feel well enough to answer a few questions?"

"I do, but Kelly's going to lie down and rest." Josie gently stuffed a small throw pillow under Kelly's head and covered her with a light blanket.

"So, there's nothing you can remember about his vehicle?" Brent asked.

Josie had been sitting with him for half an hour reviewing everything that had transpired with Abe. Her knee ached as she shifted her position in the chair. All she wanted to do was join Kelly on the couch. "No. He always showed up on foot, or the first time, on his snowmobile. He might have had one when we saw him at the restaurant, but I never saw him in it."

"Thanks. I'll just take some pictures of the crime scene, and another team might be here tomorrow to collect any missed evidence. Thank you for your time, ma—Josie."

She hadn't even thought to return to her office until Brent mentioned it, but since she couldn't remember locking her safe, she hobbled back to the room and hesitated at the entrance. Blood splatters on the floor where Kelly had fallen, the fear hidden behind Nooko's bravery, and the gun against her temple became vivid images threatening to rob her sanity. She bent over, struggling to catch her breath, and felt strong arms support and lead her to the couch before her knees buckled.

"You sit, ma'am. We'll take care of securing the room." Brent retrieved two bottles of water from the refrigerator, gave one to her, and set one on the table in front of Kelly, who hadn't stirred from the couch. "I'll be back to check on you tomorrow. I believe Officer Donnelly is on her way over, but I'll radio her and tell her to come tomorrow. You two get some rest."

"Thank you, Brent. For everything." Josie rested her head on the back of her chair and turned to look at Kelly. She looked so vulnerable, so lovely, lying on her side. Josie wanted to curl up next to her and feel the heat of her body meld with her own, loving her, grounding her.

She sighed and gently woke Kelly to help her to bed.

CHAPTER THIRTY-SEVEN

Josie woke to the sound of knocking. She checked for Kelly next to her to make sure she was okay. A voice penetrated her senses and pushed aside the rising panic.

"Josie? It's Barb."

Kelly sat up next to her and Josie stroked her cheek.

"It's Barb. You stay. I'll go talk to her." Josie stood and shuffled to the door, feeling battered and exhausted.

"Sorry to wake you, but I have some news I thought you'd want. And I'll admit I wanted to check on you both."

"Come in." Josie stood aside while Barb entered, carrying a plastic bag, and sat in one of the leather chairs. "Do you need to see the office, too?"

"No. The police have that covered. You two look pretty good considering what you went through." She looked to Kelly, who'd quietly entered the room and sat on the couch.

"I've got a few stitches, and I'm sore, but I'll heal," Kelly said. She still looked groggy but less so than earlier.

"It was pretty awful, Barb. I walked in and saw Abe with a gun pointed at Nooko's head." Josie rested her face in her hands, trying to dispel the vision. "It was awful."

"I hope my news helps a little. I found Abe's hideout. I think it's where he held Ruth, too."

"Where?"

"It wasn't anywhere near all those other cabins I told you about. I found what was more like a hunting blind than a cabin. It had a canvas roof and three sides, and this was tacked to one of the support poles." She pulled a flat piece of wood out of her bag and handed it to Josie.

Jack's Place was printed in bold red letters that stood out from the solid black background.

Josie ran her fingers over what was probably her father's creation. "I never knew he called himself Jack. He was never the same after Mom died. Maybe he wanted to escape his grief by pretending to be someone else. Are you sure this was where Abe was?"

"The police are going over it now, but I saw evidence of recent meals and bedding. I also found this." Barb reached back into her bag, retrieved a framed picture, and handed it to her.

Jose studied the photograph for several minutes before, fighting back tears, she handed the snapshot to Kelly. "That's the three of us the day before the accident. Mom had cooked a pot of soup and we ate dinner in front of the fireplace. Dad set the camera on the mantel and used the automatic timer to take this. It was the last day we shared a meal together. He may have run from the bad memories, but not from us. Thank you for bringing this to me, Barb."

"I thought you might like to have it. It would have been lost forever if Abe hadn't known about the blind and used it. It must have been your dad's for years before."

"I'm not saying I'm glad the bastard did what he did, but if the Hand of Fate brought this to me, I'm grateful."

"I'm hungry. Do you two feel up to going to the Teepee? My treat," Barb asked.

"I sure do. How about it, Kelly?"

"Sounds good. I think I slept off most of that pain med. I'll just freshen up a little and be right back." Kelly stood and walked slowly out of the room.

"I'm happy for you, Josie. And for Kelly, too."

"Thanks, Barb. You told me you were smitten once, and I don't want to hurt you."

"Kelly and I are friends. That's all I have time for right now even if I wanted something more with her. You're both fantastic and deserve each other. I like seeing you happy."

"Thank you." Josie swallowed hard. She'd better talk to Kelly before Barb congratulated her on her engagement.

"I'm ready." Kelly took her hand as they walked to Barb's car.

"After we eat, I'd like to visit Nooko."

"Me, too. Barb may want to go, too."

They sat in the car and ate their burgers, avoiding talk of Abe or kidnapping. Josie relaxed for the first time in days. "Shall we take some vanilla ice cream to our patient?" she asked.

"Good idea." Barb picked up the empty bags and made room for the ice cream.

❖

Josie followed Barb and Kelly down the hall. She smirked as the nurse who'd demanded to know who was family earlier nearly saluted Barb when she saw the uniform and pointed the way to Nooko's room.

"Hey, Nooko." Josie adjusted the bed tray and set the ice cream in front of her.

"Oh. Thank you, dears." Nooko eagerly dug into the bowl of ice cream, grinning after swallowing a spoonful.

"You look like you're feeling better," Kelly said as she scanned the monitors in the room.

"I am. The doctor wants me here overnight again, though. Did you find Abe?" Nooko looked at Barb.

"Not yet, but we found the blind where we believe he kept you hidden. Do you feel up to answering some questions?"

"Of course. I want you to catch him. That nice young trooper was here earlier. I told him all I could remember." She turned to Kelly, looking alarmed. "Are you all right?"

"I'm fine, Ruth." She patted her hand and lifted her slinged arm slightly. "See? My arm's already healing. You relax. You've been through an ordeal no one should have to go through."

Barb had her notebook out, and she perched on the end of Ruth's bed. "Was the place he had you a hunting blind in the woods?" Barb asked.

"Yes, and it was cold at night because there were only three sides and no heat. He watched when I had to go to the bathroom and we ate awful venison jerky and canned peas." She scrunched her face. "He kept babbling about his strongbox and constantly studied and fiddled with a map. Then he'd pace back and forth mumbling about his uncle Abe and how he left it for him, and he'd get what was his." Nooko paused. "Could I have some water, please?"

Josie handed her the cup of ice water. "You're doing great. You don't have to continue today. You should get some rest."

Nooko waved her off and continued. "I remember there was a sign on the blind. I noticed it when we first got there, before he sat me in a chair, tied my hands, and blindfolded me. The sign said Jack's Place."

"We found it," Barb said. "It sounds like we got the right place. The police are checking for DNA evidence, but I doubt they'll need it for a case."

"Oh. And he shot something. Or someone." She looked scared. "That was before he moved me to that blind."

"That was me, Ruth." Barb took her hand and smiled softly. "I saw him in the woods by some cabins, and he caught me trying to sneak up on him."

"Oh, dear. Are you okay?" Nooko tried to sit up and Barb gently held her down.

"I'm fine. It wasn't serious."

Nooko relaxed back on her pillow. "Thank you for visiting me." Nooko reached to her and tears rolled down her cheeks. "I'm sorry, honey." She sniffled and reached for a tissue.

"Nooko, it's over. And you certainly have nothing to apologize for. Abe is an evil man."

"Oh, Joslyn. I thought it was you. I thought you'd returned, so I went to the office to see you." Nooko's voice shook and her lip trembled as more tears fell. "He was pounding on the safe and swearing. He lifted the hammer and threatened to bash my head in when he turned and saw me. Then he grabbed me. My cane fell to the floor and he wouldn't let me have it. Then he yanked off my emergency button and stomped on it. He told me he'd kill me if I made any noise." She squeezed her eyes shut. "He dragged me out the door. I tried to fight him, but he was too strong." She sniffled and her eyes fluttered open.

Kelly grabbed her wrist to check her pulse. "You rest, Ruth. You're safe now. It's over." She moved away when the doctor stepped to the bed.

He watched the monitors and listened to her heart with his stethoscope. "You settle down, Ruth. Kelly's right. You're safe now, your family's here, and no one can hurt you. I'd like you to rest now. There's time for more questions tomorrow."

Josie stood at the foot of her bed holding her feet. "He can't hurt you here."

"And we're going to catch him soon, Ruth." Barb stood at the head of the bed, resting her hand on her shoulder.

"I'm going to give her something to help her sleep again. You all can head home. We'll take good care of her tonight." The doctor consulted with the nurse and left the room.

"Good-bye, Nooko. We'll be back in the morning." Josie kissed her cheek and stood back while Kelly and Barb followed her lead. Nooko lifted her hand in a feeble wave and dropped it back to the bed.

The ride back was quiet, with Kelly dozing with her head on her shoulder. "Thanks for driving, Barb."

"No problem. You two get some rest. I'll call you tomorrow with an update."

She and Kelly crawled out of the back seat and hugged Barb. Josie stood by the car, sudden fear gripping her heart. "Do you think he'll be back, Barb? Do you think he'll try to hurt us again?"

"I doubt it, but you could go stay at the hotel in town if you're worried. He got what he was after. The strongbox was probably the only reason he wanted your land, and what was in it is probably worth a hell of a lot more than the thirty grand he offered you. I don't think he ever really wanted your land. He probably thought he could get it cheap and scare you into selling so he could dig for the box. Of course, we can't know what's going on in his mind, but my guess is that he's hiding out, looking for a way off the island. We will catch him. I'll make sure the police stake out your place. I'll radio them right away, so someone will be here all night. Does that help?"

Barb's intensity calmed her fears. "That'd be great. Thanks, Barb, and I'll keep Dad's twelve-gauge handy, too."

"Everything looks quiet around here," Josie said as she entered the bedroom after making her nightly rounds to find Kelly lying half undressed on the bed. "You asleep?"

"No. I'm going to need a little help getting these clothes off." She spoke with her eyes closed. Her eyebrows pinched together, showing the amount of pain she was in.

Josie's heart ached as she watched Kelly protect her injured arm. Her feet were bare and her jeans were unbuttoned and pulled down to her thigh on the right side. "Did you take your pain pill?"

"I hate the way they make me feel."

"Do I need to tell you it'll help you sleep so you can heal faster, Nurse Kelly?"

Kelly opened one eye and smirked.

Josie went to the kitchen and brought two bottles of water back to the bedroom. "Here." She opened one and handed it and a tablet to Kelly. "Let's get you undressed."

"Even though my arm hurts like crazy, I love hearing those words from you."

Josie paused and their gazes locked. "I love saying them to you. Only you."

"Only me sounds pretty good, too." Kelly brushed her lips over hers.

"I can't believe how close I came to losing you, and it jogged something in me. All my fear of loving you because you might somehow be taken from me now pales in the fear of missing out on us being together for as long as we have. I mean, there's no guarantee of tomorrow, but we all hope for one. I had a friend in school who used to quote her preacher. 'Plan for the future, but live as if it's your last day.' It always reminded me of my mom dying, but now I feel differently. I want to plan for however long our forever will be with you." She held Kelly's uninjured hand to her heart. "I love you, Kelly."

"I love you, too. For our forever." Kelly kissed her and leaned her forehead against Josie's.

Josie thought back to her conversations with Nooko and her own ruminations about Kelly. Her fears and doubts were what brought her to her ability to accept the love Kelly offered and to return the feelings. A few weeks ago she couldn't have imagined falling in love. Today she couldn't imagine living without it. She wrapped her arms around Kelly and kissed her tenderly. "Let's get some sleep. I'm exhausted."

"Yeah. Me, too, but I'm happier than I've ever been in my life."

Josie gently removed Kelly's shirt and undressed before sliding into bed and covering them both. She scooched closer to Kelly and turned to kiss her. "Good night, love," she murmured softly.

Kelly snuggled close and sighed into her shoulder.

CHAPTER THIRTY-EIGHT

"Breakfast is ready." Josie carried plates to the table where Nooko's place setting sat waiting.

"I could use a hand with this, please," Kelly shouted from the bedroom, sounding frazzled.

Josie laughed when she saw Kelly with her good arm straight up in the air and her T-shirt dangling halfway over her head. She helped her finish dressing and pulled her against herself to nuzzle her neck. "Mm. I like assisting you getting dressed almost as much as disrobing you."

"I'd agree if I weren't so incapacitated."

"How's it feeling this morning?" Josie examined her arm.

"It feels better, actually. I think the pain medication and rest helped a lot."

"Good. Let's have breakfast and you can take another pill before we go spring Nooko."

Josie picked at her food, trying to chase away the vision of Nooko with a gun pressed to her head. As good as it felt having Kelly there with her, she couldn't get over the traumatic events.

"Hey. You okay?" Kelly rested her hand on her wrist.

"I will be when Nooko gets home. I can't believe she felt the need to apologize for being in the wrong place at the wrong time. I really believe Abe would've found another way to grab her if he hadn't that day. I'll put together a bag of clothes for her, and we can go." Josie carried the breakfast dishes to the kitchen as she spoke. "You know, I think he probably didn't even have a plan, other than to try to break into the safe. When Nooko walked in on him, he decided it would be easier to take her hostage, so he nabbed her." She turned to Kelly, who'd followed her to the kitchen and sat at the kitchen table. "Her increased mobility put her directly in his path."

Kelly rose to wrap her arms around Josie. "And…her new strength and flexibility has helped her make it through this. She'll heal faster and be home sooner. Let's go make that happen."

Josie drove slowly on the way to the medical center, mindful of Kelly wincing at every bump in the road. She parked in the handicapped spot of the building, shut off the engine, and sat quietly.

"You ready?" Kelly asked.

"Yeah. I can't believe we're here and Nooko's inside attached to tubes and monitors." She turned to Kelly and tipped her head. "It doesn't feel real, does it?"

"Nope. It'll take a while to get over this. Let's go see how Ruth's doing and hope she's well enough to come home."

They stopped at the door to her room. Nooko was sitting up in bed laughing and engaged in conversation with an elderly woman seated in the room's visitor chair.

The visitor smiled and greeted them when they entered. "Kelly?"

"Mrs. Robins. It's good to see you. Do you two know each other?" Kelly asked.

"Loretta and I went to grade school together." Nooko grinned and reached for Loretta's hand. "I can't believe she's here. We haven't seen each other in years."

"It's good to meet you, Mrs. Robins. How did you know my grandmother was here?" Josie looked back and forth between them. She and Nooko were chatting as though they were out for coffee instead of sitting in a room filled with IV bags and monitors.

"Oh, everyone at the home knows, dear. It's a small island with a long memory, you know. When I found out, I had to come see her. The nice man who drives the senior bus brought me."

Kelly checked the monitor and lifted Nooko's hand to check her IV. "Have you seen the doctor this morning?"

"Oh yes. He's been in twice to check on me and Loretta. I'll be able to go home this morning."

"The doctor knows Mrs. Robins is here?"

Loretta pulled her walker to her and stood. "Oh, yes. I talked to him before I came over. He's a nice man. He lets a few of us leave for the day if we're able, but I'm only supposed to stay an hour, so I'm going home."

Nooko and Loretta hugged and kissed good-bye, just as the doctor entered the room.

"I trust you two had a nice visit." He turned to Kelly, who was still watching Nooko's monitors. "You look as if you know what you're doing."

"I'm a nurse, so I've seen this before." Kelly smiled.

Josie stood at the foot of Nooko's bed, unsure if she should interrupt. Her worry over Nooko being alone was for nothing. She loved the thought of the other elders on the island remembering her grandmother. "I brought you a change of clothes."

"Thank you, honey. Can I go home now?" She directed her question to the doctor.

"Yes. I'll have my nurse go over your instructions. You take it easy for a while, and I'm going to come over to check on you in a week." He left the room and the nurse entered.

While she was talking to Nooko and removing the IVs, Josie turned to Kelly. "Why do you know who Loretta Robins is?"

"She lives at the new nursing home on the island where I worked this summer. It didn't even occur to me she might know Ruth, but I suppose it makes sense."

The conversation halted as they got Nooko into a wheelchair, which she protested until she was told it was hospital protocol, and into the car.

Once they were on the road, Josie glanced at Nooko in the back seat through the rearview mirror. She looked so peaceful as she dozed. "I can't believe they found each other after so many years. When Nooko and my grandfather left the island, she kept in touch with a few friends but lost contact with most of them. It's special they found each other."

"Connections are amazing. Ruth is special, too. It's not surprising people still remember her."

The rest of the ride was quiet, and Josie looked carefully at the lodge as she headed up the drive. She didn't see anyone or anything out of place and was reassured by the police cruiser parked next to the building. She waved at the driver as she turned off the car. She couldn't wait for this feeling of dread to go away. They helped Nooko out of the back seat and led her to the couch in the lodge. "Can I get you anything?" Kelly asked.

"No. I'm just glad to be home." She leaned her head back on the couch. "That was awful what we went through, wasn't it?"

"It sure was." Kelly settled next to her.

Josie sat in one of the chairs, listening to Nooko and Kelly talk. "Abe's gone. The police will find him and lock him away forever." She realized she was speaking to herself when she saw Nooko and Kelly sound asleep. She went to her office and called Barb.

"Hey, Josie. Everything okay?"

"Yes. We brought Nooko home from the clinic today. The doc says to keep an eye on her, but she doesn't have any broken bones or substantial injuries. Mostly bruises and dehydration. She and Kelly are resting now. Any luck finding Abe? Brent said someone might have seen him?"

"Sorry, nothing new yet. But we're not giving up. I believe the police will want to talk to Ruth. I expect they'll be calling you soon. If she's not up to it, don't worry. We can talk when she is."

"Thanks, Barb. I'll let Nooko know." Josie hung up the phone and checked on Nooko and Kelly before going to her studio. She filled her sketch pad with a rendering of a dream catcher design demanding her attention. She cleared off her large worktable and laid out the last three of her mother's eagle feathers. She searched her drawers for two equally sized small willow hoops, set them side by side above the feathers, and reverently pulled out the last of her mother's large hoops. She placed it above the two smaller rings, picturing the final creation in her mind. She checked her supply of beads and small feathers before slowly sliding the drawer closed. This would be her special gift to Kelly and herself. A symbol of their shared dreams and life together. She hoped Kelly wanted that as much as she did.

She locked her studio door and joined Kelly and Nooko in the lodge. It would be a while before she could feel easy leaving them for any length of time.

"I missed you." Kelly's eyelids fluttered open when Josie caressed her cheek. Nooko slept soundly nestled next to her.

Josie smiled back, thinking how much she wanted to be in Nooko's place. "Have any preferences for lunch?"

"You?"

"Hmm. How's the arm feel?"

"I'd love a repeat of the hot tub except I'm afraid I'd drown myself trying to keep it dry."

"Maybe we better wait until it isn't so dangerous."

Kelly's beautiful blue eyes darkened like storm clouds moving across the sky, and she longed to be drenched in their wake.

She shifted in her seat as desire flooded her senses. "I talked to Barb this morning. They haven't found Abe yet, and I expect Brent to be here any time to get more information. I won't wake Nooko until he gets here, and if she's not feeling well, we'll make him wait until she is."

Kelly redistributed her weight to rest Nooko's head gently on a pillow and lift her feet to the couch. She stood and stretched her back. "I need to move. You want to go sit on the porch with me?"

"Sounds good." Josie put her cell phone in her pocket.

Kelly took her hand, and the feeling of rightness settled her. The thought of having Kelly to share the challenges and joys of life with her soothed her unrest and replaced fear with peace.

A niggling thought crept into her serenity. Kelly had a house, a horse, a job, and a life hundreds of miles away. She lived in a place Josie had never even been to. How were they going to work this out? She couldn't ask Kelly to give up her life to move to an island that got four feet of snow in the winter. Maybe she'd go for a long-distance relationship. But she knew it wasn't what either one of them wanted. Her stomach roiled with apprehension.

"I feel you thinking." Kelly shifted to face her. "What is it?"

"I'm scared." Josie blurted the words, surprising herself.

"Of what, lover?"

"I love you, and I want us to be together, but I can't ask you to give up your house and your life." Josie grabbed Kelly's free hand.

"I want the same thing." Kelly pulled their joined hands to her chest. "I'll need to go back and make some arrangements, but we'll work things out. I've grown fond of Drummond Island, and it's where you are, so it's where I want to be." Kelly kissed her hard.

Josie returned the kiss with all the passion and tenderness in her heart. She didn't know how they'd work it out, but for now, it was enough to know it was what Kelly wanted.

❖

"I'm glad that's over." Kelly plopped onto the couch after dinner. "Trooper Brent had a lot of questions."

"Yeah. Nooko's sound asleep again. Poor thing had to relive the whole ordeal, but she's tough. She wants Abe caught even more than we do."

Kelly chuckled. "That's hard to imagine, but I suppose we'll never know what it was like to be restrained and held against your will in a flimsy lean-to in the woods." She thought about all the elderly patients she'd known through the years, and few at eighty-six compared to Ruth in strength. This would take a lot out of her, and she hoped it didn't break her spirit. She vowed to do all she could to help her stay mobile and healthy.

"She comes from a long line of strong women. My mother was a tough lady, too."

Kelly smiled at Josie's expression of pride instead of sadness when she spoke of her mother. "I'd say her daughter is pretty tough, too." She kissed her and took her hand. She loved Josie, she was sure of that, and she wanted to make a life with her. For the first time, she let herself imagine what that would be like. She'd come to Drummond Island for a getaway from work, but she had a life besides work. Questions popped into her head like popcorn. Where would she work? How often could she get south to ride Pogo and see her friends and her sister? Would Josie tire of her? The last question took her by surprise. Josie had professed her love and she believed her, but Josie's fear of commitment lingered in the back of her mind.

Josie kissed her lightly drawing her from her thoughts. "You okay?"

"It was hard reexperiencing it all. I didn't realize how traumatizing it was." Kelly trembled. "I think I'm going to have a bit of PTSD." She shook her head to dislodge the insecurities.

"You're entitled, love. It's a big deal, what we went through. Don't try to minimize the effect on you because you're a nurse. I know you've probably seen awful things, but this happened to you. And to someone you care about." Josie stood and pulled her into her arms.

Kelly leaned on her, absorbing her strength and calming her doubts. "You ready for bed? My arm aches."

"It looks pretty swollen. You go ahead. I'll bring us some water, and you take a pain pill tonight." Josie kissed her and left for the kitchen.

Kelly lay on the bed on her back cradling her sore arm until Josie returned with water and her pill and snuggled next to her.

"You feel good," Kelly mumbled against her neck before sleep overtook her.

CHAPTER THIRTY-NINE

W e got him!" Barb nearly knocked Josie over when she grabbed her and spun her around.

"Fantastic. Come in and tell us about it." Josie led the way into the lodge.

"Hi, Barb," Kelly said from one of the tables where she was sitting with Nooko. "Can I get you a cup of coffee or something?"

"I'm good. Thanks. I've got to get back to the police post and fill out paperwork soon. Brent will be in touch with you, but we caught the idiot trying to sneak onto the ferry with a fake ID. The police received numerous calls from people on the ferry who recognized him from the picture we posted everywhere. Even if they hadn't gotten there to arrest him, the folks would've never let him off the boat."

Josie sat at the table with Nooko and Kelly, happy to see Barb settle down in a chair looking completely relaxed. "Great news. I hope he goes away for life!"

"I don't know what the sentence will be, but Abe's behind bars."

"Thanks again for your help, Barb. Do you know if Abe said anything about why he did what he did?" Josie asked.

"The police are interrogating him now, but remember I told you I found an Abe Bernstein who was a member of the Purple Gang, out of Detroit? I suspect our Abe is his namesake. The gang was notorious for burying the spoils of their illegal activities all over the state, and Abe had a map leading to an area on your property. I'd guess it was his relative's, showing where the strongbox was buried. When you refused to sell to him, he probably became desperate. Turns out, he didn't know your father at all. He found his hunting blind in the woods and used it, but he never even met him. I'm not sure why your dad started calling himself Jack, but that sign he carved must have made Abe think that was his name. Yeah. That Abe is a master manipulator but a real idiot. I'm glad we caught him."

Josie glanced at Nooko and sprung from her seat when she saw tears flowing down her face, and Kelly held her hand, looking concerned.

"I'm so thankful you caught him." She spoke through sniffles. "I can sleep right again, knowing he's not still blundering about in the woods."

Josie relaxed and laughed. "So those are tears of joy." Nooko hadn't said anything about being worried, but she'd guessed by the dark circles under her eyes that not everything was okay. At least she could put that worry to bed now.

"Tears of joy are a welcome sight. I'll leave you guys alone to enjoy the good news." Barb stood and hugged each of them before leaving.

"I figured they'd catch him. He wasn't exactly a genius, and all he could focus on was finding what he considered buried treasure. Greed can cause people to do bad things." Kelly stood. "Can I get you two a cup of tea?"

"Yes, please, dear." Nooko dabbed her eyes with tissue.

"Sounds good. We'll toast to Abe's capture."

"What do you think will happen to the box?" Nooko asked. "I'd love to know the history of some of the things in it."

"Don't know. I don't care if I ever see the thing again." Josie considered it would be a nice boost to her bank account but had already decided to donate it if it happened to come back to her.

"Anyone up for ice cream?" Kelly asked after they'd finished their tea.

"Could we pick up my friend Loretta?" Nooko asked quietly, looking like a child asking for a favor.

Josie looked at Kelly, who shrugged. "Sure. We'll have to clear it with the doctor first, but let's go."

Loretta sat on the bench at the entrance of the facility when they arrived. "Thank you for calling ahead, Kelly." Nooko squirmed in her seat, obviously excited to see her friend.

"No problem, Ruth."

Josie stopped in front of the bench and watched Kelly help Loretta into the Jeep. Would there come a time when Nooko would need more help? It comforted her to know the facility was close, as long as it was affordable. She pushed aside her concerns to concentrate on Nooko and her friend.

She stole a glance at Kelly and winked as they heard Nooko and Loretta speaking nonstop as they rode to the restaurant. When they arrived and parked, Josie moved one of the picnic tables at the Teepee into the shade and helped Kelly carry the ice cream. "Two chocolates and two vanillas."

"Thank you," Loretta said. She grinned and held Nooko's hand. "This was such a wonderful surprise."

Josie listened to Nooko and Loretta chat about old times and Loretta's living conditions. She loved living at the home and went on and on about the great care.

"I'm glad Loretta's doing so well," Kelly said to Josie as she ate her ice cream with a seductive look in her eyes.

"Me, too. That nursing home sounds pretty nice." Josie focused on her ice cream, fully aware it would be inappropriate to take Kelly back to the Jeep and ravish her right there in the parking lot.

"It is. It's state of the art, with the latest technology and a great staff." Kelly grinned. "I know because I trained most of them."

"Loretta must have some major health issue, though, for her to be there, right?"

"She does. That's about all I can tell you." Kelly looked sad as she gazed at Loretta and Nooko. "But she's here now with her friend, enjoying a beautiful late summer day."

"Yes, and so are we." Josie knew their time together was ending soon. She reminded herself it was only temporary, and she pushed aside the fear it might become permanent once Kelly got home and realized what she was leaving behind.

"Can we take the long way back to Loretta's?" Nooko asked.

"Of course." Josie turned to take a route along the water.

"This is beautiful," Loretta said. "I haven't seen the bay in two years."

"Where were you living before you moved to the nursing home?" Josie smiled at the joy on Loretta's face reflected in the rearview mirror.

"I lived with my daughter south of Traverse City. We never made it back to the island. In fact, we rarely left the house. She's on her second round of chemo treatments, and her husband's a disabled war veteran." Her joy faded as she spoke.

"Then I'm doubly glad you were able to join us today." Josie drove as slowly as she could, hoping to bring a smile back to Loretta. They dropped her off, and she and Nooko hugged for a long moment, with a renewed promise to keep in touch.

Josie pulled into the lodge parking lot and turned to Nooko. "We can visit Loretta whenever you want to. Maybe she'd come over for lunch once in a while." She held her breath, waiting to see if Nooko said anything about how difficult that would be once she moved back to her home, but she simply nodded and smiled, looking lost in thought.

"I'd like that, dear."

Kelly helped Nooko out of the car and Josie followed them inside. She watched Kelly with Nooko, love tightening her throat. She blew out a breath and crossed her fingers Kelly would come back to her.

❖

"I'm ready. Thanks for taking me." Kelly stepped into the Jeep easily before Josie had a chance to help her.

"Of course I'd take you. Having stitches removed is a big deal." Josie chuckled. "I'm glad it's healed as well as it has. I think the doc will be pleased."

Kelly grabbed her hand as she drove. "I'd like to talk after I'm done."

Josie's stomach clenched. *We need to talk. Just the phrase every woman wants to hear.* "Of course. We can stop at the beach. There's a shaded bench by the water. We can talk there."

The nurse didn't bother to ask about family this trip, but Josie waited outside the exam room anyway, wanting to give Kelly some privacy. She'd barely gotten through the first five pages of a magazine when Kelly came out without her sling. "That didn't take long."

"She's healing nicely." The doctor had followed Kelly out. "Make sure she doesn't do any heavy lifting, and I suggest she keep the sling on." He looked at Kelly and shook his head. "Keep that sling on for another week." He was still shaking his head as he walked toward another exam room.

"Not following doctor's orders?" Josie took the sling from Kelly and held it until she relented and put it back on. "You sure can be a difficult patient, Nurse Kelly." Josie smiled and shook her head.

"Yeah, yeah." Kelly grinned and kissed her. "Thanks for caring."

"Wait by the front door. I'll bring the car around and pick you up."

Josie parked in the sand-covered lot and took Kelly's hand when she climbed out. The beach was empty, which didn't surprise her. The summer crowds had thinned as the days shortened and the nights grew colder. A cool breeze wafted off the water, bringing the scent of fish and end-of-summer decayed vegetation. They walked to the bench and Josie kissed Kelly's hand before releasing it. "What do you want to talk about?"

"Us."

Josie clenched her fists, fear racing through her veins.

"It's a good thing, lover. Don't look so scared." Kelly smiled and kissed her lightly.

Relief almost made her dizzy. "Sorry. Go ahead."

"I wanted to talk about my horse, Pogo. I can't leave him behind. Can we build a little paddock and small barn somewhere not too far from the lodge?"

Josie blinked, trying not to laugh. "Your horse? You wanted to talk about your horse."

Kelly looked puzzled at Josie's reaction. "Yes. I've had him since he was a foal, and I'm not moving without him."

"I'll start working on the paddock next week. You're willing to move. I like the sound of that."

"I think I was clear when I told you I want someone to share my life. I love you, and I want it to be you. Like I said, you're here, and I want to be where you are. The doctor offered me a job today. It was an unexpected surprise. He's been shorthanded for a while, and all the nurses coming to the island want to go work at the new facility. I kind of enjoy the idea of working nine-to-five and no weekends."

Josie sat back on the bench, absorbing what Kelly was saying. "You'd said you were looking for a change. This sounds as if it's an opportunity for something different. We have Pogo and your job taken care of. I want you in my life. I want to be in yours. I love you, and I want us to make a life together. I hope you'll be happy living here with me at the resort, on Drummond Island. That's what I want. What's next?"

"I think that's it, lover. I'll give my boss, Janis, notice and go home to pack." Kelly leaned against her as she spoke. "I'm not sure how long it'll take to get things settled with my house."

"When do you think you'll leave?"

"In a few days. I want this arm to heal before I start packing."

"I don't want to spend a day without you in my life, but I'm willing to try to be patient to begin our forever. It's getting chilly out here. Let's go home and tell Nooko our plans." She kissed Kelly and they walked hand in hand back to the car.

❖

They went straight into Josie's room via the back door to her bedroom, instead of going in through the main lodge the way they usually did.

"Oh, I like this entryway. It's close to the bed." Kelly pulled her toward the bed as she spoke.

"Kelly." Josie sat on the edge of her bed holding Kelly at arm's length. "If we get on this bed now, we'll miss dinner and probably breakfast, and Nooko will be standing in the doorway tapping her foot."

Kelly kissed her and groaned. "Okay." Kelly stepped back but held on to her hands.

"I'll miss you." Josie kissed her hard, wanting to memorize the feel of her lips for the time they'd be apart.

"I'll miss you, too. Maybe you can work on Pogo's fence while I'm gone."

"He's first on my list." Josie chuckled. "You come back safe to me, love."

"Plan on it." Kelly turned and pushed her back against the wall with her good arm and kissed her again.

Josie grabbed her ass and pulled her tight against her, needing to feel their combined heartbeats. She slid her hands under Kelly's T-shirt to feel her warmth and the softness of her skin. She opened her eyes, took a breath, and absorbed her sight and scent. She memorized her soft murmurs and her taste as she gently nibbled her lower lip. She reluctantly moved away when she heard Nooko's voice calling from the living room. "I guess we better get out there before she comes looking and finds us naked." Josie released Kelly and went to find Nooko.

"Did Kelly get her stitches out?" Nooko stood in the middle of the room, leaning on her cane and looking puzzled.

"She did."

"I wondered where you two went. Come sit. I want to talk. Where's Kelly?"

"Right here." Kelly came out of the bedroom and snaked her good arm around Josie's waist to pull her close.

Nooko looked at them with narrowed eyes, then with a huge

knowing grin. "It's about time. I planned to sit you two down and talk some sense into you both." She looked at Kelly, then turned to Josie. "The way I see it, you've been given a second chance from the Creator, and I'm glad you've decided to take advantage of it."

"I think you're right, Ruth. We're going to take advantage of every day we're given." Kelly looked at Josie as she spoke.

"Kelly's going to move in with me, Nooko. As soon as she takes care of things at her house."

"When are you leaving?"

"In a couple of days. I have a job lined up, and Josie's making room for my horse, so I don't expect to be gone long."

Nooko's tears began as she and Kelly stepped close to give her a hug. "Today must be the day for tears of joy." Nooko sniffled and returned the embrace.

CHAPTER FORTY

Josie stepped back and reviewed the small barn and fenced area that would be Pogo's new home. She'd researched the project extensively before tackling it, and it'd turned out better than she'd expected. She hoped Kelly would like it. Thoughts of Kelly never left her the closer it came to the day of her arrival. She'd be home in two days, and Josie wanted everything to be perfect. She put away all her tools and went to find Nooko.

"I'm in here rearranging, honey."

Jose stood in her doorway to watch Nooko unpack a suitcase and hang clothes in the closet. "I'm glad you decided to stay the winter and you're settling in. Like I told you, if you forgot anything, we can pop back to your house and get it."

"Thank you, dear. I think I'll be fine. Thank you again for taking me back to check on my house. I feel settled knowing everything is okay there." She sat on the edge of her bed. "Kelly's coming home soon, isn't she?"

"Yes. She'll be here the day after tomorrow, and she's having her horse trailered right behind her."

"I can't wait to see her. She's only been gone a few weeks, but it seems like forever."

Josie understood what Nooko meant. She'd taken her back to her house to pick up clothes and personal items, and she'd closed everything up for the winter. Then she'd finished Pogo's new lodging. Now, as she paced the lodge and longed for Kelly's touch and her kisses, the time seemed to drag. She built a fire, settled on the couch, and called Barb.

"Hi, stranger. How's everything going?"

"Good, Barb. Nooko's unpacking and settling in, and I just finished Kelly's horse's area. Any word on that strongbox?"

"I don't think there's any way you'll get to keep the gold coins, but maybe some of the rest of the stuff. The police sent it to the FBI and they'll decide what will happen to it. Anyway, they'll let you know."

"Thanks. Do we know when Abe goes to trial yet?" Josie squelched the bubbling anger that hadn't stopped simmering.

"Not yet. I'm sure he'll go away for at least twenty years. I'm hoping he gets a life sentence. When's Kelly arriving?"

"Day after tomorrow." Josie shifted the phone to her other ear and stretched her legs out on the couch and tried to relax. "I can't wait."

"I'm really happy for you, Josie. Give Kelly a hug for me when she gets there."

"Thanks, Barb. I will. Maybe next week we can get together. We'll let Kelly get settled in a little first."

"Sounds good. Take care."

Josie disconnected the call and stoked the fire before heading to her studio.

She attached the final row of beads on their dream catcher. She held it to the light and watched the beads sparkle tiny reflections lighting the way for good dreams. She swung it gently, happy with the slight sway of the smaller hoops and the fluttering of the willowy feathers suspended from them. One for her and one for Kelly. *Two together forever.* Like their love. She carefully carried it out of her studio to their bedroom and hung it on the wall at the head of their bed. *Soon, love. We'll be together soon.*

"She's here." Nooko beamed as she rose from her seat by the lodge window.

"I see her. I'll go help her unload." Josie rushed out the door.

"Hi, lover. I've missed you." Kelly stepped out of her car with her arms open wide.

"Me, too. Phone calls just didn't cut it." Josie pulled her into her arms and kissed her.

Her passion flared as their kiss deepened. She wanted to feel Kelly everywhere. She'd already claimed her heart, and now she craved to claim her body and soul. Realizing they were standing in the middle of the parking lot, she slowly moved away.

"Let's get Pogo unloaded. The rest can wait for the moving van to arrive."

Josie led Kelly to the new barn and helped her get Pogo settled, amazed at how well trained he was. "He's a good boy, isn't he?"

"Oh, yes. He's my baby. Thanks for making him such a comfortable home." Kelly kissed her and pushed her against the wall of his stall.

Josie was certain they'd have made love right there in the cold barn if they hadn't both been wearing coats. "Let's take this in where it's warm." She nuzzled Kelly's neck as she spoke and took her hand to lead her inside.

"I thought you two got lost," Nooko teased them.

"I've missed you, Ruth." Kelly released her grip on Josie's hand to hug Nooko.

Josie poked the fire to distract her from her need to immediately drag Kelly to bed. "I picked up a few pasties in honor of your homecoming. We can eat before the movers get here if you'd like. Then I have something I want to show you."

"Ah. No. May I see it now?" Kelly stood with her hands on her hips.

Josie laughed. "Come on." She reached out her hand.

Kelly grasped her hand and allowed herself to be led to the bedroom. She gently touched the new dream catcher over the bed. "Beautiful."

"One hoop for you and one for me, and a big one for us together, for our shared dreams. You like it?"

"I love it. And I love you. Thank you for making it. We are going to have wonderful dreams."

"Yep. Dreams of our forever." She wrapped Kelly in her arms and kissed her.

About the Author

C. A. Popovich (capopovichfiction.weebly.com) is a hopeless romantic. She writes sweet, sensual romances that usually include horses, dogs, and cats. Her main characters—and their loving pets—don't get killed and always end up with happily-ever-after love. She is a Michigan native, writes full-time, and tries to get to as many Bold Strokes Books events as she can. She loves feedback from readers.

Books Available From Bold Strokes Books

Breakthrough by Kris Bryant. Falling for a sexy ranger is one thing, but is the possibility of love worth giving up the career Kennedy Wells has always dreamed of? (978-1-63555-179-2)

Certain Requirements by Elinor Zimmerman. Phoenix has always kept her love of kinky submission strictly behind the bedroom door and inside the bounds of romantic relationships, until she meets Kris Andersen. (978-1-63555-195-2)

Dark Euphoria by Ronica Black. When a high-profile case drops in Detective Maria Diaz's lap, she forges ahead only to discover this case, and her main suspect, aren't like any other. (978-1-63555-141-9)

Fore Play by Julie Cannon. Executive Leigh Marshall falls hard for Peyton Broader, her golf pro…and an ex-con. Will she risk sabotaging her career for love? (978-1-63555-102-0)

Love Came Calling by C. A. Popovich. Can a romantic looking for a long-term, committed relationship and a jaded cynic too busy for love conquer life's struggles and find their way to what matters most? (978-1-63555-205-8)

Outside the Law by Carsen Taite. Former sweethearts Tanner Cohen and Sydney Braswell must work together on a federal task force to see justice served, but will they choose to embrace their second chance at love? (978-1-63555-039-9)

The Princess Deception by Nell Stark. When journalist Missy Duke realizes Prince Sebastian is really his twin sister Viola in disguise, she plays along, but when sparks flare between them, will the double deception doom their fairy-tale romance? (978-1-62639-979-2)

The Smell of Rain by Cameron MacElvee. Reyha Arslan, a wise and elegant woman with a tragic past, shows Chrys that there's still beauty to embrace and reason to hope despite the world's cruelty. (978-1-63555-166-2)

The Talebearer by Sheri Lewis Wohl. Liz's visions show her the faces of the lost and the killers who took their lives. As one by one, the murdered are found, a stranger works to stop Liz before the serial killer is brought to justice. (978-1-635550-126-6)

White Wings Weeping by Lesley Davis. The world is full of discord and hatred, but how much of it is just human nature when an evil with sinister intent is invading people's hearts? (978-1-63555-191-4)

A Call Away by KC Richardson. Can a businesswoman from a big city find the answers she's looking for, and possibly love, on a small-town farm? (978-1-63555-025-2)

Berlin Hungers by Justine Saracen. Can the love between an RAF woman and the wife of a Luftwaffe pilot, former enemies, survive in besieged Berlin during the aftermath of World War II? (978-1-63555-116-7)

Blend by Georgia Beers. Lindsay and Piper are like night and day. Working together won't be easy, but not falling in love might prove the hardest job of all. (978-1-63555-189-1)

Hunger for You by Jenny Frame. Principe of an ancient vampire clan Byron Debrek must save her one true love from falling into the hands of her enemies and into the middle of a vampire war. (978-1-63555-168-6)

Mercy by Michelle Larkin. FBI Special Agent Mercy Parker and psychic ex-profiler Piper Vasey learn to love again as they race to stop a man with supernatural gifts who's bent on annihilating humankind. (978-1-63555-202-7)

Pride and Porters by Charlotte Greene. Will pride and prejudice prevent these modern-day lovers from living happily ever after? (978-1-63555-158-7)

Rocks and Stars by Sam Ledel. Kyle's struggle to own who she is and what she really wants may end up landing her on the bench and without the woman of her dreams. (978-1-63555-156-3)

The Boss of Her: Office Romance Novellas by Julie Cannon, Aurora Rey, and M. Ullrich. Going to work never felt so good. Three office romance novellas from talented writers Julie Cannon, Aurora Rey, and M. Ullrich. (978-1-63555-145-7)

The Deep End by Ellie Hart. When family ties become entangled in murder and deception, it's time to find a way out... (978-1-63555-288-1)

A Country Girl's Heart by Dena Blake. When Kat Jackson gets a second chance at love, following her heart will prove the hardest decision of all. (978-1-63555-134-1)

Dangerous Waters by Radclyffe. Life, death, and war on the home front. Two women join forces against a powerful opponent, nature itself. (978-1-63555-233-1)

Fury's Death by Brey Willows. When all we hold sacred fails, who will be there to save us? (978-1-63555-063-4)

It's Not a Date by Heather Blackmore. Kade's desire to keep things with Jen on a professional level is in Jen's best interest. Yet what's in Kade's best interest...is Jen. (978-1-63555-149-5)

Killer Winter by Kay Bigelow. Just when she thought things could get no worse, homicide Lieutenant Leah Samuels learns the woman she loves has betrayed her in devastating ways. (978-1-63555-177-8)

Score by MJ Williamz. Will an addiction to pain pills destroy Ronda's chance with the woman she loves, or will she come out on top and score a happily ever after? (978-1-62639-807-8)

Spring's Wake by Aurora Rey. When wanderer Willa Lange falls for Provincetown B&B owner Nora Calhoun, will past hurts and a fifteen-year age gap keep them from finding love? (978-1-63555-035-1)

Children of the Healer by Barbara Ann Wright. Life becomes desperate for ex-soldier Cordelia Ross when the indigenous aliens of her planet are drawn into a civil war and old enemies linger in the shadows. Book Three of the Godfall Series. (978-1-63555-031-3)